Advance Praise for
Setting the Family Free

"Like Karen Joy Fowler's classic, *We are All Completely Beside Ourselves*, Eric D. Goodman's newest novel is droll, trenchant, political ... it operates on just about any level a reader could wish for. *Setting the Family Free* might be a fable by intention, but the what-if premise of a private zoo of exotic animals loosed on a middle American town is also a generous, boisterous, surprising read, like a tiger in your backyard.

— Jacquelyn Mitchard, author of *The Deep End of the Ocean*

"A supremely moving novel by turns ferocious and tender and funny from beginning to end. Goodman's finest book."

— Junot Díaz, Pulitzer Prize winning author of *The Brief Wondrous Life of Oscar Wao*

"What a read! Part fable, part meditation, and total page-turner, *Setting the Family Free* is a rollicking read from first sentence to last. This engaging tale of a zoo that literally opens its doors is at once funny, terrifying, and sometimes heartbreaking. What Eric D. Goodman has managed to do with the sections told by the animals is something rare and wonderful. Look for this one on the 'Best of 2019' lists!"

— Jerry Holt, author of *The Killing of Strangers* and *Rickey*

"*Setting the Family Free* reinforces Eric D. Goodman's powerful voice and imagination as one of Baltimore's most riveting and prolific writers. As with his former novels, Goodman captures the human condition through multiple and unpredictable lenses, illuminating our strengths and weaknesses in a presentation which merges past and present stories, intertwining conversations, and metaphorical geographies. However, *Setting the Family Free* takes that vision a step further, exploring the existence of the animal, both human and nonhuman, when pushed beyond its natural and enforced boundaries. The blurring between caged and free is violently, gracefully, and thoughtfully crafted, a true tale of terror—both within and without real and realized bars."

> — Katherine Cottle, author of *My Father's Speech, Halfway: A Journal through Pregnancy,* and *I Remain Yours*

"Warm, poignant, funny, and suspenseful, Eric D. Goodman's *Setting the Family Free* looks at the meaning of family from different, sometimes conflicting, perspectives. The unusual structure with its many points of view brings to life the individuals—including the animals—that make up the colorful cast of characters. This novel was a quick read: I flipped the pages rapidly, wanting to know what each character would say or do next and how that individual would affect the whole. *Setting the Family Free* is entertaining, but while reading, I also paused at particularly touching spots of the story to ponder on this messy, sometimes crazy, sometimes wonderful unit called *family.*"

> — Lucrecia Guerrero, author of the award-winning novel *Tree of Sighs*

"Wild, wonderful, well written, and highly original. An Ohio town is overrun by wild animals and it's a jungle out there in this page-turner novel."

> — Toby Devens, author of *Happy Any Day Now* and *Barefoot Beach*

"Sammy Johnson collects exotic animals on his rural Ohio property, which isn't a problem until suddenly it is, and then everybody wants in on the action. 'Dealing with the press could prove as unpleasant as dealing with wild animals,' Deputy Chuck Ellison observes. But the press is only a part of it in Eric D. Goodman's rollicking story of things getting out of control. Toss in the law, psychologists, zoologists and even an old drinking buddy, and you start to get the full picture, vivid as the nightly news!"

> — Charles Rammelkamp, author of *Mata Hari: Eye of the Day* and *American Zeitgeist*

"In an age when we humans seem hellbent on destroying the planet and everything on it, it's imperative to have authors writing with empathy about the impact our decisions have on our fellow creatures. Fiction is the perfect vehicle for this, especially in the hands of a compassionate writer. Eric D. Goodman takes an interesting premise, the release of captive animals from human control, and puts them on a more even footing with humans. Are we the same or even similar? Or are they just the "other" and must be subdued if their needs and wants conflict with ours? Goodman resists a Disney ending, and as all good writers do, manages to raise more questions than he answers. *Setting the Family Free* is a good read written by a thoughtful and skilled writer."

> — Bathsheba Monk, author of *Nude Walker*

"After nearly 150 years of "The Greatest Show on Earth," Ringling Brothers locked up the lion and tiger and camel and kangaroo cages for good not too long ago. Where did the animals go? Here, in Eric D. Goodman's latest literary circus, a good read under the Big Top of a fine craftsman's imagination. Step right up."

> — Rafael Alvarez, author of *Basilio Boullosa Stars in the Fountain of Highlandtown*

"*Setting the Family Free* creates a genre all its own. It has elements of a crime novel, a romance, and a thriller. But at its heart, it is literary fiction telling the story of a deeply flawed but good man who seeks his own fulfilment through the love of animals. Awed by the power and majesty of exotic animals—lions, tigers, leopards, bears—Sammy Johnson collects them, lives with them, and loves them. His feelings for them, and theirs for him, clash with the norms of the society in which he lives, costs him his marriage, and threatens his way of life. His solution to the dilemma makes for a gripping read. This book will stay in my mind for years to come."

> — Tom Glenn, author of *Last of the Annamese* and *The Trion Syndrome*

"Inspired by true events, and set in the 'Badlands' of Southern Ohio, Eric D. Goodman's latest novel describes the consequences of 'legal' persecution: what happens when a man who served his country in war is destroyed by tax charges and Byzantine laws.

"Usually, such men die quietly. But some—like Joseph Stack, who crashed his plane into an Internal Revenue Service Building in 2010, or Sammy Johnson, the outlaw of Goodman's book, who released dangerous predators by cutting open their cages in his private zoo—lash out one last time. They choose the 'Samson Option.' They kill themselves and take others with them.

"Every year, humans kill 50 billion animals for meat. Now, thanks to Goodman's *Setting the Family Free*, the animals are eating us..."

> — Mark Mirabello, Ph.D, professor of history at Shawnee State University, author of *The Cannibal Within*, *A Traveler's Guide to the Afterlife*, and *Handbook for Rebels and Outlaws*

SETTING THE FAMILY FREE

SETTING THE FAMILY FREE

a novel

Eric D. Goodman

Apprentice House Press
Loyola University Maryland

First Edition

Casebound ISBN: 978-1-62720-216-9
Paperback ISBN: 978-1-62720-217-6
Ebook ISBN: 978-1-62720-218-3

Designed and edited by Christina Damon
Promotion by Claire Riley
Design edits by Carmen Machalek

Photo of the author with the Bayre Lion Statue, Mt. Vernon, Baltimore, by Nataliya A. Goodman

Published by Apprentice House Press

Apprentice
House Press
Loyola University Maryland

Apprentice House Press
Loyola University Maryland
4501 N. Charles Street
Baltimore, MD 21210
410.617.5265 • 410.617.2198 (fax)
www.ApprenticeHouse.com
info@ApprenticeHouse.com

Also by Eric D. Goodman

Womb: a novel in utero
Tracks: A Novel in Stories
Flightless Goose

Learn more about Eric D. Goodman and his work at
www.EricDGoodman.com

For my family—

*Thank you for your ongoing support and encouragement,
and for setting me free to pursue my passion for writing,
unleashing me to create works like this one.*

On Animals

You've got to understand the power of these majestic creatures. Are they easy to fall in love with? Yes. Do they love you back? Maybe. Will they eventually kill if you pretend they're people? Absolutely!

— Leland Anders, Celebrity Zookeeper

I have been studying the traits and dispositions of the "lower animals" (so called) and contrasting them with the traits and disposition of man. I find the result humiliating to me.

— Mark Twain, *Letters From Earth*

Animals, whom we have made our slaves, we do not like to consider our equal.

— Charles Darwin, *Metaphysics, Materialism, and the Evolution of the Mind*

And God said, "Let us make mankind in our image, in our likeness, so that they may rule over the fish in the sea and the birds in the sky, over the livestock and all the wild animals, and over the creatures that move along the ground."

— *Genesis 1:26*

All animals are equal, but some animals are more equal than others.

— George Orwell, *Animal Farm*

I think I could turn and live with animals, they are so placid and self-contained. I stand and look at them long and long.

— Walt Whitman, *Leaves of Grass*

Look, there's no denying that it's easy to fall in love with animals. I spend a lot of time with them, I know as well as anyone. But you can't live with them in your house or enter their cages like you're part of the family. No matter how tame they might seem, they'll swat you around like a rag doll.

— Jackson Withers, Animal Protection Agency

...there is no folly of the beast of the earth which is not infinitely outdone by the madness of men.

— Herman Melville, *Moby Dick*

Only animals were not expelled from Paradise.

— Milan Kundera, *The Unbearable Lightness of Being*

Breaking

[Transcript of the local evening news broadcast in Chillicothe, Ohio, 6:42 p.m.]

Zachery Adams

We interrupt our regular report with this breaking news: authorities are warning all residents of Chillicothe and the vicinity to remain indoors. Avoid wooded areas. Eyewitnesses report dangerous animal sightings in the area. Amy Shivers is on the scene. Amy?

Amy Shivers

Uh, yes, Zachery. I'm here, just east of downtown Chillicothe, where, as you can see, chaos has broken out. Ambulances, police, medics, wildlife authorities—they're all here trying to make sense of the situation. There's already been an attack.

Zachery

What kind of attack? On a person or another animal?

Amy

People, Zachery. There are dangerous, wild animals on the loose. According to neighbors, the owner of this property, Mr. Samuel Johnson, has an exotic private zoo of wild animals. A number of them have escaped.

Zachery

If they're captive, are they really considered *wild* animals?

Amy

We're talking lions, cougars, bears, tigers—all out roaming the neighborhood. Some of the faster-moving animals could soon be in the city. Animals have already been spotted near Route 23. They may be approaching downtown as we speak.

Zachery

Can you tell us about the confirmed attack?

Amy

At this time authorities are not releasing any information, but the ambulances and medics indicate an attack.

Zachery

Any speculation on how this happened? How these animals got out?

Amy

Not yet. But I have an eyewitness, here with us, who can give us some insight. It was the neighbor, Bobbie Anne Thompson, who first noticed something amiss. She made the first call to 911. Mrs. Thompson, can you tell me what you saw?

Mrs. Thompson

Everyone's got to get their animals inside! Themselves and their pets and their animals!

Amy

What was the first thing you noticed that made you believe something might be wrong?

Mrs. Thompson

My horses. I looked out my window and noticed that my horses were acting up. Running around wild in their pen, like they were being chased. And then I saw it.

(crying)

It was the Neighbor Who First Noticed Something Amiss

Bobbie Anne Thompson worked in her kitchen, as she did most weekday afternoons. Dinner slow-cooked as she emptied the dishwasher. At eighty-two, Bobbie Anne was still perfectly capable of handling everything herself. But since her husband died a couple years back, she'd resorted to allowing her adult son to stay with her, to "watch over" her. To her mind, it was simply an excuse for a middle-aged, laid off divorcé to move back in and sponge off Mommy. But he seemed to have convinced himself—if not her—that his motives were purely altruistic.

"We'll help each other, Mom," he'd said when he suggested the lifestyle change. As though he were sugarcoating the truth of her feeble inability rather than masking his own shortcomings. "God knows you can use a man around the house, with Dad gone. And there's no doubt I miss your cooking. Who'd have thought we'd end up in the same boat?"

"Same boat," she'd hissed at the time. "Divorcing your wife of ten years is not quite the same thing as a fatal tractor accident taking the life of your loyal and stable husband of forty years!"

Dexter hadn't known what to say.

Still, Bobbie Anne realized having her son with her would be more help than hindrance. If nothing more, it would give her a new purpose in life. The center of her life had always been her dear husband and their time together. Without someone else to care for, she knew she wouldn't bother to do these things for herself. She found it easier to cook and care for two than for one. She'd been taking care of loved ones for so long, she was better at helping others than at helping herself.

"I'll pay half the mortgage," he'd offered.

"The house has been paid off for twelve years."

"Then I'll pay for all the groceries and half the utilities."

She considered Dexter a good son. Sure, his motives were not entirely focused on her wellbeing alone. But her wellbeing had prompted him to conjure a way for the two of them to benefit from one another. He was much more help this time around than the last time he'd lived at home, back when he'd been a sullen, rebellious teenager.

Dexter got off work at five o'clock. He normally walked from the unattached garage to the house's side door around a quarter past five. Now, as the soup simmered on the stove and the bread baked in the boxy machine he'd gotten her for Christmas, it was about four in the afternoon. Once she emptied the dishwasher, the bread would be ready for her to dump out of the machine and slather with butter. She liked to give it time to cool. Then she'd get half an hour or so to watch Judge Judy before Dexter arrived home.

She bent over to take another plate from the bottom tray of the dishwasher. Standing with the plate in hand, she glanced out the window as she dried the remaining droplets from the ceramic surface and placed it in the cabinet's stack. The horses were gathered together in a circle. That was somewhat unusual; strange enough that she began watching more intently than she normally might.

Another plate, another drying and peering. A saucer, a glance. The horses were running, as though startled. They whinnied and galloped.

"What's gotten into them?" she asked out loud, as though the horses were mischievous children, while she bent for a handful of silverware. She dropped the silver in one end of the towel and used the other end of the damp cloth to dry the utensils one end at a time. She placed the dried silverware in the open drawer's tray. A spoon. A knife. Everything where it fit. All the while she watched out the window looking for what nagged her, for what didn't fit. A knife. A fork. A teaspoon.

A tiger.

"Oh my Lord!" She dropped the silver—towel and all—onto the

linoleum floor. She wondered, had the tiger been there all this time? Had it been hiding in the brush and she hadn't noticed it? Had it pounced out when she was bent over the dishwasher? Or had it been there in front of her for hours, this ferocious tiger with white coat and black stripes blending perfectly in with the black and white horses? *Black and white and red all over.* She shook her head.

Rationality was hard to find as she began yelling, opening the window to demand that the white tiger stop. But the open window only let in the terrible noise. Her own screams for the animal to scat went unheard. So she rushed to the cordless and dialed 911.

"What is your emergency?"

"A tiger's attacking my horses!"

"A tiger?"

"There's a white tiger attacking my horses!"

"Are they fenced in, ma'am?"

"The horses were—the tiger got in!"

"Where are you located?"

Ordinarily, Bobbie Anne may have gotten snippy with the dispatcher at this point. She could sense that the woman did not believe her, that the woman took her for crazy. It was something she picked up on more and more often when talking with people, this assumed senility based only on her advanced years. Frankly, it pissed her off. Whether it was just something that came with the territory—young people didn't want to take their elders seriously—or her own defensive sensitivity to the oncoming possibility, she didn't know. But she had noticed it in the years since her husband had died. Normally, she may have ripped the dispatcher a new asshole for even considering for a moment that she was out of her mind. But her only concern now was to get the dispatcher to believe her and to help her.

"I'm next door to the Sammy Johnson place!"

"Sammy Johnson?"

"For all we know, there may be more than one tiger out!"

"What's *your* address, ma'am?"

She gave her address and the dispatcher assured that police were on their way.

"You've got to tell everyone to get inside," Bobbie Anne pleaded with the dispatcher, the idea dawning on her even as the words came to her mouth. "Tell the news, put out an alert! Everyone's got to get themselves and their animals inside!"

As though the dispatcher sensed the coming hang-up, she spit out the words, "Stay with me, ma'am! Don't hang up; stay on the line."

"I've got to go," Bobbie Anne cried, the terrible possibility as clear in her mind as the blood staining the tiger's mouth outside her kitchen window. "I've got to call my son!"

It was half past four in the afternoon. Dexter would be parking in the driveway in another forty minutes.

"Stay on the line, ma'am," the dispatcher urged. "Can you describe what's happening right now?"

Bobbie Anne stared out the window, but her eyes had blurred. She refocused. The horse was down, on its side, undeniably dead. The tiger fed ravenously. The bushes rustled on the other side of the fence and the horses continued their wild run.

"The tiger's eating my horse. It's terrible. At least the horse is dead, I think. It's not moving."

"Good, Mrs. Thompson. Just stay with me. Any moment now the police will be there." It seemed an unusual synthesis, the sense of urgency and requirement to wait idly by at the same time. Her mind scrambled, because she didn't know what to do and she didn't want to focus only on the atrocity in her back yard.

Black, white...and red. It echoed in her mind again. Not the image of the bloody horse, but the joke. She considered it odd, as she waited for the police to arrive, that a tired joke came to mind at a time like this. *What's black and white and red all over? A newspaper.*

Later, she would only admit the absurdity of such a thought to a reporter who asked to interview her—and only then because he wasn't like the other reporters with their aggressive urgency. Blake, calm and conversational, who would spend time getting to know her and asking how she felt about things. As though he wanted to understand, not just snatch a story.

"A joke," she would tell him during one of their meetings. "My horse being ripped apart by that monster, having her flesh pulled shred by shred off her body, and what creeps into my head? A joke."

That would come later. In between witnessing the atrocity now and this confession later spanned a lifetime of emotion and activity compacted into a few short hours. The joke was not a matter of mood, simply the reflex of a mind that hadn't experienced this sort of situation before and did not know what knee-jerk reaction to employ.

"Are you still with me, Mrs. Thompson?"

"Yes." Still on the cordless, waiting for the police to arrive, Bobbie Anne looked out the kitchen window and saw the tiger chewing away at the horse's middle. Again, she noticed the bushes between her property and the neighbor's rustling. But none of the trees were waving in the wind.

Then she spotted another set of eyes peering out from the bushes, watching the tiger from behind.

"Oh, my Lord," Bobbie Anne said. "There's another one!"

"Another tiger, ma'am?"

"Get out of there! Leave my horses alone!"

"Mrs. Thompson? What's going on?" The dispatcher faded into background noise as Bobbie Anne watched a second tiger attack a second horse.

"Ma'am?"

Bobbie Anne turned away from the window and broke free of the sight. She yelled into the phone. "Tell the news, send out a warning! Everyone's got to get themselves and their animals inside!"

Another Wild Jungle

Amy Shivers

What was the first thing you noticed that made you believe something might be wrong?

Bobbie Anne Thompson

My horses. I looked out my window and noticed that my horses were acting up. Running around wild in their pen, like they were being chased. And then I saw it.

(crying)

Carrie Mortimer turned from the television and grinned at Mac. "Oh my God, are you seeing this?"

"Whoa." Mac's eyes were glued to the tube. "That's something else." Carrie and Mac spent hours each workday scanning the little news stories in puddle-jump towns like Zanesville and Chillicothe and Portsmouth, just looking for a story to scoop up and transform into a national sensation.

Mac wasn't one for words. But the guy—overweight and underheight—was great with a camera. And who needed a man with words? Carrie prided herself as a word master, when on camera. She knew she had the chops and the looks, the voice and the body language—she had the entire package—to make it as a national news correspondent. She'd already made a big splash in New York City with a gig on a local 6 a.m. morning talk show clone, one of the many little affiliates of CNEN—the Cable News and Entertainment Network. *And as the song goes*, she often reminded herself when she watched successful anchors and morning news hosts with dreamy eyes, *if you can make it there, you'll make it anywhere.*

"What time is it?" Mac asked.

"Six forty," Carrie said. "This'll be national news at eleven."

"You think we can get a spot?"

She'd already dialed the producer, her phone ringing in her ear. "Yes. In fact, I think this'll be more than a nightly news story."

Mac's eyes widened and he looked almost as thirsty as she felt. "Morning show?"

She looked away from Mac and spoke into the phone. "Larry? There's trouble in Ohio."

Pacing the station office in stocking feet, her heels kicked off next to her roller chair, she picked up her pace as she spoke to the producer. She could feel Mac watching her long legs as they scissored one way and then another, her stride carrying her svelte frame back and forth. She dressed in clothes that asked people to look at her, so she expected it. A short skirt suit, gold stud earrings, and a simple but elegant gold bracelet on her microphone wrist. She'd clipped her hair up in a bunch at the top of her head and her makeup had worn along with the day. But it only took a moment for her to go from next-door girl to glamour girl, when duty called. More often, it felt like *she* was calling *duty*.

Carrie hung up the phone and threw Mac a satisfied smirk. "Pack a bag. We're going to Ohio to talk to some people."

Sammy's Cats

These cats are born and raised in captivity. So they're not real wildcats. They have the instinct, but they don't have the skills or socialization. It's like they're a new breed of animal. A dangerous breed.

— Leland Anders, Celebrity Zookeeper

He used to talk about starting a drive-through safari park or a zoo or something. I thought he was nuts. But then, who but a crazy dude's gonna have animals like that?

— Dexter Thompson, Sammy Johnson's Neighbor's Son

He has a lot of cats. Everyone knows it. He has tigers, lions and cougars. I always did like housecats. But he prefers big ones.

— Emily Smith, Sammy Johnson's Grandmother, *Chillicothe Gazette* Interview, 1988

Oh, he had cats, all right! Bobcats, jaguars, panthers, leopards …

— Willie Johnson, Sammy Johnson's Father

This wasn't the first time Sammy's animals got free. Lion attacked my hunting dog, years ago. Pissed the shit out of me.

— Mitch Henderson, Sammy Johnson's Neighbor

Sometimes he'd say—he could tell mean jokes, man. I mean, funny as what all. But just...wrong. Sometimes he'd say—you know that telethon for them disabled kids? And Jerry Lewis would come on and they'd call them Jerry's kids? Well, sometimes he'd say something like, "Jerry's kids would make a good snack for Sammy's Cats." Funny. But, you know, wrong.

— Mike Skaggs, Sammy Johnson's Drinking Buddy

Sammy was doing what he thought was right. "I'm doing a service," he used to say. "I'm preserving these noble beasts. They live better lives with me than they would in the wild." That man loved him some animal.

— Calvin Smitts, Sammy Johnson's Friend

I had some cats myself. Bunch of them. But they probably weighed less than Sammy's cats do, pound for pound.

— Emily Smith, Sammy Johnson's Grandmother, *Chillicothe Gazette* Interview, 1988

We didn't just *have* them—we *lived* with them. We'd let them out of their cages, especially when they were cubs. We'd watch TV and have a tiger cub between us. We even slept with them in our bed when they were young. They weren't just animals. They were our babies.

— Marielle Johnson, Sammy Johnson's Wife

There was a woman in New Jersey who had twenty-four tigers, making it the largest preserve of tigers in the United States. Sammy didn't have that many tigers. But he did have that many big cats. More, even.

— Jackson Withers, Animal Protection Agency

Lions and tigers show empathy. They can tell when I'm upset or playful or serious. They understand me. Better than people do.

— Sammy Johnson, Interview with Animal Control, 2008

Ohio has no regulations governing the ownership of exotic and dangerous animals. Exotic animals all over the state languish without adequate food, water and veterinary care. They eat rotten scraps, drink algae-laden water, and spend their days pacing on feces and urine-encrusted dirt.

— PETA, Statement issued in 2011

When I say "drinking buddy," I guess I mean "acquaintance." We talked a lot, but we never really got together outside the bar. He was a loner.

— Mike Skaggs Sammy Johnson's Drinking Buddy

…mountain lions and cougars and pumas. But those last three are all the same thing. Did you know that? Most people don't know that.

— Willy Johnson, Sammy Johnson's Father

He'd have put his life on the line for those animals. They were his family.

— Sally Johnson, Sammy Johnson's Mother

It wasn't the first time. But I guess it'll be the last.

— Mitch Henderson, Sammy Johnson's Neighbor

Getting Dinner

The Tiger hungers. For food. For the hunt. Before, food was aplenty, feedings regular and hearty, leaving time for boredom rather than want. Not now. Tiger's more hungry than bored. And now, Tiger is free.

Other tigers are about. Some remain in their cages. Others have left. One feeds in front of the cages. No need to challenge the other tiger for this kill or for hunting ground. There is more.

He has been released before, is familiar with the land around this sanctuary, prison, home. Tiger knows where food waits, smells where to go for easy kill, tastes the living meat in the air.

Tiger ambles from the row of cages to the open field, lopes toward the split rail fence. No need to hurry, zigzagging this way and that along the way. Deep breath of fresh air, free of the feces- and urine-caked dirt of the cage. Out here, the air is different: clean, crisp. He catches a scent overhead. Vultures circle. Birds perch in the branches of wind-blown trees, distracting his ears with song. A leopard drags her kill into those branches, a good place to look if food becomes scarce. Now, food is plentiful. The scent of easy meat calls.

The grass sways tall, as he likes it. His orange coat should be a blotch of color in a bland field, but his black stripes distort his shape, hide his prowl in the overgrown grass. Invisible, he reaches the fence.

On the other side, he sees now what he smelled and heard before: A man stands with three horses beyond the fence. Men are masters, strong despite inferior frames. Men use tools and machines and powers Tiger does not understand. Man cages and controls. Tiger prefers to avoid the man. Three horses forage here, too. Horses are easy prey, offer an abundance of good meat.

Nourishment is reward, but meat tastes better when hunted. Instinct overcomes inexperience. Meat normally comes served by Master. Pursuing pleases.

Which horse? Any will do. One is more than enough for him, another cat, and the scavengers above. The choice is made: the easiest reach.

Tiger stalks in the grass, steps forward. A dried reed beneath his paw breaks and Next-Door Man looks over. They make eye contact. For a moment, Tiger lowers his front—his head and his shoulders—ready to meet Man's challenge. Tiger's ears fold back like wind-blown reeds. He snarls, shows teeth. But the man turns away and abandons eye contact. Tiger feels easier, prefers the unproblematic kill. Tonight, Tiger will eat horse.

Tiger leaps over the fence. The horses whinny and gallop. Tiger selects, attacks. Intuition compensates lack of skill. No single, masterful bite to the windpipe fells this horse. Repeated batting of paw, gripping of claw, gnashing of canine. The determined clamp of powerful jaw. Dinner served.

Barned

Mitch Henderson's new horse was the best of the three. All of his horses were keepers, but Chestnut was the favorite. He was the youngest, the newest, and perhaps that was the reason Mitch regarded him so highly. But Chestnut also happened to be the least tame—hadn't even been broken yet—and the one Mitch would have to spend most of his time with in the coming weeks.

Recently retired after twenty-eight years as a federal prison guard, Mitch had a good pension and lots of time on his hands. Four years into retirement and he still wasn't quite accustomed to the idleness. He was used to putting in long hours at Chillicothe Correctional Institute, where he'd encountered some interesting characters during his career, including high-profile prisoners like Junior Johnson, the bootlegger, and Johnny Paycheck, the country music star. The concert Merle Haggard had given for inmates as a favor to inmate Johnny Paycheck was one of the most memorable moments of his career. But the look Charles Manson had given him one night, when he'd slammed the cell door shut, would stick in his mind always. It was the stare of a crazed lunatic, someone unpredictable, who you wouldn't want to trust whether encountered in a dark alley or open field.

Mitch didn't mind taking it easy, now that he'd reached his 60s. But he couldn't just sit around and watch television or read or play on a computer. He needed to do something physical. And after nearly thirty years of working inside the concrete and iron walls and bars of CCI, he wanted to do something outdoors.

He'd always been interested in animals and farming and had considered a cattle ranch. But he'd read that cows and bulls, despite their lazy appearances, could be quite dangerous. Most accidents weren't fatal, but injuries were unwanted just the same. And the majority of cattle-related accidents occurred with older men, men his age. Either inexperienced retirees trying on a cowboy hat for the first time and underestimating the power of the animals they prodded, or mature cattle hands who'd become too comfortable around the animals and who were not as quick or agile as they'd been in youth.

"Besides," a local cattle rancher by the name of Calvin Smitts had told him over barbecue ribs at the Old Canal Smoke House, "there ain't much money to be made for a small-time farmer anymore. By the time you raise the calf, buy the hay, keep up the barn, pay the vet, you done paid more on the cow than you'll get when you take it to auction. If you're not in for a few hundred head, you might as well not be in at all."

"Hell, I ain't trying to get rich or nothing," Mitch had said. "Just looking for something to do."

"You want a hobby, might as well have something easier to handle," Calvin advised. "Goats. Sheep. Llamas. Or horses. Bulls don't make good pets or good money. Them other don't make good money, but at least you got something you can play with and they ain't as dangerous. Easier to take care of."

"I wouldn't mind a horse or two."

"If I was you, I'd have fun with a couple horses before I got in with a bunch of steer. Hell, I'd get out myself if I had any sense. Once you ranched cattle all your life, that's just what you know."

The veteran rancher—who he knew from restaurant lunches and diner coffee breaks—had made sense. Mitch wanted something to do with his time—a hobby—and horses would be more fun than heifers. He could learn to break them, to ride them. There wasn't any money in it, so he couldn't pretend to be doing anything productive. But he'd been productive for a full career, so he figured he deserved a retirement of doing things he wanted.

Now, in his field, Mitch noticed his horses acting funny. Stomping their hooves and carrying on like something was wrong. He still didn't consider himself an expert on horses by any means—even his older horses, he'd only had for four years now—but it wasn't often they got to making noise and acting uneasy like this. The weather report had called for a storm later in the evening. He figured that's what they were antsy about. *Probably best to go ahead and put them up.*

The barn was about a two-minute stroll across the field. He left the horses to themselves and made for the barn at a leisurely pace. Storm might have been coming, but the sky looked clear and beautiful now, white puffs of cloud riding the wind over the lush green trees, the sun peeking in and out of them.

Inside the barn, Mitch took a red pail and filled it half up with oats. He walked back out into the sunlight toward the horses. He'd put up one horse at a time; no need to hurry. He lured Chestnut with the pail of oats, petted his velvety red side, fastened a rope around his neck, and prepared to lead him toward the barn.

That's when he heard a snap. He looked up. On the other side of the split rail fence, he saw the tall grass rustling. Wind? No, not with the movement isolated in one spot. Then he saw those eyes.

The eye contact only lasted three seconds, and Mitch hoped that three seconds wasn't enough to provoke. He'd read that eye contact to a tiger was a direct challenge. Mitch wanted to bolt and run but avoided the instinct, remembering what he'd read. The best thing to do: slowly walk to the barn without looking back.

Mitch estimated the barn at about two minutes off. The house, about four. Rope in hand, Mitch proceeded slowly with Chestnut in tow.

This wasn't the first time a tiger had stalked his animals. As pets, his horses had come as a long overdue replacement for the beloved hunting dog Sammy's tiger had killed years ago. That time, Mitch hadn't been around. He wondered how things would go this time.

He knew he needed to remain calm or at least to look it. To run or scream or do anything sudden would only provoke the tiger. Since the last incident, he'd read up on the big cats Sammy kept next door. He knew that it was unlikely he'd be able to save all his horses. But he hoped he could save at least one of them—maybe two—and himself.

Unable to resist, Mitch peeked over his shoulder, over Chestnut's back, to see the tiger still in the tall grass, its tail flickering back and forth, crouched and excited. Mitch was halfway to the barn. He looked ahead to the red barn and its white door. Mitch's target.

Funny, he thought, how he was able to pretend he lived in a normal, rural farmland neighborhood, even though he knew all too well that a lunatic lived next door. From the far side of his own land, up a hill, Mitch could even see the cages in the right light—the lions and tigers and bears and cougars and panthers. He could hear them roaring when they were hungry. At night, he could hear the howling of the wolves. And yet, he still confidently strolled around in his yard without considering that, at the mercy of his nutty neighbor, he could be left in a situation like this at any time: only a split rail fence between himself and death by mauling.

He'd voiced his concerns to the Sheriff before, had complained of the potential danger and the instability of Sammy Johnson. But the Sheriff acted like there was nothing he could do.

"I'm sorry, Mitch, but my hands are tied. He's not breaking any laws that we can stick to him."

"How can it be legal to have a passel of wild beasts in your back yard?" Mitch had asked. "It's one thing to endanger yourself or the animals. But what about me and the other neighbors? Poor old Bobbie Anne Thompson? There's a baseball field not half a mile off. What about the school? The safety of the public?"

"I know," Sheriff Roscoe Roy had commiserated. It sounded like he agreed. "But the law's the law. We've got to find something to stick to him."

Perhaps the most frightening beast next door was Sammy Johnson himself. Once, when Mitch had confronted Sammy about his animals, Sammy had shot him a malicious look that he would never forget. It was the look of a crazed lunatic, someone unpredictable, who you wouldn't want to cross in a dark alley or an open field.

Mitch had led Chestnut nearly to the barn door when he looked back once more—just in time to see the attack. The tiger leapt over the split wood fence, its hind legs projecting it a good six feet high and twelve feet across. The tiger landed in Mitch's field for only a split second, took aim and then launched into another, shorter pounce, this time landing on the backside of one of his horses—Champ. His other horse—Charlie—bolted into a gallop toward the barn. Champ had no hope of escape as the tiger dug his fishhook claws into horseflesh, clamped down onto his neck, and pulled him down like a rodeo star pulling down a roped steer.

Mitch slid open the barn door and ushered Chestnut in. Once inside, he let his newest horse go and turned back, hand to door, ready to shut it should tiger fur be in close proximity. Charlie romped around the field, not seeming to realize that he needed to come to the barn, feeling instinctively safer in the open field than caged in an enclosure. The tiger was occupied, no longer in attack mode, clamping down on the fallen horse. His jaw opened and closed again on Champ's neck two or three times before he appeared satisfied. The tiger stood over his kill and licked his reddened mouth. He looked to his left, casually, and then to his right, his tail waving back and forth more lazily than it had been flicking in the tall grass on the other side of the fence. After a moment, the tiger sniffed at the horse's middle and then tore into his belly.

Still standing at the barn door, his hand ready to slide it closed, Mitch called out to his spooked horse. "Charlie! Charlie! Get along now, Charlie!" Charlie continued to trot to and fro in the field, keeping a distance from the tiger but not comprehending the sanctuary before him in the darkened barn.

"Gotta get him myself," Mitch said under his breath. To be safe, he went inside and led Chestnut to his stall and closed the gate. He then went back to the open barn door, judged the distance between Charlie and himself and between Charlie and the tiger. Then Mitch headed into the field with a rope and a bucket of oats. The tiger wasn't paying any mind to Mitch or Charlie, contentedly feeding on his kill. Mitch reached Charlie, calmed him with the oats, and looped the rope around his neck. "There, there, Charlie. It's all right. Let's go in." He began to lead his horse toward the barn. About halfway there, he looked back to see the tiger feeding, completely uninterested.

It was then that he heard a bellowing growl and looked beyond the tiger, beyond the fence, to notice the big brown grizzly bear.

The bear climbed clumsily over the fence and then lumbered toward them in a slow gallop, one leg hitting the ground at a time so that it almost appeared to be skipping. Mitch froze for a moment as the horse jumped back and nearly broke free of his grip. But Mitch grasped the rope tightly and reasserted his control, leading the horse to the barn. The grizzly was much slower than the tiger, and that was their advantage. Mitch led Charlie toward the barn door as the bear continued to gallop toward them. Mitch got Charlie into the barn, dropped the rope and the pail of oats, and turned to slide the door closed. He locked it just in time to hear the bear claw at it, scratching grooves into the blanched wood. Mitch guessed the huge bear must have been close to half a ton of muscle and fur. He prayed, as the bear scraped slowly at the door, that it didn't charge and bust its way in. Mitch believed that if the bear figured out how to do it, he certainly could break through.

Mitch penned Charlie up in the stall next to Chestnut. Then he climbed up the rickety ladder to the hayloft for his own safety. He inched open the upstairs loft door, where hay was hoisted in for storage, and peeked down at the bear and the tiger. The bear only halfheartedly pawed at the barn door from time to time as he paced back and forth along the front of the barn. Eventually the bear sat down, as though giving up...or considering a new strategy.

Mitch looked out toward the Johnson property from his safe perch. The tiger continued to feed on Champ, although his urgency seemed to have tapered. Mitch looked further on, beyond the fence, and he saw a leopard off in the distance, walking about in Sammy's field. He remembered that leopards knew how to climb trees. Could a leopard just as easily scale the side of a wooden barn?

It occurred to Mitch as he was imprisoned in the barn that this was what it must have felt like for Junior Johnson and Johnny Paycheck and Charles Manson. This was what it felt like to be locked up. That's when it occurred to Mitch that he should call the police.

Reactions in the Local News

If we'd have known, we'd have shut it down. We on the council would have found a way. Shut the whole nasty business down.

— Mark Vernon, Mayor of Chillicothe

Oh, they knew all right. There's no question about that. I don't know how many times I reported it.

— Mitch Henderson, Sammy Johnson's Neighbor

Everyone knew Sammy had pets. You know, a person can snap and you end up with a shooting in a movie theater or a school or mall. But you don't lock up the people who *might* crack one day, because you don't know until it happens. Same thing here. Sammy's zoo was never dangerous. Until it was.

— Mike Skaggs, Sammy Johnson's Drinking Buddy

I always feared something like this might happen. I just didn't imagine it would be so bad.

— Roscoe Roy, Ross County Sheriff

"Show no fear," he used to say. "Show no fear and the animals won't bother you. But let them smell the fear on you, and it's like tenderizing a cut of steak."

— Morris Jones, Animal Caretaker

I never saw this coming. Never.

— Marielle Johnson, Sammy Johnson's Wife

When I get there, he tells me, "You'll have to sign a waiver before you come on my property." I laughed, but the dude was serious! He talked like they weren't dangerous, but he knew they were.

— Stanley Rodgers, Property Appraiser

Sammy's a collector of things. Always has been, even as a child. Toy cars, then army men. Little toy animals, then real ones. Then bigger ones. He collects cars, guns, medals. And, of course, animals.

— Emily Smith, Sammy Johnson's Grandmother, *Chillicothe Gazette* Interview, 1988

It's like the tax evasion charge on Al Capone. It was just an excuse, Sammy's guns. The ones they got him for, never even shot. Like an antique from the Civil War, a musket or some shit. Really? That's all you got on the guy and you're sending him to prison? If you ask me, they took a guy already on the fence from the war and the animals, and they pushed him over with that year in prison. And then the wife bails. Sheesh.

— Mike Skaggs, Sammy Johnson's Drinking Buddy

I think she left him because she got scared. I mean, with eighty vicious animals running around, wouldn't you?

— Bobbie Anne Thompson, Sammy Johnson's Neighbor

Yes, I knew about Sammy's preserve. And I wasn't happy about it. But he wasn't breaking the law. I tried to convince him to turn them over to the zoo or a non-profit preserve, where they could be properly cared for. He refused, insisted that he provided better care. From his point of view, he did. Some of his animals were rescues from other owners who couldn't keep up with them.

— Jackson Withers, Animal Protection Agency

Maybe if there'd been stricter gun control laws, he wouldn't have had so many guns. And maybe if there'd been stricter animal regulations, he wouldn't have had so many vicious animals. Between Sammy's guns and animals, I'd say I lived next door to the most dangerous man in Chillicothe.

— Mitch Henderson, Sammy Johnson's Neighbor

In our last year together, he spent more time with the animals than he did with me. After a while, the novelty wears off and you want to settle into a normal life. I didn't bother to say "it's either me or the animals." I already knew who he would choose.

— Marielle Johnson, Sammy Johnson's Wife

Yes, he loved his animals, but he loved his wife, too. I think it broke his heart when Marielle left him. That's the straw that broke the tiger's back.

— Sally Johnson, Sammy Johnson's Mother

The boy didn't know when to quit. With some, it's the booze. Some, it's the dope. Some fall to gambling. And like always, it's those around the addict that suffer most.

— Willie Johnson, Sammy Johnson's Father

We can only make guesses, but we can make fairly educated guesses. We have a man in control of his own life, in control of beasts stronger than himself, and he finds himself watching that control slip. He lost his guns. Lost his wife. There were liens on his property, so the threat of losing his home and land. All of that piled onto his war experience. A man can only take so much. This man broke.

— Dr. Minnie Fields, Professor of Psychology, Shawnee State University

Authorities are warning all residents of the Chillicothe and Columbus areas to remain indoors. Exotic animals may be on the loose, and residents should remain safely inside.

— Zachery Adams, Chillicothe Evening News

It sounds like a terrible horror movie, residents of central Ohio trapped in their homes and workplaces. Dangerous animals are on the prowl, and no one is safe outdoors.

— Carrie Mortimer, CNEN-TV

How could this have happened? I shouldn't have left him alone with them.

— Marielle Johnson, Sammy Johnson's Wife

The animals you see with me on television are trained animals under the care of a trained professional. Sammy's animals were domestically kept, but not trained or under control. Avoid them at all costs.

— Leland Anders, Celebrity Zookeeper

CAUTION: EXOTIC ANIMALS—STAY IN VEHICLE

— Road signs along State Route 23 and Interstate 70

Deputy Shot

Looking back, Deputy Chuck Ellison wondered why he had been so casual about the whole thing, as though it were just another routine traffic violation or fender bender requiring him to take a report. Little did he know, at the time, that he was embarking on the incident that would encompass the rest of his days. That would change him. Make him the man he became. Little did he realize, as he cruised along in his Crown Victoria, that he would come to compartmentalize his life in terms of pre-incident and post-incident. That he would never look at his wife or his kids again without fearing for their lives, lest a wild animal or unstable person attack.

Mitch Henderson asked Chuck in the days after the incident, "If you want to forget, why do you talk about it so much?" Chuck didn't know how to answer, so he continued to tell Mitch about how things transpired in that string of terrible hours.

Chuck Ellison was just about to start the late shift that afternoon. On his way from home to work, already in uniform, he sat outside the corner store in his patrol car. His shift started at five. At half past four, as he took that first sip of coffee, Delores, the dispatcher, came over the radio.

"There's a tiger loose on the Johnson farm," Delores said. "Bobbie Anne Thompson on Rural Place Road called it in. A tiger attacking her horses."

"Don't that beat all," Chuck said under his breath. He took another sip of coffee and slid the paper cup into the cup holder hanging on his door. He picked up the radio piece. "I'm on it, Delores," he told her. "I'll be there in two shakes of a tiger's tail."

He flipped on his siren, flashed red and blue lights, and picked up speed on Route 23, passing traffic in the median when he could. Not more than ten minutes later, he arrived. Chuck took his clipboard and left his police cruiser for Bobbie Anne Thompson's front porch. He didn't have to knock on the door; she must have been waiting at the window, because as soon as he stepped onto her front porch, the door opened.

"Get in, quick!" she insisted.

"I think we're just fine here, Mrs. Thompson."

"There're tigers in the yard! No one's safe out here!"

To humor her, he stepped inside and allowed her to close and lock the door. He flipped open the metal cover of his clipboard and clicked his Skilcraft ballpoint. "Now, where did you spot the tigers?"

"They're right out here!" She darted to the kitchen. He followed her through the house. As soon as he came to her kitchen window, he looked out and saw the unbelievable. His jaw dropped, along with his clipboard.

Two tigers relaxed in the back yard, their mouths drenched in the blood of Bobbie Anne's two fallen horses. The horses seemed to have deflated, their middles emptied of their innards, as though only their heads and rear ends were really there. Chuck knew tigers were solitary creatures, that they hunted alone. The horses had drawn them together here, but they were not partners in this crime. One tiger looked like what he normally pictured when he thought of a tiger: orange with black stripes. The other must have been an albino or some other breed, white with black stripes.

He also knew that, according to what he'd heard, Sammy Johnson had multiple cats. If these two had escaped, he wondered how many others might be running amok. Living horses still trotted nervously about in the back yard. He decided he would have to go next door and confront Sammy Johnson.

"Mrs. Thompson, you stay in here and call if you notice anything else, any other animals coming. I'm going next door to talk with Mr. Johnson. So we can get this taken care of."

"My Dexter is going to be home in another half hour." Worry danced around her words. "He's not picking up his cell phone. He's always letting the battery die. Can you stay here and make sure the tigers don't get him?"

"I have to get to Sammy Johnson's place now to make sure no more animals get out. But I'll call for someone to get out here right away. All right?"

He could see in her worried eyes that it was not all right. After he got to his cruiser, he radioed for backup as he drove to the Johnson place.

"I've got two tigers out here feeding on Mrs. Thompson's horses. I'm going over to talk with Sammy Johnson. Can I get someone out here with Mrs. Thompson? She's worried about her son coming home and getting attacked. I can use some backup anyway. We may have to put these tigers down, unless we can get a vet out here with some tranquilizers."

"Chuck," Delores called. "We've got another call from the Henderson place on the other side of Sammy's. Mitch Henderson is trapped in his barn. There's a bear. His wife is frantic, but I told her she had to stay inside the house."

"Oh, shit," Chuck said. "We better get on the horn to Roscoe."

"I'll call Roscoe," Delores replied. "You better help the Hendersons."

Delores was right, Chuck realized. He was already in front of the driveway to the Johnson place when he put down the radio. From the road, he could make out the cages along the edges of the private drive. He couldn't be sure from the distance, but at least some of the cages appeared to still contain animals. Clearly, some of them were empty. Chuck's heart raced, but he took a deep breath to calm it. He had to remain calm. He floored the accelerator and sped for the Henderson place. On the way, he passed three wolves. Confused, he didn't know whether he should stop and shoot them, or proceed. "Hell, I should've killed those tigers before leaving," he said aloud. He stopped his car and aimed his Glock, fired three times, and hit one wolf in the back haunch. It lumbered into the woods on the other side of the road; the other two had already vanished from sight.

Chuck considered going after them. But no, the most important thing at the moment had to be getting Mitch Henderson out of his barn—or rather, getting the bear away from Mitch.

Days later, Mitch told Chuck that he'd heard those three shots and had wondered what it had been. Bears? Lions? Tigers? Sammy Johnson waging a war of his own? Mitch told Chuck that he feared Sammy more than he feared the bear on his doorstop.

Now, as Chuck approached the Henderson place, he got on the radio again. "Delores, I'm definitely gonna need immediate backup. Tigers, bears, wolves so far. All out. Who knows how many animals may be running loose? We've got to contain them."

"Backup is on the way," Delores assured. "Roscoe's coming."

"Good. I'm at Mitch Henderson's place. I'm going in."

Chuck took another deep breath as he clutched the Crown Vic's door handle. He exhaled, threw open his door, and darted for the front porch. He rang the doorbell, knowing that a knock may draw animals—including the bear. Mrs. Henderson was quick to answer.

"Oh, thank God! You've got to get that bear! Get that bear!"

She pointed, and Chuck darted through the house until he came to the kitchen's back door. He saw the bear through the back door window, clawing at the barn. The scratch marks were visible even from the house, the white paint stripped down to bare wood. He readied his Glock and left the safety of the house for the back yard.

When Chuck later briefed authorities about his actions, when asked why he didn't take his assault rifle with him from the cruiser, he didn't have an answer. He wasn't cognitively deciding so much as instinctively acting. He'd never had to shoot a living creature before, and as much as he knew it was a possibility in his position, his first instinct was to get to the bear. It wasn't until he stood in the back yard, a huge grizzly bear charging him, that he realized his mistake.

The bear was huge and heavy, and the bulk was mostly muscle. As the bear charged, Chuck took aim with his .40 caliber Glock. He knew he'd only have time to fire twice, maybe three times. He hadn't been at the top of his class at marksmanship, but he'd passed.

Days later, Mitch Henderson told Chuck, "I saw a bullfight once when I was on vacation in Spain. Hell of a sight. But watching that bear charging you must have been the most frightening thing I've ever seen in my life. And if I was scared, watching from the loft of the barn, I can only imagine how terrifying it must have been for you."

Now, Chuck fired. The bear slowed for a second, maybe two, then proceeded at a quickened pace. Chuck fired again. The bear slowed, but kept coming. Chuck fired a third time, hitting the bear in the head. The bear collapsed on the grassy ground before him...not more than five feet away.

"Oh my God!" Mrs. Henderson screamed as she fell out of the back door, crying on her hands and knees.

"Oh, for Christ's sake," Mitch Henderson sighed from the open loft of the barn.

Chuck looked up at Mitch, then over at Mitch's wife, who cried with a combination of shock and relief. The deputy's adrenaline rush still pulsed within him. He didn't have to step toward the bear to see the crimson-red blood stain in the beast's head. The heap of brown fur and muscle was right in front of him, so close that he could feel its body heat. He lowered his Glock, still holding it with two hands. He knelt in front of the bear and began breathing rapidly, only now noticing that he dripped sweat. "You don't know how lucky we were," he said to the Hendersons. "Damn lucky."

Then he heard gunshots in the distance and he realized they weren't so lucky after all. A bloody-mouthed tiger off near the fence had been startled to his feet by the distant gunshots. Now, the tiger looked directly at Deputy Chuck Ellison.

Wired

Blake was no Luddite—he knew how to use a computer and spent more time sending emails and doing Google searches than he did writing letters or opening encyclopedias—but he still preferred paper to pixels. An old newspaper man, he preferred the feel of a printed newspaper or magazine or book in his hand to reading headlines on a computer or tablet or smartphone. Youngsters could keep their Kindles. He wanted to hold the makings of kindling in his hands.

He realized that's what his work amounted to: kindling. As an investigative reporter, his stories were printed, read, and thrown out. Seldom remembered the next day. A Pulitzer nomination one day for reporting on the Bush administration and government defense contracts being granted to companies with ties to friends without going through the proper bidding procedures...then forgotten the next year when no breaking story emerged that trumped the importance of a celebrity's breakup or reality show's shocking results.

But to Blake, it was about the process, not the result. That's why he'd rather take on a news item that lent itself to a series than a quick one-story wonder. He'd been offered beats in the past that could have catapulted to the front page. But he passed on those for stories that allowed him to delve deeper and learn more, to see a story from multiple angles. To investigate, explore, discover. Such stories seldom came along, that the general public cared about at any rate. But when they did, they were more than print on paper. Such stories evolved and lived as they were reported.

He'd just turned in a story on the art world, prompted by the surprising sale of Munch's *The Scream* for an unprecedented $119 million. He was no art expert, but he found it fascinating that a canvas with some oil splattered on it—a simple image that could easily be imitated by a high school art student with middling talent—could sell for such an extravagant amount of money. It was a story more about the concept of value than about art or money or markets—a story that asked why gold was worth its weight in gold, why diamonds were considered valuable when they really weren't that rare in their DeBeers stockpiles, why animal furs were held in high esteem when better materials were available, and why fiat currencies not tied to a gold or silver standard maintained any value at all. When it came down to it, with the exception of food, land, weapons, shelters and natural resources, nothing was intrinsically worth anything unless coated with one important element: faith.

Blake considered it an interesting concept, something he wished he could explore further. But he knew his readers—and his editor—would not ask for more. As it stood, his story would be buried in the middle of the arts section. And even when lucky enough to make the front page of the arts and entertainment section or the front page of the newspaper, these days it didn't mean what it did ten, twenty years ago. Newspapers had become little more than kindling.

But newspapers were what *he* valued.

He was about to punch out for the day, having spent twelve hours in the hustle-bustle offices of the *Cleveland Plain Dealer*, but decided to get one more cup of coffee. That's when he noticed something coming over the AP wire. It wasn't unusual to hear something come over the wire, and normally it didn't warrant a walk over to see what it was—nothing that couldn't wait until tomorrow. But he felt inclined to mosey over and check it out.

> FIVE EXOTIC ANIMALS DEAD IN OHIO—
> Chillicothe, Ohio—Officers responded to calls reporting
> wild animals on the loose in Chillicothe, Ohio (popu-
> lation 22,000), and immediately shot and killed three
> tigers, a wolf and a bear. Local authorities say the ani-
> mals escaped from a private zoo and that other exotic ani-
> mals may be on the loose. A hunt is underway for other

animals; residents are advised to remain indoors. As many
as 70 animals may have been kept at the private zoo on
the outskirts of Chillicothe and may be free. Chillicothe
is 60 miles south of Columbus, Ohio's capital.

The news was bad, but Blake couldn't help but feel an excited buzz.
Not that he wanted anything fatal to happen, but if it was going to happen, he wanted to report it. He ran to his editor's office.

"Simon, this is the kind of story I can really feel," he crowed. "Let me
cover this."

Simon glanced at the report, then up to his eager reporter. "Blake,
the story's probably over. They shot the animals. Call a few sources, do a
telephone interview or two, write it from here."

"I need to be there," Blake insisted. "This is ongoing. Dangerous animals on the loose in a city—just an hour's drive from the state capitol?"

"What about your bit on the tenth anniversary of September 11?"

"Every columnist and her sister will be writing about that," Blake
griped. "I'll hit the road tonight, be there before the sun."

"You really know how to screw a budget. All right, go. Call me when
you get something. No! Email me. I don't want you waking me up at five
in the morning."

"You got it!" Blake smirked. "I'll dig up some skinny on Chillicothe,
Columbus, the general area, then I'm on the road. This kind of story's why
newspapers still exist."

Notes on Chillicothe

Just an hour north of Portsmouth, an hour south of Columbus, Chillicothe is a beautiful area, nestled at the foothills of the Appalachian Mountains. Populated with trees like you wouldn't believe. It's God's country.

> — Mitch Henderson, Sammy Johnson's Neighbor

Chillicothe was the first *and* third capital of Ohio. Due to political infighting (politicians didn't get along any better than they do now) the capital was relocated from Chillicothe to Zanesville for just a couple years. Then it went back to Chillicothe. To avoid the constant back and forth, they agreed on a more central location—Columbus—in 1816.

> — Dr. Charles Humphries, History Professor, Ohio State University

Population of Chillicothe in 2000: 21,797
Population of Chillicothe in 2010: 21,901

> — United States Census Bureau

Chillicothe is a designated "Tree City USA."

> — National Arbor Day Foundation

Chillicothe's name comes from the Shawnee name Chalahgawtha. It means "main down," and was called so because it was a major settlement.

As we tended to do in those days, we drove the natives off and created our own settlement.

> — Dr. Charles Humphries, History Professor, Ohio State University

We're a tight-knit community. Everyone looks out for one another.

> — Bobbie Anne Thompson, Sammy Johnson's Neighbor

I can tell you this: if anyone in Chillicothe or the vicinity is in any danger whatsoever, we will do everything we can to respond swiftly and effectively.

> — Roscoe Roy, Ross County Sheriff

The First to Go

The Bear has been out of his cage before. But never unsupervised like this. Only with Master, from his cage to a fenced-in area of the field where they played. Master's friends would wrestle with Bear. Bear knew Master's wishes, had known his ways since he was a cub. Bear played with the visiting men, wrestled, but didn't hurt them. No claws or teeth. Just some pawing, knocking, growling. Play.

This is new. The cage left open and no man here. For some time, Bear remains in his cage, unsure. Then, he decides to exit, to enter the open field. He knows the way to the fenced area where men come to wrestle. No one is there.

Bear has not eaten today. What Master provided yesterday was too little. He sniffs the air and smells horseflesh. He growls, moans, and lumbers toward the fence in the distance.

The tiger's kill explains the fragrance of flesh and blood. Bear's sharp sense of smell hones him in on the target. He won't challenge the tiger for the fallen horse. But there are others in this field: horse and man. Horse will offer less challenge and more meat. Bear climbs over the split rails, in the direction of man and horse.

They head toward shelter. Bear must pick up his pace if he wants to eat. He stands for a moment, showing his full height, and growls. He breaks into a trot and hurries toward them.

The man and horse begin to run. Bear quickens his pace. The man reaches the shelter and cages himself and the horse inside. Bear tries, but his huge paws and sharp claws cannot open the wood cage. Bellowing, he begins scratching it. Keeps scratching it. Wood splinters fall. Keeps scratching.

The tiger, in the distance, roars, purrs, lying in the grass next to the remains of his meal. Bear sniffs the air and considers approaching, considers taking a bite from the fallen horse. Not wise to challenge Tiger. Better to keep scratching away wood.

A change in the air, in the smell. The opening of another door. Two other people, male and female. The scent of the woman fades. A man, out in the open air. Bear turns from the wood and shows his eyes what his nose already knows. The new man steps closer, into the grass. The man holds something in his hands, something Master sometimes holds. The thing that makes loud noise and the smell of burnt sulfur.

Near the far-off fence, Tiger looks at Bear, at the man, at its kill, then glances into the distance and yawns.

Bear sniffs the air. The man's smell has grown stronger, saltier, as he comes closer. Bear stands on his hind legs, bellows, then breaks into a gallop toward the man. Bear can see it happen before it happens: he will get there and, without slowing, will swipe at the man's neck. His paw, bigger than the man's head, will cover the face, neck, part of the chest. His claws will rip in, fasten, and stay—they will yank at the neck and kill instantly. A second swipe might be needed, might not. Bear is ready to make a meal of man.

Bear is close. The thing in the man's hands points at him and cries. The bear feels a sting in his shoulder. It startles him, slows him, but does not stop him. He lifts his paw—won't need his front right paw to hit the ground again before swiping at the man. Another sound from the man's tool, another sting, this time to his chest. It slows him. But this is not a race, and he is already upon the man. Bear pulls his paw back, claws extracting, mouth open and growling.

Another explosive sound, the strong smell of sulfur and metal, a cloud of smoke. Bear feels the impact to his head. It stuns him, stops him. He falls.

Overtime

Roscoe lounged in his home office, paying bills. He'd received mailers from two different cable companies and was considering a switch. *Why is it that cable costs me twice as much as it used to even though there isn't much of anything worth watching?* If it were up to him, he'd just get rid of it altogether, pick up some movies at the vending box, and do a little more reading. But with two kids and a wife—all with their own television needs—he knew that was a hopeless battle. He'd locked up crooks for less serious offenses than doing away with a good family's cable service.

"Dinner's in ten minutes," his wife called.

"Be right down," he called back.

His phone buzzed and chimed. That always startled him. Why didn't they just ring like they used to? He picked it up. His daughter had sent him a text. *Meatloaf for dinner. Yuk.*

Roscoe smiled. He clumsily texted back, trying to type with his thumbs, wishing he had a full keyboard. *If you pretend to like it, I will take you and Cal out for ice cream later. Tell Cal.*

A second after he sent the text and put his phone down, it buzzed and chimed again. *Who doesn't love meatloaf?*

Roscoe smiled. How did these kids text so fast? His daughter would make a great typist, if such a position still existed in the modern world. But then, most teenagers with smart phones or laptops could type and text paragraphs around him these days.

He went back to the bills. Cell phones were worse than cable. A few years back, he considered thirty dollars too much to pay for him and his wife to have cell phones. Now, with four cell phones in the family, with data plans and unlimited texting and what not, they paid close to $300 a month. No wonder middle class families struggled. The essentials that had once been luxuries were expensive.

Internet service seemed an entirely new essential. A decade ago, the internet was something they could do without at home; he had it at his office, and his wife had it at her work. Now, with two kids in school doing research projects (whoever heard of a library or a book or an encyclopedia?), they absolutely needed the internet. Even he and his wife spent more time online, when home, than they used to.

He sighed and wrote out checks for the cable and cell phone and internet bills. He waited to lick the envelopes right before dinner, so the food would wipe away the gluey taste. It wouldn't be long, he figured, before he'd be paying the bills on the internet, too. Chuck, his deputy, sang the praises of online bill pay and all the stamps he was saving. That's why the postal service seemed to be laying everyone off and was talking about closing on Saturdays. Thank God they could count on crime as something that wasn't going away. They'd always need a Sheriff.

"Dinner's ready," his wife called up again.

"Coming." He rounded up the kids, each glued to a screen (she a smart phone, he a tablet), and they all marched downstairs, into the dining room, and took their seats.

"Mmmm!" Janie said with mock enthusiasm. "Meatloaf!"

"Yippee!" Cal cheered.

Carol laughed. "You sound suspiciously pleased."

"We all love your meatloaf." Roscoe took his place at the end of the table, close to the window since he didn't mind the draft. His cell phone rang before he had a chance to lift his fork. He knew he'd better pick up when the dispatcher's name appeared on his phone. "Hello?"

"Roscoe? It's Delores. Listen, we have a situation."

"What is it?"

"The Hendersons and Thompsons have both called to report wild animals on their properties, killing their horses. Mitch Henderson's trapped in his barn. Bear and tigers. Two of Bobbie Anne's horses are dead. Chuck is on location and already asked for backup. Not sure how many animals may have escaped from Sammy Johnson's place."

"All right, I'll scoot on over there."

Roscoe stood and started away, then looked back to his family. "I got to go back in. Got to get my uniform back on."

"You haven't even had a bite," Carol called to him.

"Just keep a plate for me. I'll nuke it when I get back."

"Do we still have to eat the meatloaf?" Cal asked.

"Yes," Roscoe said, and he went upstairs to put his uniform back on— Glock and all.

It wasn't until he sat in his cruiser, headed for Rural Place Road on the eastern outskirts of town, that he realized he hadn't even taken a bite or a drink. The sticky taste of envelope glue remained on his tongue, and he couldn't smack it away. He'd get a cup of coffee to take care of it after tending to this business. Sammy Johnson was a pain in the ass to deal with, but he figured it would be a simple enough confrontation, peaceful with the exception of some choice words.

First, he turned into Bobbie Anne Thompson's place. He got there to find her son, Dexter, standing with his back pressed against his car, as though backing away from something. Roscoe parked his car in the drive next to Dexter's, then got out and stood. Only then did he notice what Dexter was staring at: a Bengal tiger. Bobbie Anne stood in the open doorway yelling, "Scat!" The noise distracted the big cat from his business. The cat's tail thrashed back and forth, as though ready to make a kill but unable to decide whether to attack the larger, closer man, or the more distant, more feeble woman.

Roscoe didn't want to wait to find out. He aimed his Glock and fired. Two shots, and the tiger fell. Dexter ran for the front door, embraced his mother, then picked her up in his bear hug and put her inside. Roscoe approached the fallen tiger, nudged it with his foot, then checked the neck for a pulse or any signs of life. Certain the tiger was dead, he looked around and darted up to the porch. Dexter was closing the door as Roscoe approached it. Roscoe pushed inside, before Dexter secured it.

"A close one," Dexter huffed. Roscoe caught the scent of urine, and noticed the spot at Dexter's crotch. No laughing matter, of course. What man wouldn't piss himself when caught, unarmed and defenseless, face to face with a giant killing machine?

"There's another tiger out back," Bobbie Anne warned. Roscoe went to the kitchen window to see. The second tiger paced next to a half-eaten horse. Roscoe weighed his options. He didn't want to kill the cat. Weren't Bengals on the endangered species list, or close to it? But what could he do? Try to catch it? Taser it?

He went back to his cruiser to get his assault rifle, then crossed back through the house and stepped out the back door. He set his scopes on the tiger and held it. Roscoe hesitated. Then, he heard another car pull into the front drive, heard the car idling, then the engine cutting off. He heard the door open, then slam shut. Another door open and shut. The tiger's ears twitched atop his head. Tigers had better hearing than humans, Roscoe realized. The tiger's tail began to thrash as it looked at him, then over to the front yard where other people undoubtedly made easy prey of themselves. That made Roscoe's decision easier. He realigned the tiger's head in his scope and shot. The big cat fell next to the horse. The buzzards overhead descended. It was then that Roscoe noticed how many of the scavengers waited patiently in the nearby trees. *Not a good sign.*

Roscoe went back inside and found Bobbie Anne and Dexter talking to two of his deputies—Toby and Tom. The backup that Chuck had called for. "Boys," Roscoe greeted them.

"That's a hell of a tiger out front," Toby said.

"There's another out back," Roscoe said.

"We just came from the Johnson place," said Tom.

"What'd Sammy have to say for himself? He'll give us hell for downing his animals, but we didn't have any choice."

"We couldn't find him," Toby informed. "We honked, got out and knocked on the door, no answer. Saw some animals still in their cages, and some of the cages were empty. But we hurried back to the car, because there were tigers and wolves roaming around."

"I shot one of the wolves," Tom said. "But at least two more went into the woods."

"Should we try Sammy's place again?" Toby asked.

"No." Roscoe thought for a moment. "We'd better get to Mitch Henderson's ranch. I think a bear's out. Chuck's there, but we'd better check on him." Roscoe turned to Bobbie Anne and Dexter. "You two stay indoors for now."

Toby sneered at Dexter. "And put yourself on a fresh pair of pants."

When the two police cruisers arrived at Mitch Henderson's place, they saw Chuck's Crown Vic still there. Roscoe went to the front door, Tom walked around to the right, Toby to the left. Roscoe knocked, rang the doorbell, pounded, and then—finding it unlocked—let himself in. He crossed directly to the back of the house, where he found Mrs. Henderson at the open back door. She screamed as Roscoe approached, startled by his presence, as though he were another wild animal making an attack. He took her in his arms and she sobbed. But only for a moment, for she quickly pointed to the back yard. "Tiger!"

Roscoe stepped into the back yard. He heard the gunshots before he saw anything. Chuck stood with his Glock in hand, but it hung down at his side, limp; the shot fired had not come from him. In front of Chuck a giant grizzly bear slumped on the ground. It had been dead for some time, flies buzzing, a buzzard circling nearby. Mitch stood ten feet out of the open barn door, two horses visible in the shadowy interior, both of them in their stalls, whinnying with worry. Tom was just coming into the yard from the right. Then, Roscoe looked to the far left where he saw Toby standing, his gun still aimed; he saw the tiger, swaying back and forth, trying to stand, finally falling over. Roscoe noticed the horse, half eaten, next to the tiger. Toby looked over at Roscoe. Roscoe could see that Toby was shaken. Truth be told, they all were.

Mitch ran away from the barn, looking back and forth as though for more animals, and made it to his wife at the back door. She cried into his chest as he hugged her.

Chuck holstered his Glock and stepped slowly toward Roscoe. Toby and Tom slowly walked toward them, looking around, cautious.

"I didn't want to kill it," Chuck confided to Roscoe. His eyes glistened as he looked at the bear. "But it was him or me."

Roscoe put an arm around his deputy, patted his back. "You did what you had to. None of us would have done any differently."

"I'm just fine," Mitch was saying to his wife. "We're all fine."

"Mitch," Roscoe called. "You two better get inside."

"You should, too," Mitch said. "Other animals may be out."

"Oh, they are," Toby assured.

"We've got to contain this." Roscoe rubbed the back of his neck. "Let's get back over to Sammy's place."

Chuck, Tom and Toby went to their two cruisers. Roscoe went back inside the house. "Mitch, keep your doors locked, but keep an eye out. Peek out the windows every few minutes, would you? Here's my cell number. You see anything, call me directly."

"Will do. And Roscoe? Tell your guys thanks."

In his Crown Vic, Roscoe heard gunshots coming from Sammy Johnson's farm before he got there. He imagined the worst: Sammy Johnson had flipped and was holed up in his house, shooting at his deputies.

But when Roscoe got there, his deputies were the ones who were firing. Right there along the private road, three fourths of the way from Rural Place Road to Sammy's house, Tom had shot a Siberian tiger and Toby had downed a mountain lion. Their carcasses lined the two sides of the drive. Roscoe rolled down his windows. "C'mon." He lifted off the brake and let the car slowly cruise toward the house, Chuck, Toby and Tom walking alongside it. When they arrived at the house, Roscoe laid heavy on his horn. He took out his megaphone. "It's the Sheriff, Sammy. Come on out now."

Of course, Sammy didn't answer. Roscoe didn't expect the stubborn bastard to make it easy. Roscoe cut his engine and got out of his car, carrying his assault rifle with him. By now, they'd all retrieved their rifles, their Glocks holstered for backup only. For the first time in his career, Roscoe believed they might be insufficiently armed. Uneasily, Roscoe took a deep breath to calm his pounding heartbeat. He adjusted his wide-brimmed hat. Then he looked ahead and focused.

They stood together on the wooden porch. "We'd better go in," Roscoe said. "Toby, you stay here and watch out. Tom, Chuck, let's go in. Tri-formation."

Chuck and Tom nodded. Roscoe kicked open the wooden door. The three men walked forward, their backs to one another, on the lookout in all directions for animals. As they entered the living room, the house filled with screeching and screaming. The sound was so disturbing that Roscoe wanted to drop his gun and put his fingers in his ears. Monkeys ran wild, hanging off the ceiling lights, bouncing on the couch, rummaging through the kitchen cupboards. A chimp lay dead on the living room floor, his innards spilled out on the rug, his genitals eaten away, a large gaping hole where the crotch belonged. "A tiger, I'd guess." Roscoe looked carefully around. "Be alert."

Over the screeching and screaming of chimps and monkeys, they heard a gunshot from outside, then another. Staying in their formation, they made their way back to the front door. But the front door had been kicked open; they had no way of sealing it. The chimps and monkeys were of little concern at the moment.

"Got another mountain lion," Toby said. "Came from the warehouse over there."

"I don't think Sammy's in the house," Roscoe said. "If he is, he's either dead or sealed away in a hidden bunker. You saw that chimp, or what was left of it. Let's go check out the warehouse."

The warehouse, about eighty feet from Sammy's home, towered twice the size. Most of Sammy's animals lived in the warehouse, and in the cages along the private road that approached his house. The cages along the drive were all empty. Either that meant they were temporarily caged in the warehouse...or they had been let out.

The warehouse doors were wide open. It was dark enough inside that they could not see in from where they stood. The four men moved from the house to the warehouse in diamond formation, back-to-back, rifles at the ready. Even before they could see, they could hear: the roaring and howling and growling and whimpering and screaming and cackling and bellowing that came from the warehouse was unnerving enough to drive them away. But they had to see for themselves. If they were lucky, these animals would still be in their cages. Dusk's cover made it impossible to tell.

"Toby, shine a light in there," Roscoe ordered. Toby relaxed his rifle and took out his flashlight. He shined it inside, and it reflected off what looked like a hundred eyes. They inched closer and closer until they could see more than the reflective eyes of big cats. They could see the cats themselves: lions, tigers, panthers, cougars, leopards. They could see wolves and bears. Hyenas laughed at them nervously. Most of the animals remained in their cages. Some of them lounged in the center of the warehouse floor, looking at the intruders inattentively, lazily. Four lions fed on a slain zebra. Two tigers pawed at prey, one at a chimp and the other at a monkey.

Off in the shadowy distance, they could make out the legs of a man. The body was concealed, tucked away in a stall and blocked by a wooden wall. Roscoe couldn't make out who it was, or whether it was even human—it could have been a scarecrow, a decoy, a chimp dressed in human clothing, anything. But chances were, it was Sammy Johnson. Most certainly dead. Protocol would be for them to go in and retrieve the body, check vitals. But to walk into that barn would be suicide. They had to find another way.

"Nice and easy," Roscoe said, "let's back away and figure this out."

Roscoe considered it a miracle that they were able to back away at all. Maybe the light startled the animals enough to hold off an immediate attack. Maybe they'd already been fed this day and weren't hungry enough to attack. Maybe the animals they'd already killed—the monkeys and apes and zebra and who knew what else—had been enough to satisfy their bloodlust for the evening, or for the moment. Or, Roscoe pondered, maybe God was watching over them, blessing them, saving them for the challenge He had planned for them this coming night. Whatever the reason, Roscoe, Toby, Tom and Chuck slowly backed away and made it to their cruisers. It wasn't until they were safely inside their cars that one of the tigers charged, denting Roscoe's metal door. They watched as the four lions moseyed out of the warehouse and into the field beyond. The lions plopped into the tall grass where they relaxed together as a family.

Roscoe thought of his own family. He thought of Cal, who was probably playing baseball with the neighborhood kids right now, not more than half a mile away. He thought of the high school and elementary school, each less than a mile away, and the after-school sports and activities that may just be letting out. He thought of the nursing home just a few streets over, the old folks reading their books and having their rocking chair conversations on the patio and porch. Roscoe spit. How was it that the taste of envelope glue remained on his tongue, but they couldn't make a chewing gum that kept its flavor more than five minutes? He got on the police radio.

"Delores, we need to get a warning out pronto. *Caution: Exotic Animals—Stay Indoors.*"

"Right away," Delores said.

"Soon as you do that, I need you to get me four people on the horn ASAP."

"Who?"

"Morris Jones, the guy Sammy had taking care of his animals. Jackson Withers of the Animal Protection Agency. Leland Anders, that TV zookeeper. And the Mayor."

"Right away. Is it that bad?"

"Worse."

Sensational Carnage

Carrie Mortimer stood in a prime location between the Siberian tiger and mountain lion. She checked her makeup (perfect) and hair (even better) and looked at Mac. "Let me know when you're rolling. We'll do two or three takes."

"All right." Mac pointed his camera. "Five, four..." he resorted to fingers, signing *three, two, one.*

Carrie

Carrie Mortimer here in Chillicothe, Ohio, on the scene of a terrible nightmare unfolding. I'm standing on the front drive of a farm owned by local resident Sammy Johnson. Johnson is just like any other American, except for one thing: he keeps exotic animals for pets. Lions, tigers and bears, to begin with. Secluded in this rural area, it is something that most people wouldn't even notice. But today, people notice—because today, these deadly animals are on the loose, stalking the residents of Chillicothe.

Carrie motioned for Mac to stop filming. "How's that for starters?"

"Looked fine." Mac gave her a thumb up. "But do you think you could give me a little more drama?" He smirked.

"Let's do the next bit, smart ass." She fluffed her hair, wet her lips, held the microphone close to her face, and proceeded.

Carrie

It's astonishing to see this beautiful mountain lion here on the side of the road, shot down in cold blood. And just yards away, on the other side of the drive, this majestic Siberian tiger, shot dead. Authorities aren't saying yet, but a person may have been killed here on the premises, as well as some other exotic animals. This terror in Ohio is not limited to a rural farm area, but may potentially reach into the city of Chillicothe and along the highways, perhaps as far off as the state capital of Columbus. All of Ohio—and the entire nation—will continue to watch as we wonder why there are animals running amuck in Chillicothe, and what sort of person would have such a dangerous arsenal of man-eating beasts to begin with.

Carrie held her microphone to her side, her arm limp. She took a deep breath. "Okay, Mac, let me do one more bit."

"Just keep monologuing, Carrie," Mac said, camera still rolling.

Carrie lifted her mic to her face once more, took a deep breath, and stared down the camera.

Carrie

What's perhaps just as disturbing as the potential peril that may come to people who are out and unaware that these wild animals are on the hunt is the carnage that has already taken place. I'm talking about the brutal massacre of these beautiful animals. Here, to my left, you can see a cougar, or mountain lion, that has been shot down and left to rot on the side of the drive. And almost immediately next to it, on the right side of the road, is another disturbing sight (you may want to shield the eyes of your children): the body of a rare Siberian tiger, shot down by local authorities.

Standing here and seeing these majestic creatures, these beautiful beasts, and to think about how they were just gunned down without any thought given to alternative ways to contain them...it's just disturbing.

But what local police are concerned about now is not the lives of these animals. They are on a mission to hunt down and mow down the rest of these animals before the beasts attack the human residents of Chillicothe and beyond.

Carrie motioned for Mac to stop filming. "That's fine for now. Get some close ups of the animals before Sheriff Taylor and Deputy Fife drive us away. Then we'll interview the neighbors and get this in the can in time for the morning broadcast."

"I'm on it." Mac filmed the animals in close up. "You think the human angle—the danger to locals—may be the better way to go?"

"Who's the reporter and who's the cameraman?" Carrie snapped. "Only the locals care about the locals. The world is going to care about these rare animals being murdered. Mark my words. Viewers are going to mourn these animals, if I have anything to do with it."

Mac was filming the body of the tiger when Carrie saw the headlights approaching in the distance. The country bumpkin Sheriff, driving toward them from the house where the police had the area blocked off. "Quick, get me next to the Siberian." She took up her microphone and kneeled next to the tiger.

Carrie

People around the world are wondering how far local authorities will go as they hunt down and murder these rare and exotic animals.

In these dark hours ahead, the question on everyone's mind is: what sort of man would collect such a menagerie of dangerous animals in the first place?

The Sheriff arrived, his gun unholstered, as though ready to use it if necessary. "I'm gonna have to ask you to leave. It's not safe here."

Carrie smirked. "You just don't want us exposing this brutality."

"Ma'am, I just don't want you to get brutally attacked. We've got to protect the people. That includes you. Where you guys from, anyway? Columbus? Cincinnati?"

"New York." Carrie showed off the label on her microphone and read it to him. "CNEN-TV."

"All the way from New York City?"

"I'm here to put Chillicothe on the map."

"You do realize we've got dangerous animals roaming around out here, don't you? You two are putting yourselves in harm's way, being out here."

"That doesn't matter," Carrie said. "This is a big story."

"Not for us, ma'am. It's a lot more than a story to us. Now get on out of here before I have to lock you up for your own safety."

What Sort of Man

Sammy always marched to his own tune. Did things his way. I'm not saying he was a lawbreaker. But he was no fan of authority.

— Mike Skaggs, Sammy Johnson's Drinking Buddy

Always shocked me how Sammy knew them all by name. He'd walk right into the cages, call them by name, and they'd come and lick his hand or let him pet them. He knew them all, and they all knew him.

— Morris Jones, Animal Caretaker

Sammy Johnson was a classic obsessive-compulsive personality type. He didn't set out to amass such a large collection, but he didn't know when to stop. He wanted to have the biggest, the best, the most. So when he collected guns, he had to have a hundred plus. When he collected cars, he had to have dozens of them rusting in his field. And when it came to his animals, he wanted to have the most powerful, most unusual animals he could get. In the end, he just got more than he could handle.

— Dr. Minnie Fields, Professor of Psychology, Shawnee State University

We used to cruise around for hours at a time scavenging road kill. When he had a few, it wasn't so bad. But with all of those animals, it became a big job to keep them all fed. Some of these cats eat twenty to thirty pounds of meat a day. So we'd drive around in his pickup and scrape dead deer, raccoons, squirrels, dogs, cats off the side of the road, toss them in the back, and throw the carcasses in the cages. Not exactly legal. But what else could we do? We had to feed the animals.

— Morris Jones, Animal Caretaker

After the first accident, we began routine inspections of the animals and the facilities. We did put down the cat that attacked the woman. But we couldn't force him to get rid of the others.

— Jackson Withers, Animal Protection Agency

My friend had her arm in the cage, trying to pet it, and the tiger snagged her. She had to get stitches. She was pretty scared. That's the main reason Sammy never went through with his plans to open a zoo or safari park, to share his animals with the world. Maybe that's why, in the end, he decided to share the world with his animals.

— Marielle Johnson, Sammy Johnson's Wife

Willie always got mad when Sammy he came home with another pet.

— Sally Johnson, Sammy Johnson's Mother

Mice, hamsters, rats, ferrets, birds, cats, dogs...

— Willie Johnson, Sammy Johnson's Father

To feel the power of love from such a massive beast is amazing. People think I'm crazy or something for having these guys. But if you love your dog or cat, you know what I'm talking about. These are my pets, my family, and I love them. There's nothing like a relationship with a big cat.

— Sammy Johnson, Interview, *The Columbus Dispatch,* 2003

...tigers, lions, cougars, panthers, leopards...

— Willie Johnson, Sammy Johnson's Father

A six-year old tiger weighs about five-hundred to six-hundred pounds. There's a reason they're called *big* cats. Even if they want to get frisky with you the way a house cat does, they can rip your head off with the playful bat of a paw.

> — Leland Anders, Celebrity Zookeeper

There's no doubt he cared more for our animals than he did for himself.

> — Marielle Johnson, Sammy Johnson's Wife

...bears, wolverines, wolves, coyotes, horses, zebras, bulls, bison...

> — Willie Johnson, Sammy Johnson's Father

His first was a tabby cat. I'm the one give it to him.

> — Emily Smith, Sammy Johnson's Grandmother, *Chillicothe Gazette*
> Interview, 1988

...snow leopards, black bears, brown bears, grizzlies, Kodiaks, foxes...

> — Willie Johnson, Sammy Johnson's Father

He was a good guy. I think animals helped him cope with hard times. Considering his experiences in Nam, he did pretty well, if you ask me. But some things you just can't control. He was at the end of his rope.

> — Mike Skaggs, Sammy Johnson's Drinking Buddy

The guy was unstable. A danger to the community. I mean, how many times do your tigers and lions need to get free and attack other people's animals before you realize you're in over your head? Two? Three?

> — Mitch Henderson, Sammy Johnson's Neighbor

A bad man? No, not exactly. He wasn't trying to hurt people or create trouble. But he wasn't a pleasant man to deal with.

— Roscoe Roy, Ross County Sheriff

I can't imagine what he was thinking. He had to know that setting them free would be signing their death sentence. I just don't know.

— Sally Johnson, Sammy Johnson's Mother

The man was full of love. I can tell you that. He was just a big teddy bear, full of affection.

— Marielle Johnson, Sammy Johnson's Wife

What kind of man was Sammy Johnson? I don't much know and I don't much care. I know what he caused. And based on that, Sammy Johnson was a selfish ass.

— Chuck Ellison, Deputy, Ross County Sheriff's Department

Cages

Deputy Chuck Ellison could still see the bear's startled expression, could almost feel the impact as the bear fell—dead—in front of him. And his heart ached for the tiger and mountain lion he'd shot down. But he had a feeling he was going to need to get used to such unpleasantness. As he waited for backup, along with Sheriff Roscoe and Deputies Tom and Toby, as they watched the lions in the field for any sudden movement and kept watch over the warehouse to make sure additional animals didn't escape, he knew they were in for a long night.

A cheetah began to step out of the warehouse. Chuck fired and struck the ground just in front of it. The cheetah darted back inside.

"Morris Jones is on his way," Roscoe said. "Can't reach Leland Anders yet. Jackson Withers is in Cincinnati, so he'll be two hours or more. Mayor's been informed, but hopefully he'll just leave us alone to do our jobs."

The four of them had parked their three Crown Vics bumper to bumper, creating a sort of semicircle barrier between themselves and the warehouse full of animals. Off to the side, they could still see the lions in the tall grass, rolling around, nudging against one another, could almost hear them purring like giant house cats. The men had their Glocks holstered at their sides and their assault rifles in hand.

"Why don't we call some local vets to come out with some tranqs?" Chuck asked.

"Delores already has," Roscoe said. "What veterinarian wants to come out here and risk life and limb to face off with tigers and lions and bears?"

"One with kids playing outside," Chuck shot back. "Or one that might give a damn about animals."

"Just stay calm," Roscoe said easily. "Way I see it, we don't have much choice at the moment. It'll be dark in another hour. We can't let any more animals loose. We're going to have to lock them up if we can. And if we can't, we'll have to put them down."

Chuck looked into the shadows of the open warehouse. "And what did Jackson Withers have to say about that?"

Roscoe huffed. "He's coming with tranquilizers. But even he said we may not be able to use them. You put a pride of lions in an open field and try to tranq them, it could be ten minutes before the medicine knocks them out. Lions can do a lot of damage in ten pissed-off minutes."

Chuck sighed heavily. "Guess so."

Tom spit between his teeth. "I'm more worried about *us* getting killed than the animals."

Toby laughed. "Hell, they got the claws and teeth, but we got the guns and ammo."

"We've got to think about all the nearby civilians," Roscoe said. "We can't let these animals off this farm."

The men stood there behind their wall of metal and motor, watching the warehouse and field. Then, a police cruiser and ambulance arrived within minutes of one another. The medics rushed from the ambulance to where the four policemen were gathered behind the barricade.

"Where's the body?" a young medic asked.

"You'd better just wait in your van," Roscoe instructed. "You can't get to it right now." He motioned with his head toward the warehouse. The roars and growls and moans of wild animals emanated from it. "We've got to clear it out before you go in. Or we'll be calling another ambulance to get you."

"I see." The medic flushed. "We'll wait in the ambulance. Let us know when we can do our jobs."

By the time the medics had returned to their ambulance, the two newly arrived police officers—Mickey Ketchum and Cybil Jackson—had reached them.

"Evening," Ketchum greeted.

"Is this the party?" Cybil asked.

Roscoe nodded.

"What've we got?" Ketchum asked.

"We've got to secure that warehouse," Roscoe ordered. He briefed the new arrivals. "This could get ugly. We don't want to kill them unless we have to. Our best-case scenario is to go in, rifles at the ready, and latch all of the gates to their cages. For the ones that are still in their cages, at least."

"Looked like more than half of them were still caged, when we were up close," Chuck said. "About twenty minutes ago."

"The rest," Roscoe continued, "we ought to try to lure back into their cages and close them up. If we can't, we shoot them."

"Sheriff?" Cybil asked. "How do you persuade a half ton of bear into a cage?"

Roscoe sighed. "Like I said, we may have to shoot them."

"How many are there?" Ketchum asked, bobbing and swaying his head and examining the shadowy darkness of the warehouse interior. Ketchum was the most experienced person here for a job like this, and Chuck appreciated this fact, in spite of the guy's arrogance. Ketchum had been a sharpshooter in the Marines. Then, when he got out and returned home after twenty years of service, he joined the local police force. He was the best sharpshooter they had. The best at squeezing in and out of a tight place and getting a tough job done. Chuck liked Roscoe and would follow his Sheriff anywhere. But he and his boss both knew that Ketchum was the tactical expert here now.

"We didn't get an accurate count," Roscoe said. "We shined a light in, saw at least a couple dozen animals loose, and backed away. It's a danger zone in there."

"Morris estimated about fifty in the warehouse," Tom said. "That's if all the animals were still in there, which we know they're not."

Ketchum adjusted the bulge in his lower lip, then spat out a brown liquid. "That means we're looking at a good twenty or more that are loose in the warehouse, a good thirty or so that need to be locked up?"

Roscoe rubbed his neck. "That's about the look of it."

Ketchum squinted and peered into the warehouse's darkness, looking a bit animalistic himself. "If we have any hope of caging the ones still in, we've got to start by shooting the ones that are out. Before we even go inside. Aim from outside."

"I don't like that," Roscoe said. "I hear where you're coming from. But some of these animals might be endangered species. Rare tigers. We don't want to kill them if we can avoid it."

"It may be a choice between endangered species and endangering people," Ketchum said.

Roscoe nodded. "And if it comes to that, no question. We'll put them down. But now that we have some people and some gun power, let's go in there and see what we can do. They may be easier to control than we think. They *have* been living as pets all their lives. They could be docile."

"Wouldn't count on it," Ketchum said. "But we'll try it your way first."

"Good," Roscoe said. "But no question about it: you feel like you're in danger, or any of us are in danger, you don't give it a second thought. Shoot to kill."

"No doubt," Ketchum said.

"But no need for us to get trigger happy," Chuck threw in.

"We've got company." Toby pointed back toward the private drive. "We may want to get rid of Lois Lane before starting the war."

"Good idea," Roscoe said. "I'll be back in a few. Get yourselves ready for action."

Dealing with the press could prove as unpleasant as dealing with wild animals, Chuck figured as he watched Roscoe drive away the pair. He'd already driven off Amy Shivers from the local news; Amy was next door with Bobbie Anne Thompson now, and that may not have been the best place for her to go. The man and woman in the drive now, between two dead animals, were not locals—they appeared to be from the city—and that meant more scrutiny when it came to the tough decisions the Sheriff would have to make regarding the animals. Chuck was glad Roscoe was taking care of the press. Chuck was nervous enough trying to handle the animals.

On the way back from driving off the press, Roscoe stopped by the ambulance. As Roscoe walked back to their barricade of cruisers, the ambulance pulled closer in and aimed its bright headlights into the open doors of the warehouse. The eyes of big cats reflected back and large shadows spilled onto the ground and walls behind them.

The six officers walked in v-formation, Roscoe in the lead with Ketchum beside him, the others fanned out beside and behind them.

"Morris mentioned that Sammy used to feed them in their cages every evening." Roscoe's calm voice was almost a whisper. "Even the ones he let out. He'd yell 'dinner, dinner, dinner,' and they'd go in their cages and eat. When we get in there, if we try cooing that, maybe they'll go back in their cages."

Ketchum nodded, but Chuck could see even from behind that the sharpshooter didn't buy it.

Once they were inside the warehouse, lighted by headlights, they could better assess the specifics of their situation. A dozen animals remained in their cages. A dozen others were loose, in plain sight. That meant about two dozen here—fewer than anticipated.

"Oh, shit." Roscoe pointed. "A back door. And it's open, too."

Tom sighed. "They've been getting out the whole time we've been standing guard."

"Let's deal with what we've got here now," Ketchum said.

Cold sweat broke out on Chuck's face. "But the civilians, the kids outside—"

"We have alerts out everywhere," Roscoe reminded. "Nothing more we can do out there now."

"We're here, now." Ketchum looked at Roscoe, then Chuck. "Stay focused."

They eased in, their assault rifles aimed and ready to fire. Roscoe began calling, "Dinner, dinner, dinner." The bobcat and panther got back in their cages, then a cheetah. Five lions, seven tigers, and a bear were already in their cages when they walked in. The hyenas must have fled out the back door, along with the wolves. Three lions were feeding on their zebra, paying the intruders little attention.

"Easy, everyone keep aim on the animals," Roscoe whispered. "Let's move into the room and get to the cages."

Keeping their formation, aiming at the animals, they did as the Sheriff instructed. Chuck closed and latched a cage with two leopards in it. The company inched deeper into the warehouse. Toby closed the cage to the panthers. In deeper. Cybil closed the cage to the bear. Deeper. By now they were halfway into the large room, at its center, between walls of cages. The lions, in the middle of the floor, looked up from their zebra, their mouths stained with blood. These lions could attack at any moment. Or they could be shot dead.

Further into the warehouse, the stall doors were open—stalls that undoubtedly held the zebra and some horses at one point. A man's legs, covered in blue jeans, leaked from the far stall. From here, in the dark, they still couldn't tell whether they were really human, or perhaps a straw scarecrow or dummy. A decoy.

Sweat trickled down Chuck's face. His palms sweated, and he worried that his rifle would not aim true. But they were halfway in, and he had more hope now than he did when they'd entered. He hoped they might not have to use their guns at all.

In deeper, he shut the cage of a cheetah, then a wolverine, then a few cages of tigers: Bengal, Siberian, white. He shut them, one by one. The lions, in the middle of the floor, licked their mouths, as though considering dessert.

It wasn't until Toby was closing and latching the last cage that Chuck noticed the green-handled bolt cutters on the ground near the blue-jeaned legs. At virtually the same moment, someone else noticed something, too.

"Guys," Cybil called. "The doors aren't any good. The sides of the cages have been cut open!"

Their company emitted a nervous energy. If Chuck could sense it, he knew the animals could smell it, too. Chuck wanted out of that room fast. They all did.

"Stay calm." Ketchum barely sounded calm himself. "Everyone just stay calm. Let's ease on back out of here. Just the way we came in. Nice and easy."

The caged animals began coming back out of their cages.

"Keep your aim, but stay calm," Ketchum said.

A leopard—they hadn't even noticed it—fell from the rafters above and landed right on Cybil's back, taking her down to the ground. Immediately, the leopard went for her neck, clamping down on her windpipe. Toby fired at the leopard and shot it in the head. Whether Cybil had been killed by the leopard or not, they never found out, because a tiger took over where the fallen leopard had stopped. The tiger dug his claws into Cybil's leg and pulled her across the floor. Tom shot the tiger, and it slumped over Cybil's lifeless body.

That's when all hell broke loose and all of them fired their weapons, and animals started jumping and attacking and falling, and nobody knew whether anybody would get out alive.

Last Leap

The Leopard is a climber. Stuck in a cage most of the time, it's easy to forget skills and techniques. But set free, instinct takes over. She is out of practice but still knows her claws. She can scale a tree or the beam of a barn or warehouse as easily as she can pace a dirt floor or sever a carotid with a swipe at the neck.

She is not sure why she has been cut free, but she's free. Would she choose freedom over captivity? Perhaps. But she knows her cage, feels secure within it, and is uncertain about the outside. So she takes her time. She begins by placing her head out of the cut-open wire. Then her front paw, out and back in. Then both front paws, out and in. She paces inside her cage as she considers her next move.

Lights intrude, shining in. She stays put and watches to see what will happen next. Some men stand outside, looking in. They retreat as quickly and calmly as they approached. The lights fade. The men, now barricaded behind metal on rubber.

Hunger eventually drives Leopard out of her cage. Hunger and curiosity. Master is off limits. The lions dominate the dirt floor of the warehouse. The zebra is spoken for. Monkeys and chimps swing to and fro, but Leopard isn't keen on chasing them around the rafters, at least not yet. She senses something about to happen, hears the sounds of man's noise, organic and mechanical. Flashing lights appear. A large vehicle in the far-off distance, a woman talking into a stick in front of a man with a large box on his shoulder. Many strange goings on. Leopard is hungry, but content to wait and see what is about to transpire.

She climbs a beam and finds a comfortable place in the rafters. She knows if she makes a kill it will be easy for her to drag it up here, up the beam, or up a tree if she decides to drag her kill outside. She will kill. She must kill. Hunger dictates.

She can smell them and hear them before she can see them. A pride of people, five men, one woman, slowly ambling into the warehouse. They move forward and backward, forward and over, like a large beast, eyes all around it. They begin closing the cages. But only the doors that close. This beast of many faces does not notice the openings on the backs and sides of the cages that Master has made for them. This beast with many eyes appears blinded by fear and uncertainty.

To take a single one of them will be easy. She calculates the ease of killing one and then dragging the carcass up the beam before one of the remainders can attack her. Many other animals roam about, her brothers and sisters, those she considers kin, those she considers enemies, those she doesn't consider at all. Will they attack, too, if she strikes first? Will they distract the many while she hauls the one up to safety where she can feed on fresh flesh?

The humans are deep inside the warehouse now. She can smell their sweat, a trickle of urine. She smells the fear as distinctly as the moist hands on gunmetal. The female will be the lightest, the easiest to carry up to the rafters. The female has endurance and skill and cognitive power, yes. But less mass to contend with makes her the obvious choice.

Leopard takes another look at Master in the corner, at the lions protecting their zebra, the bear scratching his back on the intact side of his cage, the tiger roaring in his cage. Leopard looks once more at the people, then hones in on the female.

Leopard leaps from the rafters and hits her mark.

The Half of It

Morris Jones already had a headache when the call came. He seldom got headaches—maybe once or twice a year—but when he got them, they were whoppers. And they always seemed to come at exactly the wrong moments, as though precursors to bad news. Animals could sense changes in the weather and atmosphere. Dogs had almost a sixth sense when it came to directions, had been known to walk home across nations. Was it so hard to believe that he, Morris Jones, could somehow sense when something bad was about to happen? Headaches always seemed a sign of bigger headaches to come.

When his cell phone rang about twenty minutes into his headache, he already anticipated a bad-news call. Could it be his mother? She'd been sick with the cancer for more than a year now. Was it his ex with bad news about one of the kids—trouble at school or something? Or his girlfriend of three years, ready to dump him? Maybe Sammy felt the need to chew him out for not cleaning the cages this week. It could have been anything, really. Apprehensively, Morris picked up. "Y'ellow?"

"Mr. Jones? This is Delores down at the Sheriff's office."

"Yeah?" The possibilities raced through his mind.

"Roscoe wants you down at Sammy Johnson's farm. Some animals escaped and he needs your help."

"Oh." Morris sighed relief. "No problem. I'll be over in a few."

"Right away," Delores pushed. "They need you."

So it isn't a big deal after all, he remembered thinking at that moment. And he remembered wondering: *why the headache?* Had whatever powers that usually brought on the throbbing pain before troubled times gotten confused by a call that came from the authorities? He slipped on his overalls and boots, threw on his cap, grabbed a shotgun and headed out to his pickup truck. *No big deal at all.*

His headache was pounding when he arrived on Rural Place Road. It was nearly ten to six, leaning on twilight. As he passed the Thompson place, he could see news vans parked outside and floodlights, like umbrellas, cast over well-dressed reporters. When he got to Sammy's place and turned into the drive, he sensed the panic, the uncertainty. He saw the flashing lights of ambulances and police cruisers. In the headlights, he could see a gurney being carried from a cluster of people over to the ambulance.

The scene was so lit up that he almost didn't notice the tiger and mountain lion sprawled out on each side of the drive. Other fallen animals decorated the distance, where the policemen were fidgeting with their pointed rifles, huddled behind a barricade of Crown Vics, focused on the open doors of the warehouse in front of them.

On the way here, Morris had thought about stopping by the corner store for some aspirin. But he knew they wanted him in a hurry and figured the headache would pass. As he came up the drive and toward the mayhem, his headache grew even worse and showed no signs of subsiding.

Then it hit Morris like a six-hundred-pound gorilla: the cages that lined the drive were all empty. That must have been why Delores had asked how many animals Sammy owned.

Morris pulled up to the collection of vehicles. He cut his engine but left his headlights on; that seemed to be the protocol here. He grabbed the shotgun from his passenger seat and jumped out. He approached the Sheriff and his men. "What in Sam Hill is going on here?"

"I was planning to ask you the same thing, Morris," Roscoe said. Roscoe and Ketchum and Chuck appeared unscathed. But others were being treated for wounds—scratches and bites, from the looks of it. "We've got a slew of animals loose in there."

"We ought to get them back in their cages," Morris suggested. "If we could get some fresh meat in the cages, that'd lure them back in."

"The cages are cut open," Chuck told him.

"That's what got us into this mess," Roscoe snapped. "We shut them in, they came out the other end."

"Who the hell would've done that?" Morris glared at Roscoe. "Where's Sammy?"

"We've got a body in there." Roscoe jerked his head toward the warehouse. "We think it may be him."

"Sammy's smarter than that," Morris said. "When it comes to his animals, anyhow. I'll bet he's holed up in the house."

Roscoe shook his head. "We were in there and didn't find him."

"Maybe he didn't want you to find him." Morris rubbed his temple. "He does have his hiding places, you know."

Roscoe looked at Chuck and Ketchum.

Ketchum spit out a brown stream. "I'll go with him."

"All right," Roscoe said. "Morris, we've been in there once already. Animals everywhere. Mostly monkeys, but possibly some big cats, too. See if you can find Sammy, then get back here."

"What, have I been deputized?" Morris asked. "Do I get a salary?"

"You get to avoid the additional loss of human life." Roscoe frowned. "Now get!"

Morris led the way, but he did so with Ketchum in front of him. That is, once they were in the house, Morris told Ketchum where they should go, which rooms to check out, which closets Sammy used for hiding. But Ketchum, known for his swift marksmanship, stood between Morris and any animals they came upon. Monkeys and chimps screeched loudly around them. Morris took Ketchum to the basement and shined a flashlight in the crawlspace, revealing a stockpile of weapons and rations. Behind what looked like a utility closet, another secret room was fully stocked with ammo, perishables, and a bar.

"I could use me one of them when this blows over," Morris joked, tilting his head toward the booze.

"Focus," Ketchum said. "We've already got one officer down."

Morris stiffened. "That's just nature. It's what they do." He led Ketchum back up to the ground floor. Morris winced at the sound of screaming monkeys. He tried to pet one, tried to calm it with a hushed voice. The little monkey bit his finger, drawing a pinpoint of blood. Morris hissed, put his finger to his mouth and sucked it.

Ketchum scoffed. "A baby chimp?"

Morris waved his injured finger. "Shows what you know about animals. Put you in the ring, unarmed, with a chimp, he'll chew you up."

"That's why we're armed."

Morris shook his head. He looked around the living room. "I guess Sammy's not here."

Ketchum fished the wad of tobacco from his lip and flung it to the floor. "That's one screwed up shithead."

"Sammy marches to his own tune," Morris said. "But let's get the facts straight before we jump to conclusions. We don't know what's going on yet." The two men cautiously exited the house and made their way back to the barricade of vehicles.

Ketchum approached Roscoe. "Nothing."

"Just got off with Delores," Roscoe briefed them. "Still can't get ahold of Leland Anders. We think he's in Columbus. Jackson Withers, from the Animal Protection Agency, is en route now, should be here soon. Delores has contacted a good two dozen vets, Chillicothe to Columbus to Portsmouth, and none of them are equipped to deal with this. I'm afraid we don't have much choice. We tried caging the animals and just can't do it. We've got to take them down before they take down people."

Morris released a heavy sigh. "Can't we hold them in, until Jackson or Leland or an expert gets here?" He couldn't bear the thought of all these pets being murdered.

Roscoe shook his head sympathetically. "Look, Morris, I don't want to kill these animals any more than you do. But we're out of options. The back door's off and they're drifting out as we speak. We just went in not thirty minutes ago and got our asses kicked. I'm not sending anyone back in there again without a shoot-to-kill order."

Morris couldn't vilify the authorities. On the way here, he'd passed a teenaged couple holding hands by the pond, had waved at farmers in their fields. Of course, human life had to be put first. But after years of working with these animals, helping Sammy take care of them, feeding them day in and day out, cleaning their cages and petting them and talking with them and coming to know them as loveable pets, he just couldn't bring himself to shoot them. He wished Sammy were here to take care of everything. Or even those pains in the ass, Leland Anders and Jackson Withers.

Morris held his place behind the police cruisers as Roscoe and Ketchum led the others—Chuck, Toby and Tom—back to the front of the warehouse. Morris hadn't been here, but he could envision what must have happened last time. He understood the truth of the matter: what had killed the officer was Roscoe's very choice not to shoot unless attacked. After that first attack, after the first gunshots, the animals must have gone ape shit.

This time, regrettably but necessarily, it would go easier, Morris figured. They'd start shooting with their assault rifles before they even got to the doorway. Except for the few that had gotten out the back, they'd be able to down the whole lot of animals in a matter of minutes.

Morris wanted to close his eyes as he listened to Roscoe and his deputies opening fire. But he kept his eyes opened because he didn't want to be caught off guard when a leopard or lion jumped over the heads of the officers and landed in front of him—or on top of him. Growls and roars and screeches and moans filled the air, accented by gunshot after gunshot. His splitting headache thumped and he feared a vessel in his forehead may burst.

Sure enough, a mountain lion made it through, leapt, and came to stand between Toby's back and Morris's front. Toby had other beasts to contend with in front of him and continued aiming into the warehouse. The cougar paced the ground, looking at Morris, flicking its tail, then looking at the back of Toby and the rampaging men. The cougar saw easy targets and crouched down, preparing to pounce. Morris knew what he had to do. He aimed his shotgun and fired. The cat turned to him and charged. Behind the vehicle, Morris discharged the casings and reloaded. The mountain lion came slowly his way, already weakened by the buck-shot. Morris aimed and shot again. The cat fell.

Moments later, the gunfire ceased. Morris dropped his heavy weapon to the dusty ground and looked at the men, who seemed to have been reduced to animals themselves. Roscoe breathed dust deep into his lungs and coughed it back out. Chuck stared numbly at the carnage before them and panted. Ketchum stretched his neck one way, then another, and let out a heavy sigh. Staring blankly at the carcasses, Toby took off his hat and wiped sweat from his brow. Tom stepped to the side of the warehouse and threw up. They all looked as dazed as Morris felt.

"It's done." Roscoe released a heavy breath.

"Don't forget the pride of lions out there," Ketchum said. Morris looked in the direction Ketchum pointed and saw them there—four or five—in the tall grass, still within the parameters of the split-rail fence.

"And we've got two or three wolves out there," Toby reminded.

Morris didn't want to, but he stepped inside the barn to bear witness. Lions, tigers, cougars, bears, panthers, cheetahs, leopards, chimps, hyenas...all dead, their corpses carpeting the dusty dirt floor. Morris wanted to cry.

Roscoe pointed. "There's the body."

Morris saw the legs coming from the zebra stall, brown boots and blue jeans. He recognized them as Sammy's.

As Roscoe walked toward the stall, a roar erupted from it. Out came an orange tiger with broad black stripes. Its mouth drenched red with blood, the tiger snarled at the men. Sniffing the air, it seemed to take in the dead animals all around it and understood his own life was endangered. The tiger bolted. Roscoe aimed and fired, but missed. By the time Ketchum had his rifle aimed, the tiger had managed to escape out the back and was out of view. Ketchum ran to the open door, took aim, but didn't bother firing.

"Out of range," Ketchum said. Roscoe sighed.

Gingerly, Morris walked toward the stall, careful to avoid any other animals that might be lying in wait. "Yep," he confirmed. "It's Sammy, all right." It looked like his old boss, but at the same time, it didn't. His genitals were gone, a huge gap of blood and flesh where his groin should have been. His belly ripped open, his intestines oozing out the side. His forehead and scalp were gone, the skull cracked open, puncture marks from the tiger's teeth all over his face and head and neck and shoulders. Claw marks had shredded his arms and chest and legs, the clothing and the flesh, where the tiger had dragged the body from wherever it had been to the seclusion of this stall. Not far from the body were a gun and bolt cutters. These details confused Morris.

"I guess we'd better get to those lions." Roscoe stared out into the field. "Let's pile up in the back of Morris's pickup and drive out. Safer, shooting from the bed of the truck. Morris, you fit to drive?"

"Huh? Oh, I guess."

Roscoe put an arm on Morris's back. "I know it ain't easy. But we've got to. We don't have a choice."

Morris continued staring at the animals in the warehouse. He counted, then counted again. He looked up at the Sheriff. "Where's the rest of them?"

"The rest? There must be thirty animals down."

"Thirty?" Morris wanted to laugh it off but didn't have the capacity to laugh right now. "Did you see how many cages are in here? Did you see those empty cages along the drive? Where are the rest of the animals?"

Ketchum approached them in the center of the barn, Sammy's mutilated body staring up at them with empty eye sockets. "You mean there's more of them out there?"

"More?" Morris slumped over at the sight of the animals around him. But the animals that were *not* dead on the ground troubled him even more. "You don't know the half of it."

Leaks

Authorities have confirmed two dead, one of them a police officer.
As many as thirty exotic animals may be on the loose in and around
Chillicothe. These large cats are nocturnal hunters. Please heed
the warning to stay indoors as local authorities work to restore safe
conditions. Stay tuned for more details as they become available.

— Amy Shivers, Chillicothe Evening News

Sammy Johnson had a long history of trouble with the law, not always
leading to conviction, but often leading to warnings that should have
tipped off authorities to the possibility of a tragedy.

— Article Excerpt, Blake Hartle, *Cleveland Plain Dealer*

It's terrible. It breaks my heart to see so many wonderful animals—some
of them rare and endangered—gunned down like this.

— Leland Anders, Celebrity Zookeeper

We'd already lost one officer when we made the decision to euthanize the
animals. What we need to focus on now isn't the dead animals—it's the
living ones, still out there.

— Roscoe Roy, Ross County Sheriff

Further indication that local authorities aren't handling the treatment
of these animals ethically is their banishment of free press. Ross County
Sheriff Roscoe Roy threatened to have reporters arrested and imprisoned.

This blatant violation of first amendment rights is sure to bring the Sheriff and his department under even more scrutiny.

— Carrie Mortimer, CNEN-TV

Our first goal is the protection of people. We don't restrict the press or withhold any information. We've got nothing to hide. We just wanted to save *their* hides.

— Chuck Ellison, Deputy, Ross County Sheriff's Department

Don't kill my babies! Don't kill my babies.

— Marielle Johnson, Sammy Johnson's Wife

We fully support our Sheriff's office and know they are doing all they can to protect our fine citizens. It is with a heavy heart that we kill anything. But we may need to put down another animal before we let an animal put down another human being.

— Mark Vernon, Mayor of Chillicothe

Well, yes, I guess if it comes down to the life of a person versus the life of an endangered species, we have to put human life first. Surely, there had to be another way.

— Leland Anders, Celebrity Zookeeper

Another way? If there was another way, I wish he'd told us about it. We didn't want to put down the animals. But it was us or them. People or predators. We're open to ideas, because we're out of them.

— Roscoe Roy, Ross County Sheriff

Sammy had a mean streak in him. I mean, he didn't go looking for trouble. But if he felt like he was backed into a corner, he could lash out.

— Mike Skaggs, Sammy Johnson's Drinking Buddy

As someone who loves animals, someone who has spent his entire life trying to protect them and gain support for understanding them and preserving them, this is a terrible day. But I can't criticize what they did. We have to look forward.

— Jackson Withers, Animal Protection Agency

Ohio needs stronger animal laws to prevent something like this from happening again.

— PETA

You have to show them love. Give love, and you'll get love back. Show them hate, and they'll hate you. Animals are like people, only more pure. They'll show you what they're really feeling. They don't hold back.

— Sammy Johnson, Interview, *The Columbus Dispatch,* 2004

Nothing like this has ever happened before. It's like Noah's Ark just shipwrecked in the middle of America.

— Leland Anders, Celebrity Zookeeper

Tranquilizer

Jackson Withers wasn't prepared for what he found when he got to Sammy Johnson's animal preserve. Flashing lights pulsed from police cruisers and ambulances. As he idled up the drive, he saw the bloodied and mutilated animal carcasses sprawled out on the ground. A tiger. A bear. A mountain lion. Then he got to Sammy's giant warehouse of a barn. When he stepped in, he was astonished.

Nearly thirty animals—Bengals, Siberians, bears, panthers, cougars, leopards—had been gunned down. Sammy Johnson's body was here, too, half eaten away—by a tiger, from the looks of it. If it had been one or two animals, that could easily have been chalked up to self-defense. But this looked more like mass murder. Brass shell casings, scattered across the ground like chicken feed, were the only items in greater supply than animal corpses.

As he stood in the barn with his head hung, Jackson heard gunshots and jumped. He heard the revving motor of a truck in the field. Lots of shooting. He could even make out the sound of shell casings hitting metal, of lions roaring, monkeys screeching from an enclosed area.

Jackson ran outside to see the truck in the distance, five men in the back, firing away as though at war. But these weren't redneck hunters. Jackson knew these people. Sheriff Roscoe Roy and his men.

Jackson had visited Sammy Johnson's preserve before, had put in formal requests to have this makeshift zoo shut down and to have the animals shipped to approved rescue shelters and preserves like the one he ran. But the Sheriff always shrugged it off. "I wish I could, but my hands are tied. The law is the law and rights are rights." And the Sheriff was right. Sammy hadn't broken any laws, and he had the legal right to his animals.

Now, the animals were paying the price.

The gunfire ceased and the truck plowed back to the barricade of police cruisers behind which Jackson now stood. Jackson waved his hands, calling out, "Whoa, whoa, whoa," lest they mistake him for an animal and open fire. Jackson hadn't been to war and he hadn't been in any sort of battles, but he had read enough to know that when men got themselves worked up in a situation like this, they could get a little trigger happy. He didn't want to be counted among the casualties tonight. He hoped to prevent more casualties.

"It's about time," Roscoe called down from the back of the pickup.

"What in God's name are you all doing? Can't we go about this humanely?"

"That would be great." Roscoe jumped from the back of the truck. The others slid out, and Morris came from inside the cab. The men huddled together between the headlights. Roscoe shook hands with Jackson. "Wish we could."

"Maybe we should move out of the light," Chuck suggested.

"Doesn't make any difference, really," Jackson said. "Cats see better at night than in the day. We're the only ones who wouldn't be able to see."

Ketchum spit. "We're really up shit creek without a paddle, ain't we?"

"How many animals are we talking about, and where are they?" Jackson asked.

Morris massaged his temple with thumb and forefinger, as though this helped him think. "Unless a few are dead and unaccounted for, we're figuring on about twenty-two animals still roaming, not including the chimps and monkeys."

"What types of animals are we looking at?" Jackson asked.

"Six lions."

"Same pride?"

"Yes," Morris said. "They'll be traveling together. Then there's two Bengal tigers."

"Are they a pride?" Roscoe asked.

Jackson and Morris looked at each other and smirked.

"No," Morris said. "Tigers are solitary creatures. Most of the animals we're dealing with are loners. But lions hunt in prides, as a team. That may make them the most dangerous."

"True, because of their number," Jackson admitted. "But tigers are arguably more dangerous as individuals. They're stronger cats."

"Don't matter what's more dangerous," Toby said. "Any of them could kill easily enough."

"True." Jackson looked at Toby's assault rifle. "Just like people."

Morris continued. "One Siberian tiger. Two bears—a grizzly and a Kodiak."

"I downed a grizzly," Chuck reminded.

"I'm not counting the ones already killed," Morris said. "So that's two bears, two leopards, three mountain lions. Then we've got three wolves, two or three coyotes, a bobcat, a Komodo dragon..."

"What's that, a lizard?" Ketchum asked.

"Biggest lizard you've ever seen," Jackson said. "It can drop a water buffalo in the wild. It could drop one of us."

"Let's see," Morris continued, "I already got the bobcat..." He scratched his head. "Oh, yeah, and the ligress."

Jackson shook his head. "Leave it to Sammy to not be satisfied with normal tigers and lions."

Ketchum squinted. "What're we talking about?"

Morris smiled, as though proud. "We crossed a tiger with a lion."

"That don't sound right." Tom stared at the ground as though trying to picture the animal there.

Morris chuckled. "It's just a giant sweetheart."

Roscoe looked at the men. "We've got our suspects."

Ketchum cracked a smile. "Not the *usual* suspects."

Roscoe scoffed, then addressed Jackson directly. "Think we should go into the woods to look for them, or just patrol the rim?"

"I don't know anyone who's ever had to go on a hunt like this one," Jackson began. "But I'd say our best bet is to cruise the perimeters of the woods abutting the property here, to begin with. After once or twice around, we keep a couple guys patrolling while the rest of us go in."

Roscoe nodded thoughtfully. "Sounds like a plan."

Jackson said, "And when we spot something, if it's not attacking anyone, we wait and watch. I have my case of tranquilizer darts. If we can bring one in alive, that's what we want to do."

"Agreed," Roscoe said. "You don't have a police radio, do you?"

Jackson shook his head. "No."

"You ride with me. Everyone, let's spread out and cover this area."

•

Roscoe briefed Jackson on all that had transpired over the past couple of hours. The two men seldom made eye contact, Roscoe alternating from looking at the road ahead and the trees beside them; Jackson keeping his attention on the horizon and the ground, looking for tracks or the animals that made them. As Jackson listened to Roscoe's account of the evening, he came to better understand it.

"The press is already having a field day with this." Roscoe sighed.

"I know." Jackson nodded. He understood the unfortunate situation. But he still didn't like what was going down.

Roscoe peeked out his side window, then back at the road ahead. "It looks bad when you only see the surface. It's kind of like a politician trying to explain how much worse things would be if the other guy won. It may be true, it may not, but there's no convincing people. They only see what it looks like on the surface, without the defining details."

"We should be more worried about saving people and these animals, if we can," Jackson said. "In hindsight, maybe it would have been a good idea for you to stockpile tranquilizers at the station. It's not like it never occurred to anyone that this could happen. Especially with Sammy's history."

"We always figured between you, Leland Anders, and the local zoos and preserves, we were covered. But we couldn't get anyone here on the double."

"I'm here now."

Roscoe nodded and smiled.

The sun had set behind the distant trees, but twilight still offered some light. After about ten minutes of driving, Jackson spotted something. "Stop." Roscoe did, and Jackson jumped out to look. On the side of the road, in a puddle of mud, he found a clear mark. "Tiger track." he pointed.

"Better get your darts ready," Roscoe said. Then he got on the radio and called for backup. Roscoe readied his assault rifle and stepped out of the car. Jackson loaded the appropriate dart—different sizes for different-sized animals—and put a few spares in a small case, which he jammed into a shoulder bag.

"We may not find it, mind you," Jackson said. "But it's a lead."

"We'll take it," Roscoe said. By the time Jackson made out another track in a spot of grassy mud, Ketchum and Tom were with them. Roscoe looked around at the darkening surroundings. "Let's go in."

Quietly and carefully, they entered the woods, following the tracks and subtle disturbances in the tall weeds and grass, broken sticks decorating the path along the way. Jackson found that he was more excited than he'd expected. Exhilarated. He'd hunted animals before in the wild, with a camera. But not a tiger in Chillicothe with a tranquilizer gun. And not in a situation where they may find themselves face-to-face with a killing machine, instead of from a carefully planned safe distance. But along with the excitement came a nervousness that he forced himself to swallow. He knew he was out of his natural element.

Jackson kept his face forward, looking at tracks and disturbances in the foliage, scanning the distance before them. "Look very carefully, scan very slowly," Jackson whispered to the three men behind him. "You may not think it to look at them, but tigers blend right into their surroundings."

"Don't worry, professor," Ketchum quipped. "I think I'll notice a big orange blotch if we come across it."

"No," Jackson said. "You think so, but you won't if you scan quickly like you would for a deer or a fox. The black stripes of a tiger distort his body when he's in the grass or behind trees. He'll blend in, and be on top of you before you even knew he was there."

"There he is!" Tom called in a hushed voice, without pointing.

Good kid, Jackson thought. *Knew not to make a sudden movement.*

"He knows we're here," Jackson advised quietly, carefully, as they all stood completely still, their guns aimed at the orange and black tiger they all could now see. "He could smell us long before we could see him. And he can hear us whispering. The idea isn't to sneak up on him. It's to make sure he doesn't see us as a threat. We want to remain slow, motionless, quiet."

"Take your shot," Roscoe whispered.

Jackson aimed his rifle. He knew it was one shot or not at all. If he missed, if the dart hit a bone, or did not hit a good portion of muscle, the medicine would not take effect and the tiger would just get angry. Even if he did hit his mark perfectly, no one knew for sure how the tiger would react. It was unpredictable. It could lie calmly as it waited for the medicine to take effect. Or it could thrash and roar and attack.

Jackson aimed for the back haunches and pulled the trigger. It hit.

"Good shot!" Ketchum cheered.

Whether it was the dart alone, or the dart combined with the sudden commotion and movement, they would never know for sure. But the tiger did not calm. It stared them down with an angry snarl, showed its teeth, let out a loud and gravelly roar, and then crouched, and launched itself a full twenty feet in their direction with one powerful leap.

"Open fire," Roscoe ordered. Jackson didn't have time to load another dart, and there was no point in doing so. Roscoe, Ketchum and Tom all fired at the cat, and each man hit his mark. The tiger twitched, groaned, and fell in the leafy opening between them and the foliage that had concealed it.

"It's done," Roscoe said. "Good try, Jackson. We did our best."

"Sure." Jackson looked at the beautiful tiger that had just threatened their lives.

"Tom," Roscoe said, "geo-tag this place on your GPS so we can come back to retrieve the carcass."

"Should we haul it back now?" Ketchum asked.

"No, we'd better just focus on finding more of them on our way back to the road. Unless we run across something else on the way, we'd better get back to cruising and looking for animals."

When Roscoe and Jackson got to the cruiser, Delores was on the radio advising that Leland Anders had arrived at Sammy Johnson's preserve.

"He wasn't too happy about what he saw," Delores informed. "But he said there's no use trying to tranquilize the animals now, with it being dark and there being so many on the loose. Said 'nightfall makes it their home game now,' or something like that."

"Oh, great," Jackson mocked. "Mr. Celebrity Zookeeper has come to grace us with his sound bites."

Roscoe chuckled. "We can use all the help we can get." He looked at Ketchum. "You keep patrolling and let us know as soon as you spot something. Jackson, let's go bring Leland up to speed."

"For now," Ketchum said. "But I have a bad feeling. Before too long, we won't have to look for the animals. People will be calling us to report their sightings, or worse."

What's Your Emergency?

As a teenager, Delores Maxwell had always enjoyed talking on the phone. But she'd never had aspirations of making a career of it. When her cousin, on the force, told her about a position opening for a dispatcher, Delores decided to give it a try. She figured she'd be a natural at it. Eighteen years later, she still spent much of her time on the phone. Only now, it was paid work. These days, she avoided the phone when not on the job.

"Email me, or visit me—just don't call me," she joked with her friends. "I'm liable to answer, 'what's your emergency' instead of 'hello.'"

This evening, she had her work cut out for her, taking more calls in one shift than she'd ever taken before. And they were not pleasant callers.

"Nine-one-one, what's your emergency?" she answered over and over. She'd gotten good, over the years, at remaining calm during the most strenuous situations. A child could be trapped in a house with a burglar downstairs, a man could be screaming over the sound of gunshots, a woman could be crying into the phone over a dead mother or husband— Delores knew how to talk to people so that she could extract information gently and get help on the way.

"Wolves!" a young woman screamed into the phone. "A pack of wolves, attacking us!"

"Where are you located?"

"Western View." Short of breath, she sounded as though she was running. "Western View Park. Three."

"Three wolves?"

"And people! Us." She sounded young, like a teen.

"Help is on the way."

⠀⠀⠀⠀⠀⠀⠀⠀⠀⠀·

Not ten minutes later, the line beckoned again. "What's your emergency?"

"Help! There's a tiger!"

"Where are you, ma'am?"

"Strawser Park. A tiger, pacing in the trees!"

"Don't run, ma'am. Try to back slowly away. Don't look the tiger in the eyes."

"It's looking at me!"

"Try to remain calm, ma'am. Help is on the way."

⠀⠀⠀⠀⠀⠀⠀⠀⠀⠀·

A few sips of coffee, another call. "What's your emergency?"

"Need an ambulance, quick! Foothill of the Appalachians! Me and my wife. Mountain lion! Drove it off, but it's still..."

"Where exactly are you?"

"In the Goddamn mountains! Hiking trail, at the bottom! Scioto Trail Park!"

"Are you in a safe place, sir?"

"No! There's a mountain lion!"

"Help is on its way, sir."

⠀⠀⠀⠀⠀⠀⠀⠀⠀⠀·

"My boyfriend's being attacked!"

"What's your location?"

"Yoctangee Park," she cried. "A bear!"

"Are you out of harm's way?"

"I'm in a tree. My boyfriend's rolled up on ground, in a ball! The bear's gonna kill him!"

"Sit tight. Don't try to approach the bear. Your boyfriend's doing the right thing. I've got someone on the way now."

⠀⠀⠀⠀⠀⠀⠀⠀⠀⠀·

"I seen a bunch of lions running along the freeway."

"Is anyone hurt? Or in danger?"

"I'm in my car. But I mean, there's *lions* out running along Route 23. That's an accident waiting to happen."

"Which way are they going?"

"They ducked into the woods, but they were headed north."

•

"Delores," the Sheriff called over the radio. "Those incoming calls are priority number one. But when you get a second, get on the horn to the police in Columbus and Portsmouth, Ironton, Zanesville, everywhere within an hour's distance. We're going to need their help. And they're probably going to need ours."

"Will do," Deloris said into the radio as the phone rang again.

•

"I think it's a bobcat," the caller huffed. "I remember it from the cub scouts. Didn't even know the things were real. A bobcat. What's next, a Webelo?"

•

"A Komodo dragon, that's what it was. Nearly bit the boy's hand off. It crossed from their yard into mine. A Komodo dragon, just like in that Godfather movie with Ferris Bueller. Some kind of endangered species."

•

"They were cheetahs."

"No, leopards."

"My girlfriend thinks they were leopards. Headed up the road."

"Down the road."

"Down the road, headed in the direction of Ironton."

"No, Portsmouth."

"I mean Portsmouth. Two or three of them."

"Two—give me that. Ma'am? There are two leopards running like the wind, headed south. Thursday night means a bunch of drunk college kids around Shawnee State. Do leopards run long distances, or are they just sprinters, like cheetahs?"

"I don't know," Delores admitted.

"I don't know, either. But they were running fast, like they knew where they were headed."

·

"Help! My husband's being attacked by a cougar!"

·

On a night like this, even a pro like Delores could barely keep up. She longed for the cherished days of pleasant phone conversations.

Family Outing

The lions don't like it out here. They didn't like their cages, but this tension is not what they expected to come with freedom. The tall grass just outside the compound is pleasant. But they sense the need to vacate as the other pride arrives. As more men arrive. Death smells strong in the air around them. They relinquish the field to the other pride and enter the woods.

They down a deer and have a snack. Rest for a moment. Then, the pride walks on at a steady pace, looking for somewhere safe to settle. They are uneasy in these woods—too many sounds are too close. From a far-off distance, they hear the other lions falling, the explosive echoes of the men and their toys, the roaring and moaning and silence of their cousins from the compound. Vacating when they did was the right choice. But now, a sense of restlessness troubles them like the stink in the air.

The forest seems thin, too close to the loud open spaces. Too close to people and their noise and toxins. The lions search for deeper forest or vaster field—a place where they can relax without fear of meeting man.

Their journey brings them to the hard black path where men travel in glimmering shells faster than cheetahs. The lions walk along the path for some moments, but the shells whiz by and nearly hit them. The path feels rough on their paws. They step off on the other side and continue to walk in the direction of the road—north—the sun already beneath the horizon, but still lighting the sky along the rim.

They come to one of man's metallic shells, stopped where two black paths cross. The leader of the pride, Alpha, approaches the casing (the others backing him up) and he attempts to break it. But it is not flesh and blood. It *contains* flesh and blood, screaming out typical human noises of fear and desperation. But the shell is hard and cannot be penetrated. It rumbles and speeds off, leaving a cloud of fumes around the lions. Alpha snorts, sneezes, and leads the pride back to the edge of the thin forest, alongside the black path.

The further the lions walk, the less likely freedom from man seems. It is as though their natural habitat is gone. Nature has been hollowed out.

Alpha's internal compass drives him to lead the pride north. In the north, there must be a wide-open space, free of man, where they can rest.

Celebrity Zookeeper Shoots to Kill

Leland Anders arrived at Sammy Johnson's property to realize his worst nightmare: lions and tigers and leopards and cougars and bears and panthers and so many beautiful animals...murdered. He removed his leather fedora for a moment and took a deep, quivering breath. He could feel the tears coming on, but he knew he had to keep it together. This nightmare might very well get worse.

He'd known Sammy. Didn't much like him, but had met him, had even worked with him. As younger men, Sammy and Leland had both worked at the Columbus Zoo. Sammy used to feed the animals. But they'd let Sammy go because he kept getting in the enclosures with the animals, something strictly forbidden.

"You can't do that," Leland had told him the first time he saw Sammy alongside a tiger. "That's suicide."

"Not suicide," Sammy had responded. "These animals are just like us. They want to eat, sure. But they want love."

"That thing could kill you before you knew what hit you."

"But so could you," Sammy had said. "Just because the animal *can* kill doesn't mean it will. They're like people. If you keep them fed, keep them happy, and don't screw with them, they're not going to screw with you."

Another time, at the zoo, Leland caught Sammy in with a pride of lions. The four lions were pawing one another, playing, resting in the sun. Sammy sat on a rock next to them, not actually frolicking with them, but in harm's way.

"Get out of there, now!" Leland had insisted.

"You see?" Sammy slowly exited. "Look at them. A perfect, happy family. They don't want to hurt me any more than you do."

"But look at them play," Leland griped. "One friendly bat of the paw, and you're dead. Not because they intended it. Because you're not a lion, and they are."

That was decades ago. A few months after that, Sammy had been fired. Shortly after, he shipped off to Vietnam. Years later, Leland encountered Sammy again, when he'd heard about Sammy's plans to open an exotic animal zoo and safari park. It never happened because Sammy never got the permits—in part because of Leland's expert testimony against it. The only thing they had in common was a love for animals, even if expressed in different ways.

Leland didn't hate Sammy. He knew that Sammy really did love his animals. Sammy seemed like the kind of guy who needed to possess the things he loved. Leland didn't feel the need to control. Better to admire the animals from a distance, to allow them to roam free.

"If I end up getting killed by an animal, I guess I deserve it," Sammy had said, years ago, from the lion enclosure.

"No, you didn't deserve it." Leland hunched over a tiger's corpse. "But it was bound to happen sooner or later."

Headlights lit up the drive, illuminating the animals and the blood. Leland wiped away his tears and faced the oncoming vehicles. He'd met them before, but never looking so disheveled. The Sheriff, Roscoe, and his number one, Chuck, looked like they'd had their souls sucked out of them.

Jackson, who sometimes criticized him for taking animals on live television, had beaten him to the scene. Regardless of any differences, Leland knew they were all on the same team now. And their unfortunate goal: to take out more of these magnificent creatures.

Roscoe tipped his hat. "Good evening."

"Not too good, by the looks of things." Leland motioned to the carcasses, then looked squarely into the eyes of the men who had killed these animals.

Roscoe gave Leland a looking over. "Things are going to look a lot worse before we're done." He proceeded to give a count of the animals missing.

Leland took it all in. "You're going to need a press conference."

Roscoe feigned a smile. "My priority is to get these animals off the street before they start killing people."

"I agree," Leland said. "But you've got to get out in front of this story. You don't want to issue a statement *after* the carnage begins. You need to be out in front of this."

Jackson shook his head. "Leland, I think the Sheriff's department has more important things to do than to worry about public relations."

Roscoe sighed. "We've already got warnings on the lighted road signs, and local television and radio are broadcasting warnings."

Leland persisted. "The public needs to see their Sheriff or someone of authority in charge of this."

Roscoe walked to his vehicle's radio. "Delores, get me the Mayor." He looked back to Leland and Jackson. "You tell Mayor Vernon what you're telling me. Let's let the politicians handle the bullshit while we handle the bulls."

"That's fine." Leland took the radio. "As long as someone gets out there with this. But by morning, you'll need to face the press."

Chuck looked down at Leland's boots. "After tonight, I doubt any of us will care much."

Leland rode up front with the Sheriff. That seemed to upset Jackson, who'd been annexed to Chuck's cruiser. As Roscoe drove and they looked for signs of animals along the edges of the wooded areas, they listened to the Mayor's address on the radio—a broadcast of what aired on all of the local television and radio stations in central Ohio.

"Although we are warning everyone to stay indoors, I want to express my full confidence in the cadre of experts out there dealing with this situation. Sheriff Roscoe Roy and his fully capable team, including animal experts from the zoo and from the Animal Protection Agency, are working together as we speak to find these animals and keep our citizens safe. Everyone should stay indoors. If anyone spots one of these animals, call 911 right away."

Leland looked at Roscoe, who appeared worn out. "At least it's a full moon," Leland said. "Makes it easier to see them."

"I'll tell you, it was just devastating to have to kill those animals, Leland. We took no pleasure in it. None of my guys did. We..."

"I know." Leland looked at the dashboard. "You just did what you had to."

"We're not going to be able to go in after them in the dark, are we?"

"Not easily. But we probably won't have to. They'll come out to us."

"That's what I was afraid of."

The first attack: a mountain lion in the foothills of the Appalachian Mountains, in the outskirts of Chillicothe. The Sheriff put on his lights and siren and sped off, the others in their cars and Morris in his truck all following behind. Another emergency call came only minutes later: a bear attack in Yoctangee Park.

Roscoe called into his car's police radio. "Chuck, you and Jackson and Ketchum go take the bear. Toby and Morris, keep patrolling and stand by—I'm sure another attack or sighting will come any minute. Tom, Leland and I will get the mountain lion."

"On it," Chuck said. Leland looked behind and saw two of the vehicles pull out of their caravan and rush off in the other direction.

"Guess we've got to shoot it." Roscoe seemed to be asking as much as telling.

"I don't think we have much choice," Leland agreed. "If we're lucky, it'll still be there. A mountain lion can kill its prey in seconds—the average is less than a minute. Just a death grip to the neck and then they drag their prey away and hide it in the brush."

"The husband's fighting it," Roscoe reminded. "Maybe he drove it off."

"I doubt it." Leland drew on his lifetime of knowledge. "Mountain lions are stubborn sons of bitches. Once they get their mind set on something, it's like a chemical trigger in the brain. The thing they have their mind on—prey—is all they can think about, and they'll risk their lives, beyond reason, to keep it."

When they arrived on the scene, medics were standing by—but not daring to approach. Leland exited the car as Roscoe did, each of them with a standard issue assault rifle loaded and ready.

The mountain lion had its teeth locked on the woman's head, bottom teeth in the area of the eyes on the face, the top teeth sunk into her hair, into her skull. The woman struggled with her hands on the mountain lion's face, feeling her way and cramming her fingers into ear and eye and nose wherever possible. The man stepped forward and back, avoiding the swats of the cat as he beat on it with a heavy stick. The only thing saving him was the cat's single-minded focus: to keep his prey at any cost.

"They're doing everything right," Leland admitted as he and the Sheriff took aim. Leland didn't fire, unconfident of his shot given the close proximity of human and puma heads. In an instant, as though distracted by their presence and threatened by more challengers to the prey, the mountain lion let go of the woman's head. Roscoe fired, but the mountain lion leapt out of the line of fire quickly, hooking his front claws into the man, causing him to drop his blunt stick and tumble to his back. Leland noted how the man quickly protected his face and head with his forearms even as the cougar bit into his arms and violently shook him.

"It felt like I got hit by a truck," the man would later tell Leland.

"I knew I was dead," the woman would say to reporters as she recovered in her hospital bed, stitches all over her face and shaven head, her arms and neck and shoulder. "I'd probably have given up, but my husband kept yelling for me to resist, for me to put up a fight. So I did—I started cramming my fingers into its nose and eyes and beating its face. We bought ourselves enough time for the police to come and kill the cougar."

"They were extremely lucky," Leland would later tell reporters in one of the hundreds of interview he would give regarding this and the other animal incidents of the ordeal. "A mountain lion may seem a smaller cat, only about one-twenty to one-forty pounds. But it can cover forty feet in one leap and can take down more than ten times its body weight in one swipe. It typically kills prey in forty-five seconds, cutting off the air supply. Had they not fought back, they would have been dead when we arrived."

That was later. But even if he was never questioned about it or asked to recount it, Leland would never forget that mountain lion moment. Right after Roscoe missed his mark, after the mountain lion traded one victim for another, after the mountain lion sank his two-inch canines into the forearms of the man before them, Leland fired his weapon. The mountain lion fell on top of the man. The victim still had the wherewithal to throw the animal off before slumping back down next to his wife. The medics looked to Leland and Roscoe for the go-ahead, received it, and rushed to help the wounded couple.

"Nice shot." Roscoe patted Leland's arm and stepped back into the cruiser.

"Not nice," Leland sighed. "But necessary."

By Moonlight

The wolf does not need to look to the sky or sniff the wind or listen to the birds to determine whether there will be moonlight tonight. He knows instinctively that a full moon will light the sky, like one who habitually wakes moments before the rooster crows. It is in the air, in the ground, in the trees, in the water, in the wildlife. In the time itself. The wolf knows tonight the pack will have an easy hunt. Because tonight, they will hunt by moonlight.

The Alpha wolf leads the pack through the wooded land. It has been days since they have eaten meat. Master fed them only dry food of meal and artificial flavoring two days ago. Alpha had considered attacking the men who arrived, but caught the scent and sound of guns firing. Alpha led the pack into the woods. Now they move swiftly.

Three wolves make up the pack: Alpha, another male and a female. They have been together since they were pups, but they have only known the cage. Where they are going, the wolves do not know. But they wait for the night to cast itself over the horizon, and for the moon to fill the sky and give them a reason to howl.

Alpha finds animals here in the wooded land that it does not know. Large, svelte creatures on four legs with white bushes for tails and large, multi-pointed antlers. Smaller, slyer red creatures, like little dogs or cats, slinking between the bushes with pointed ears and long, bushy tails. Little creatures with four legs, but two of them like hands, collecting nuts, evade the wolf's snaps as they scurry up trees.

The animals that the wolves know are the ones they've lived with for years. Tiger. Lion. Bear. Bobcat. Cougar. Leopard. Man.

Man will be the prey of the night, the object of the hunt. Man who is not protected in car or house or cage. Man who is out in the open, without gun. Under the light of the moon, vulnerable.

The moon has come. The wolves howl. The hunt begins.

Nightmares at Daytime

Chuck drank bourbon and thought over things as they happened, and as they might have happened. Ketchum sat beside him at the bar, remaining silent.

Chuck had only been doing his duty, doing exactly what he had to do. But well after the ordeals of that night and day, the terrible images sizzled in his mind. Nightmares nearly every day of his life. But not in sleep—in daytime. He could no longer go to a school baseball game without looking for a lion to pounce the field. Or visit Yoctangee Park without seeing a bear maul a man half to death. He could no longer drive along Route 23 without seeing the line of fur shaved off the back of a tiger by bullet. Or patrol Rural Place Road without seeing thirty dreadful carcasses.

He was following orders, still in a daze, when he and Jackson and Ketchum raced to Yoctangee Park to respond to the call. When they arrived, they saw a bloodied, barely recognizable ball of clothing and flesh on the ground, a plaything for the Kodiak bear. When Chuck fired at the Kodiak, he only enraged the bear further. It turned toward him, but then saw the woman—the girlfriend of the man being attacked. The bear mistook the woman for the marksman, and charged her instead.

The woman had watched what the bear did to her boyfriend as he lay in a mutilated ball on the ground. She didn't seem convinced that he was doing the right thing, Chuck could see in her panicked expression. She must have been thinking, *Can so much shredded flesh and spilled blood be a best result?* So, instead of doing what her boyfriend had done, she turned to run. The bear caught up with her, knocked her over, and went to town on her face, her neck, her gut.

Ketchum shot. So did Jackson. Chuck fired again. They all hit, crimson corsages flowering black fur. The bear bellowed and strained to move forward, toward his attackers. The bear fell. But so had the woman.

The ball of shredded clothing, skin and flesh remained rolled up. It quivered and tightened when the medics touched it, then eventually relaxed and opened. It was a young man, perhaps thirty.

"He did everything exactly right," Leland Anders would later say, praising the young man for his quick thinking. "Mr. Billings avoided certain death by protecting his vitals, rolling himself up into a ball so the bear could only get to his back. He'll be sore for a few weeks—lots of bruises and scars—but he'll be fine. He's lucky to be alive to show off those scars."

"What's he talking about it for?" Jackson had griped. "Leland wasn't even there."

"He's the talking head everyone wants to hear from," Roscoe had said, which seemed to agitate Jackson even more.

Chuck knew Mr. Billings had more than physical scars to contend with. Mental anguish was sure to haunt him for the rest of his life. The trauma of being mauled half to death by a bear. And worse, finding out that his girlfriend had been mauled all the way to death.

"We made it," the guy had said when the medics stirred him and placed him carefully in the ambulance. It wasn't until later, after the surgeries, after he woke from the anesthesia, that they informed him. Chuck imagined that's when the real pain must have begun.

"We got it," Ketchum had said after the bear fell.

Chuck registered the actions of the medics. The extra attention devoted to the man. The sheet placed over the woman's head. Chuck understood that the bear had killed the woman. And that the only reason the bear had attacked her was because he had opened fire on the bear without first making sure the woman was safe.

"That's nonsense," Jackson had said when Chuck suggested it was his own fault for prematurely opening fire. "That bear would have killed them both without our interference."

"The bear was focused on the man," Chuck said. "We should have gotten the girl safely out of there and *then* opened fire."

The surgery had lasted six hours. The physical pain and the permanent scars would last far longer. For Billings and for Chuck.

Chuck visited Billings in the hospital. "I'm sorry," he said, "about your girlfriend. I'm sorry the bear got her."

"I know," Billings said, still protecting himself within an emotional ball. "Thanks."

Thanks, Chuck thought. *Thanks for getting my girlfriend killed.*

The bear was only doing what bears knew to do. The enemy wasn't a villain, just a foe.

And the tiger. Chuck would never forget the tiger. Chuck and Ketchum just happened to be in the right place at the right time. They'd been startled, standing at the edge of the road under the light of the moon, when a deer shot out of the patch of forest to their right. They'd raised their assault rifles instinctively, then sighed relief when they saw it was just a deer. But, only a moment later, out of the woods leapt a tiger, right on the tail of the deer. The tiger did not run so much as fall out of one springing leap and into another. Chuck watched as the tiger hit the ground several feet behind the deer, then sprang up with such force that it projected itself into the air over the deer and batted its paw into the deer's shoulder. The claws locked in like fishhooks, and the tiger sunk her long canines into the deer's neck. The mass of tiger and deer had tumbled to the ground before Ketchum or Chuck even registered what was happening, before they'd even had time to lift their weapons and take aim.

Resting in the overgrown grass with its kill, the tiger turned her head sideways to rip shreds of flesh from the belly of the deer. Amazing, how easily the tiger ripped apart the animal, like pulling apart an overcooked game hen.

Ketchum had already fired on the animal and hit it in the shoulder. The tiger jumped up and growled at the two men. Chuck took aim, as the tiger rushed toward them, and hit the beast as it was landing on its front paws with its hind quarters airborne, not more than twenty feet away. The bullet overshot the tiger's head and hit just between the shoulders, and Chuck could clearly see the bullet—as though in slow motion—slide across the surface of the tiger's back, along the spine, for about three inches, shaving off a strip of orange-black fur, revealing the red muscle normally hidden beneath. The snake of fur and skin twisted in the air and then fell to the ground. The tiger, whether reflexively carrying out the action already initiated or consciously continuing her attack, proceeded toward them. She leapt up, big paws and sharp claws coming right at them. Chuck and Ketchum both fired again, hitting the tiger in the head and chest. They cleared the way and the tiger fell, dead, right between them.

"Don't get much closer than that," Ketchum said.

Chuck remembered lot of close calls from that night and the next day. Even worse, the visions of things that might have happened, seared into his brain.

The pack of lions scouting out the easy kills of the nursing home, where the men and woman often sat outdoors listening to the Cleveland Indians and Cincinnati Reds on their radios, reading books, rocking in chairs and talking about the upcoming holiday season and visitors. The pride of lions discussing nothing, joining them on the lawn, killing the easy meat. The rest home's restless screaming, deaths coming sooner than anticipated and under far less humane conditions than expected.

The mountain lions coming across the Boy Scout troop camping in the woods near the Appalachian Mountains. They'd decided to rough it and had unplugged, not listening to the radio, not watching television, not checking internet headlines on their phones or laptops. They were out in the wild, pitching tents, building campfires. Chuck considered it a miracle that they had survived unscathed, not even aware of the potential dangers until they'd been reached by Roscoe and Leland, worried parents and spouses having informed the authorities of the unaware campers. The boys had been sent home before any real damage, but Chuck couldn't shake images of what might have been.

At the bar, sitting in silence for eternal minutes over their bourbon, Ketchum patted Chuck's back. "If you need to talk, I'm all ears."

"What's there to say?" Chuck tossed back his Jim Beam.

"Plenty." Ketchum sipped on Wild Turkey. "I know how it is." He finished off his shot. "More than you guys realize."

The bartender, Dennis, refilled their shot glasses, their two favored bottles in easy reach.

"What do you mean?" Chuck looked over at Ketchum.

"I mean I've suffered the aftermath of war. I live the nightmares, the flashbacks, the hallucinations. I know all about PTSI." He paused. "And I think you're beginning to know something of it, too."

"PT-what-now?"

"Post-traumatic stress injury."

Chuck grew red in the face, as much from embarrassment as anger. "I need a drink, not a shrink." He slammed back another.

Ketchum sipped. "I don't mean nothing by it. Just that I'm here if you need to talk. We've seen some horrific things. No need to keep them bottled up."

Chuck looked at Dennis and pointed to his empty glass. He caught Ketchum's frown in the mirror. Ketchum sipped on his half-full glass, smacked his mouth to taste, and made a benevolent face. He put his hand on Chuck's shoulder. "Just let me know if you want to, that's all."

Chuck looked down into his refilled glass, then closed his eyes. He wanted to explode, but he managed to maintain his composure for the people around him. For himself and Ketchum. Eyes closed, the bar and people faded away and other visions appeared.

Tigers in the tall grass beyond the softball fields and playgrounds, distorted and unseen, stalking, waiting to leap into that long-jump run, penetrate prepubescent flesh, supple neck and soft abdomen. Little league uniforms and a rainbow of play clothes marooned with blood.

Mayor Mark Vernon's Tapes, Volume VI, Tape 124

Conversation between Mayor Vernon and Sheriff Roy

Sheriff Roy: No, we don't have things under control. We're managing as best we can. We're hunting them down, responding to calls, eliminating them. But there's a hell of a lot of them. If help came, I wouldn't turn it down.

Mayor Vernon: Calling out the National Guard is not something to take lightly.

Sheriff Roy: Does this seem like a light matter to you? It sure as hell doesn't to me.

Mayor Vernon: I'm just saying we should be reasonable. We don't want to cry wolf.

Sheriff Roy: Mark, if there's ever been a good time to cry wolf, this is it.

Mayor Vernon: Look, if we can take care of this ourselves, that's the way we should do it. With or without outside intervention, it's not going to be pretty. This reeks already. Do you realize what the political ramifications will be? For me and for you?

Sherriff Roy: That's why the people like you so much, Mark. Your selfless dedication to people over politics.

Mayor Vernon: Oh, get your head out of your ass. You know what happened last time we called in the National Guard. If we had just let the protest taper out on its own, I might be running for President instead of screwing around with this rinky-dink bullshit.

Sheriff Roy: It ain't my fault you got called for jumping the gun. This isn't a peace demonstration. These animals are eating people! It's bigger than your aspirations and my career. I've got people dying out here, and there's still a bunch of animals on the prowl.

Mayor Vernon: (sighs) Are you telling me that your team can't handle them? Because, if that's what you're saying, I'll ask for help. I've already been in touch with the Governor and the White House. With any luck, the National Guard can be here before dawn.

Deputy Ketchum: (muffled) We're better off without them, Roscoe. Get twenty, thirty battle-geared Army soldiers in here and it could get ugly.

Sheriff Roy: Just a second, Mark.

Deputy Ketchum: (muffled) I know what I'm talking about. A few more men would be fine, but we get an army out here, we'll drive them off before we find them. This ain't a lockdown situation. We've got to track and hunt these bastards.

Sheriff Roy: Mark?

Mayor Vernon: Yeah, Roscoe.

Sheriff Roy: Can we get them standing by? We may not need them yet. But, if things don't start looking up in the next few hours, I think we'd be fools not to send out a distress signal—no matter what the reaction might be.

Reaction

I was so relieved when the cops brought Michael home. He's always loved camping, always been into scouting. But after this, I don't know. I just don't know.

— Lizzie Wilson, Parent of Cub Scout

I don't think I'll be swinging on the porch for a few weeks. I'll just stick with the parlor.

— Lulu Simmons, Meadow Brooks Nursing Home

I'm not afraid. I mean, there's always animals around. They know to stay away from people, mostly. If a few more got away, they'll just learn to live in the forest like they're supposed to.

— Michael Wilson, Cub Scout

The Sheriff's Department did what it had to do. When you have dangerous animals like these—nocturnal predators—and it's nighttime, and they're near large populations of people, you don't have the luxury of trying to humanely trap them or bring them in. Human life was at stake. There would have been carnage in Chillicothe.

— Leland Anders, Celebrity Zookeeper

CARNAGE IN CHILLICOTHE, SAYS LELAND ANDERS— America's favorite animal activist, Leland Anders, says that by killing dozens of rare animals, the Chillicothe Sheriff's Department was avoiding carnage in Chillicothe. But others are saying that the shootings *created* carnage in Chillicothe.

— Carrie Mortimer, CNEN-TV

What I want to know is, what kind of man collects all of these wild animals? I mean, how was he able to acquire them all? How did he feed them? And why didn't the police do anything about it?

— Dexter Thompson, Sammy Johnson's Neighbor's Son

A crazy guy, that's who. Someone who just doesn't know when to stop.

— Bobbie Anne Thompson, Sammy Johnson's Neighbor

Was Sammy Johnson a little crazy? Well, sure, I guess you could say so. But look, aren't we all? I mean, I got me a good nine hundred records. Does that make me a little crazy?

— Mike Skaggs, Sammy Johnson's Drinking Buddy

This just makes it worse for the rest of us. Those of us who have exotic pets, but who care for them responsibly.

— Juls Metternich, Exotic Pet Reserve Owner

It's easy for you and I to look at a case like this and think it's extreme. But when you're moving from one thing gradually to another, it doesn't seem that way. He started out with regular house pets, worked his way to more exotic pets, then ended up with what he had. Adding one more pet to the collection is not a big deal. Until one day someone from the outside comes in and says: you've got an entire zoo here.

— Dr. Minnie Fields, Professor of Psychology, Shawnee State University

I never got so many calls at once. I don't know what was worse: the calls about animal attacks, or the haters calling to criticize us for killing the animals.

— Delores Maxwell, Dispatcher, Ross County Sheriff's Department and Chillicothe Police Department

He made friends with a monkey in Nam. Said it would sleep in the tent with him, and he taught it to do tricks and stuff. He liked watching animals in the wild. But he liked having them as friends even better.

— Mike Skaggs, Sammy Johnson's Drinking Buddy

I got my son a tiger cub for a pet. Once it got big, we just couldn't keep it. Bit off more than we could chew. Sammy took it in for us. He rescued a lot of animals like that.

— Lilith Robinson, Chillicothe Resident

They killed my babies. Think of having your house pet shot down by the police. Fifty times over.

— Marielle Johnson, Sammy Johnson's Wife

I knew he had wild animals. But I never realized just how many. And I can't wrap my head around how a guy ends up with that many animals. Shouldn't be legal.

— Mitch Henderson, Sammy Johnson's Neighbor

How do you even get into something so weird? I mean, when do you wake up and decide, "I want to be the guy with a bunch of wild animals?" How does that process even begin?

— Dexter Thompson, Sammy Johnson's Neighbor's Son

How it Began

"When did you become interested in animals?" a guest once asked Sammy Johnson. He hadn't known how to answer. When had he *not* been consumed by an admiration of such noble creatures?

By age five, Sammy spent an hour or more each Saturday watching animals behind glass walls and barred cages. Saturday was shopping day. Next door to the grocery store, in the same strip mall, beckoned the local pet store. That's where Sammy spent his time while Mom shopped. Other kids were picking out their favorite cereals and snack cakes while Sammy put fingers in the hamster and mouse cages, petting their delicate little heads, playing with dogs and cats, ferrets and chinchillas.

By the time Sammy turned six, he understood this wasn't a zoo. Once he learned that people could actually buy the animals and bring them home, he felt as though a completely new world had erupted. "Please" became an important word in his vocabulary, followed by "can I have" and "why not?" To Mom's credit, at first she succeeded at keeping a pet-free house, in part because of Dad's insistence. But in time, Mom couldn't help but give in to Sammy's sweet, sincere affection for animals. By the time Sammy reached seven and a half, he had a hamster. Then a couple of mice. A ferret. A lizard. A tarantula.

Part of what convinced Mom (and eventually Dad) that perhaps Sammy was the sort of boy who wouldn't lose interest after a couple weeks and leave the caretaking duties to the parents was the little collection of unapproved pets for which Sammy already cared: caterpillars and frogs and insects. Before ever obtaining store-bought pets, Sammy took matters into his own hands, sneaking pets of his own into the house. He marveled as a caterpillar morphed to a beautiful butterfly. He caught flies and lightning bugs to feed his frogs.

By nine, Sammy graduated to barn cats. Dad had a particular disinterest in cats, because his mother-in-law had so many of them. But being in rural farm country, stray cats abounded. Whenever a stray would happen by, Sammy lured it with saucers of milk and morsels of lunchmeat and hot dog. By the time he turned ten, Sammy cared for six outdoor cats that had never, to his knowledge, been inside a house.

For his eleventh birthday, Dad finally relented. "Mom and I have noticed how well you've been taking care of your pets, Sammy. So we figure you earned this." Dad left the room and returned with a thumping box tied up in ribbon. Air holes decorated the sides and top, and the box thudded and jerked as Dad tried to balance it in his hands. When Dad placed it on the kitchen table, the box barked.

Sammy nearly burst with happiness as he frantically removed the ribbon and threw off the lid to find a young beagle wagging inside. Sammy couldn't believe it! Dad's and Mom's smiles were barely in his peripheral vision, his eyes affixed to the puppy as he lifted it from the box and cuddled it in his arms. The dog jerked and flopped, tail wagging, tongue slapping his neck and face. The beagle acted the way Sammy felt inside. He wasn't allowed to keep it in the house, but when weather was nice, Sammy would sleep in barn with his beloved dog.

Later in life, Sammy had the same glowing sense each time he went to greet a new exotic pet. Every animal he adopted took him back to his eleventh birthday, Mom's and Dad's approving smiles in his peripheral vision.

As a teenager, Sammy began showing up at a neighbor's farm where he helped out with the horses, cows and chickens. At fifteen, he worked as an animal caretaker at three local farms. He drove a tractor long before he drove a car, and that's how he would get from one farm to another. Tasked with feeding the cows, bulls and horses, scattering feed for the chickens, collecting eggs in the hen house, and feeding the dogs, it didn't feel like work at all. Being around the animals brought Sammy peace and pleasure. Sometimes he had to be reminded to get to work, to stay busy, because he found it easy to fall under the spell of an animal and waste hours playing with or petting a favorite horse or dog.

When Sammy wasn't in school or working with the animals on one of the nearby farms or playing with his own collection, he enjoyed looking through picture books about animals, reading *National Geographic*, or tuning into programs like *Mutual of Omaha's Wild Kingdom*. He'd already read *All Creatures Great and Small* twice.

As each school year wound down, Sammy's classmates were excited about getting out of school—but for Sammy, summertime meant zoo season. In the last month of school, Sammy wouldn't let Mom and Dad forget, consistently asking "when are we going to the zoo?" and "which one will we go to first?" every few days until he got concrete answers. Then he reminded them of the plan daily. "June 22, we're headed to Cincinnati!" Sammy got specific about such visits. "Can we leave home early, when it's still dark, like a fishing trip, and stay until they close?" He pulled out his maps to the zoos so he could lead the family on their safaris. "If we hit the big cats first, then the monkey house, we'll have time to hit both of them again at the end of the day, after dinner with the elephants."

Sammy considered such visits magical, mesmerized by the exotic animals—especially the chimps, wolves, bears and big cats.

"Is there any animal you don't like?" his father once asked in jest as they sat at an outdoor picnic table enjoying oversized turkey legs and soda.

"I don't know," Sammy mused. "Pink flamingos, maybe? I could do without them. And vultures are kind of icky." But on zoo day, Sammy insisted it essential they hit every animal in the zoo, even the icky ones.

When Sammy made it halfway through high school, his father finally allowed a dog and cat in the house. Then, in a matter of weeks, Sammy's private zoo of domesticated pets migrated inside. Sammy cleaned after them so there would be no reason for his father to kick them back out.

At age seventeen, Sammy's childhood dream came true: he applied for a job at the Columbus Zoo and got it. Sure, his main duties included shoveling elephant and rhino poop, but it was a job with zoo animals, and he was electrified by the future prospects.

Leland Anders, an animal keeper who had interned as a veterinarian and had worked at the zoo for four years, had burrowed himself into a mammal management career. Leland had a reputation for being the Zoo Director's pet. About six years older than Sammy, Leland had a flair for saying witty things, and he'd begun doing segments about animals on local television talk shows. Sammy imagined a future in which he could do the same, perhaps working along with Leland. Sammy didn't really want the spotlight, didn't feel the need to be on camera, but he imagined being an animal handler for Leland or someone like him, helping to care for the beautiful creatures before and after they took the stage.

Sammy tried to make friends with Leland, had lunch with him at the zoo picnic tables and admired the lions and tigers with him. But Leland wasn't giving Sammy any special treatment. Sammy could count on Leland to be there with a smile and friendly animal chatter, but Leland couldn't be counted on to help Sammy in his career.

Sammy still loved his own animals—his cats and dogs, hamsters and mice. He relished the local farm animals he helped care for, even the mundane cows and sheep. But at the zoo, getting close to animals such as tigers and lions, bears and panthers was a new kind of thrill. He lived for the moments when he could feed the cats, and he even crossed over into their cages at times—although not allowed—so he could pet them. The day he hugged a bear was magnificent: he felt empowered, as though the bear transferred some of her strength to him as they embraced.

Sammy only entered the tiger cage after he'd fed them and they'd eaten their fill. He joined them carefully, crook in hand for protection. He seldom needed to raise it. He spoke softly to them, crooning, "That's a good tiger." In most cases, he could approach a caged tiger and perhaps pet it behind the ear, but little more. The tigers seemed wary of him. But the afternoon when a tiger cub came to him, rubbed her head against his leg, sat in his lap and began purring—the parents looking on, unconcerned—Sammy knew that he wanted to be around these sorts of animals all his life. This was the feeling of family.

"Hey, get out of there!" Leland insisted when he caught Sammy up close with the animals. But what Leland and other keepers didn't understand was the intimate connection Sammy had with the animals. He could feel them, could understand them. And Sammy was certain the animals understood him. These lions and tigers and bears were not mean. They *could* kill him, yes, just as a human walking down the street or driving a car could kill him. But he felt certain they would not.

The more times Leland and other keepers caught Sammy sneaking into the cages, the fewer times Sammy was allowed to feed the exotic animals. So Sammy knew he would have to find another way to get close to them. He began asking around, and he discovered *Animal Trader Monthly*, a newsprint circular advertising exotic animals for sale. He considered it shocking, how easily someone could buy an exotic animal.

"Absolutely not!" Dad barked after Sammy made his proposition. "You're not bringing a wild animal here!"

"I can keep it caged up in the back yard!" Sammy was almost eighteen, but still felt like a child when he tried to persuade his parents.

"No, Sammy." Mom took Dad's side. "We can't live with a wild animal. People just can't live with wild animals."

"You're already exhibiting hoarder tendencies as it is!" Dad griped. "You've got to be careful."

"Now, Willie," Mom said in her calming voice. "Sammy seems to know how to take care of the animals he's gotten so far."

"Yes, that's what you used to say about your mother," Dad yelled. "If he's not careful, Sally, he's going to end up just like her!"

Sammy realized that in another year he wouldn't need permission. He could get his own place and do his own thing. He had a job at the zoo to afford it. Leland had been talking about leaving the zoo to do a television show full time, which would mean another opportunity for promotion. Sammy felt as though his dreams were on the cusp of coming true.

Until they began to crumble.

He lost his job at the Columbus Zoo after being caught one too many times with the big cats. A few weeks later, a coyote killed his very first house cat, a ten-year-old tabby. And then, about six months after Sammy turned eighteen, he was drafted. Sammy abandoned his pets and his family for the first time in his life, and shipped off to Vietnam. His grandmother took his cats.

Pet Hoarding—a Johnson Family Tradition

For Exotic Animal Owner Sammy Johnson, Hoarding Animals was a Family Affair

by Blake Hartle, Part of a continuing series for the *Cleveland Plain Dealer*

CHILLICOTHE—People across the nation, from reporters to investigators, are trying to understand why 63-year-old lifelong Chillicothe resident Sammy Johnson decided to amass a collection of 83 exotic animals, and why he unleashed them into the community. Investigators and psychologists continue to search for answers. A good place to start: a look at Mr. Johnson's family history.

"I always feared he'd end up like his grandmother," said Willie Johnson, Sammy Johnson's father, after the attacks. "His grandmother was a pet hoarder, too."

Emily Smith, Sammy Johnson's maternal grandmother, spent eight years of her life, in the 1960s and 1970s, as a hoarder of cats. Neighbors knew her as "the Cat Lady." Many communities have a cat lady, which has become somewhat of stereotype. But for Emily Smith, who died in 1994 of congestive heart failure, collecting felines had crossed over into a psychological dysfunction.

Pet hoarding is a dysfunctional behavior that will likely gain more attention after the high-profile case of Sammy Johnson. Most pet hoarders collect common housepets, such as dogs and cats and birds. But there are those who collect feral dogs, big cats, wolves, foxes and animals that are more dangerous. Pet hoarding has no known diagnosis or treatment. It is the compulsive need to accumulate and control animals in large numbers.

It is usually dangerous to the health of both the animals and the hoarder. It is estimated to affect households in virtually every community across America. And in many cases, it is illegal.

"Guess you could say we're both cat people," Mrs. Smith said during an interview in 1988, when her adult grandson's escaped tiger attacked a neighbor's dog and made local news. "I love house cats, he loves big cats."

Emily Smith's collection started small enough. According to her family and neighbors, she started out with a cat she acquired at a local pet store. Within a year of getting that first cat, she had seven others.

"Once she had more than a few, she kind of got a reputation as a cat person," said Clyde Henderson, a previous landlord. "People would bring her their kittens or unwanted cats. Then, they'd just start dropping them off in her yard."

Within a few years, Smith had 80 cats living in her two-bedroom home. When Smith called the landlord to repair a faulty toilet, he was shocked.

"The walls were not just scratched; there were deep grooves all over the drywall where the cats had gone to town on them. The place stank of cat piss and crap. Litter boxes filling half the living room were packed, but the cats still had poop and vomit all over the place—on the carpets, kitchen linoleum, all over the washer, dryer, sink, toilet tank, you name it. I just had to get rid of her. Those damn cats were causing way too much damage," Clyde Henderson told reporters after her eviction. "I had to take her to court to pay for the damages. Pretty much had to gut the place after she and those cats were out. Security deposit didn't come close."

For some, the prospect of an eviction and losing one's home might be incentive enough to get rid of so many animals, but that was not the case for Emily Smith. In fact, once she obtained a larger house on the east side of Chillicothe, her feline hoard swelled nearly twofold.

"When it was 80 cats, we could pretend it was normal," Smith's daughter, Sally Johnson, said. "But then, more people kept dropping off cats, and strays would come around, and the cats kept getting pregnant, and she couldn't afford to fix any of them. Well, they multiplied like rabbits."

Smith's cats took over her entire three-bedroom house, and she kept only the living room for her own use, sleeping in a reclining chair in front of the television. One bedroom was devoted to the food and water, one to the enormous collection of litter boxes, and one was covered with pillows, sheets and blankets to form a mass pet bed.

Smith's own bed, unused and unmade, had become stained with feces and urine, as had most of the furniture in the home, including the chair in which Smith spent much of her time watching television and sleeping.

"The ammonia smell was overpowering," said a neighbor who wished to remain anonymous. "You could smell it from the end of the drive before even walking up to the house. I don't know how she lived with it."

The ammonia, in fact, caused damage to Smith's lungs and contributed to her onset of respiratory problems. It may have been a contributing factor to her heart attack years later.

"It got to where I couldn't go to my mom's house. It always stank, hard to breathe," said her daughter, Sally Johnson. "Poop and throw-up everywhere, had to be careful not to step in it. That's not the way she raised me."

"The old bat's crazy. We couldn't even take Sammy over for fear that a cat would infect him," said Willie Johnson, Smith's son-in-law, in a previous interview. "There's disease everywhere. You can see the stains on the furniture and the floor and walls. The wallpaper's hanging off the walls in nasty shreds. No good for her or the cats."

"You can trust cats more than you can trust men," Emily said when asked about her pets. She lost her first husband in her late twenties, then had a string of boyfriends in the years that followed.

"Owning the cats," Smith later speculated after giving the cats to the Humane Society, "may have been a sort of defense mechanism. Least that's what my shrink told me. Protecting myself from getting my heart hurt by making it so no man would ever want to come over. People break your heart and let you down. Cats don't do that."

When her collection grew to 180 cats, her family intervened. "I knew we had to do something," Sally Johnson said. "But I didn't know what. When I'd bring it up, she'd get all defensive."

"She just didn't know where to draw the line between care for the cats and disregard for herself," said Willie Johnson. "She'd be on the phone with Sally and say things like, 'The cats peed on me again last night,' or 'I'm just going to hose out the bedroom instead of trying to scoop and scrub everything up.' Terribly nasty. People say bad things about their mothers-in-law. But I had every reason to."

Emily Smith explained she'd been forced to give up her pet cat as a young child when her own family relocated from a mining town in West Virginia to take up farming in Chillicothe. Emily's daughter believed that the experience of having to abandon her cat as a child made her feel responsible to care for abandoned cats later in life.

"How do you tell someone who is doing something out of the goodness of their heart that it's wrong?" Sally Johnson asked.

Eventually, it would take an accident, and the law, for Emily Smith to get rid of her cats. All of her income (she worked at a gas station and received an insurance pension from her first husband) went to feeding and taking care of her cats. She sacrificed her own meals and health for her pets. It was only a matter of time.

Police responded to a phone call from a neighbor complaining about an odor coming from the Smith residence. The neighbor knew that Smith had cats, but had no clue that there were so many.

"That house needed to be condemned right away," Sheriff Ward Howard said of the Smith home. "It just reeked of ammonia; you could barely breath at the front door." They evacuated Smith to Southern Ohio Medical Center for respiratory treatment. Animal control came later in the day and attempted to catch the cats. For the rest of that day and most of the next, animal control worked with the Humane Society and caught a total of 163 cats. The cats were inspected and treated. It's estimated that another ten to twenty cats got away.

"We tried to place as many as we could with homes and animal shelters," said Jessica Silverberg of the Humane Society. "But, unfortunately, many of them had to be put down. They were disease-ridden or missing eyes or had severe respiratory problems. We placed a few, but most people didn't want to take them. It takes a special person to take care of special animals."

Emily Smith spent four days in the hospital. She was not allowed to return to the house, which required major renovation. She went to live with her daughter and son-in-law for nearly a year before getting her own apartment. With the intervention of her family and a therapist, Emily Smith decided that she should not get any more cats or house pets.

"The nice thing is, I didn't really need house pets any longer. Sammy had animals, and I could always visit his," Smith said.

It may be a stretch to say that Sammy Johnson collected his exotic animals because his grandmother was once the community cat hoarder. But there is no denying the similarity. Someone close to Johnson—who had lived with him for some time and had been a regular part of his life—was a compulsive collector of cats. Since early childhood, Sammy Johnson had an interest in collecting animals. His grandmother's obsession with collecting cats may have, in part, influenced Sammy Johnson's compulsive trait to collect bigger, stronger animals.

The connection has been made before. Emily Smith herself, in an interview in 1988, said, "His first was a tabby cat. I'm the one give it to him. After that first, he caught himself a taste for cats. From then on, it was always his dream to get a tiger. We shared a love for cats."

###

Evening Stroll

The moon shone full in the clear sky. The perfect evening for a walk. Elise and her two children put on their shoes and went to the wooded area behind their house for an after-dinner stroll.

"Look, there's the Big Dipper." Elise pointed. "And the Little Dipper."

"Isn't one of them supposed to look like a bear?" asked her son, Colin.

"Well, I think the tails of the bears make up the handles of the dippers—the Great Bear and the Little Bear. Connect the dots and you can make a lot of shapes. You can even make up your own constellations."

"Cool," Colin said.

It *was* cool, nearly chilly. And it was *cool*, in the way that Colin meant it, for them to hang out together. So many of Elise's friends with ten- and twelve-year-olds had already been deemed "uncool" and their kids didn't want to be seen with them. Her kids still wanted to go for evening walks with her.

Ally, her daughter, noticed the animals first, darting out from the edge of the forest abutting their property. Birds scattered from the treetops above the three silhouettes. At first they took the trotting figures to be dogs, a few strays from a nearby farm or home. But it soon became obvious that these were not dogs; they were wolves. And regardless—dog or wolf—they were not friendly. Ally broke the evening's silence with a shrilly scream.

Elise knew that wolves were social animals; showing the alpha who was boss might drive the wolves away. But when the alpha wolf snapped at her ten-year old son and when she saw the blood gushing from his leg, Elise lost all rationality. She forgot what she knew: that screaming and crying and running would show the wolves weakness instead of driving them off; that wolves were smart enough to hunt for vulnerabilities in prey, like going for the youngest and weakest prey first.

The wolves had approached slowly, but with purpose. The alpha stood in front of the pack, his eyes flitting from Colin to Ally to Elise and back to Colin. The alpha attacked first, aided by the other two.

Elise didn't know what to do. Blood rushed to her head as she watched the wolf bite Colin's leg. The two other wolves bit into Colin's other leg. The alpha jumped up and clamped down on Colin's forearm, slipping off after shredding his flesh. It wasn't one dog to one person; it was every dog to whichever human the pack focused on at a given moment. If Elise and Ally had been lesser animals, they may have fled and left the weakest link here to be dinner for the pack. Instead, Elise launched a counter attack, and Ally followed her lead. The two women kicked and screamed at the wolf as it latched onto Colin's lower leg, opened for a better grip, and latched on again, splattering blood on the dark grass.

"Get away!" Colin screamed.

Elise needed to avert focus from her son. She kicked a wolf in the side, then all three wolves turned to her. They snarled at her with blood-stained teeth and bore into her with intense eyes. The alpha clamped onto Elise's leg and the companions did, too. Elise cried out at the sting. Her son took his opportunity to run, and as they bit her, she could feel the pain Colin must be feeling as he tried to move through the injuries. As quickly as they'd attacked her, they turned to chase her limping son, perhaps encouraged by the trail of blood he left in the grass. The snarling wolves snapped at the backs of his legs and bit his hips and butt. Ally picked up a stick and clobbered one of the wolves in the side. The animals counterattacked, biting the offending arm and hand. When Colin took his turn, throwing rocks at the wolves and drawing them back to him, Ally ran out of harm's way.

"Call 911!" Elise screamed at Ally. Thank God, Ally had her cell phone with her, even though Elise usually encouraged her to leave it behind so she wouldn't be distracted by texts from her friends during their walk. Ally called 911 and Elise charged toward the wolves, drawing them away from Colin with a yell and a running kick to the side. A wolf yelped, but quickly joined the other two in attacking her.

"Go!" Elise yelled. She wished her children would run to safety and let her contend with the wolves and their stinging teeth and claws. But her kids wouldn't leave her. They fought the wolves as a family, just as the pack stuck together in their attack. Two families of three, fiercely fighting. Her yoga pants dripped with blood and where her legs did not sting, they felt sticky. The wolves bit into her fleshy calves and threw their heads from side to side in efforts to bring her down. She and Ally and Colin kicked the wolves in the heads and underbellies, hit them on the backs and in the sides and on the heads with heavy tree branches and rocks. The fur around their mouths and on their front legs were matted with blood. The wolves were weakening.

By the time the police responded to their call, they had more or less driven the wolves off. The wolves were still here in the large field at the edge of the woods, but it was as though the wolves had taken a break to reconsider. Fight or flee? After all, this wasn't the vulnerable, weak kill they had expected.

Fight or flee was no longer an option when the police arrived. The two policemen—Toby and Tom, she would later find out as they introduced themselves at the hospital to take a report—opened fire on the wolves with their assault rifles, and the wolves fell. Elise was afraid to look closely at her legs, afraid to touch her deep wounds. But she inspected Ally and Colin to see if pressure needed to be applied.

"We made it!" Elise smiled at them and placed her sticky red hands on their heads, bringing them in for a hug. "We're going to be all right."

By the time the ambulance arrived, the whole ordeal hadn't taken more than fifteen minutes. It seemed like hours.

It was only later, in the ambulance, that Elise would find time to question why wild animals would attack humans. *Isn't it easier and more natural for wolves to go after smaller animals, like rabbits and squirrels, perhaps deer or foxes?* She didn't suspect there were many wolf attacks on people. None that she'd ever heard of. *Wolves tend to avoid humans.*

In the hospital, she learned of the news she had not yet seen break— exotic animals on the loose. These were not wild animals after all. They didn't see people as a threat.

"They most likely came to you, originally, with the intention of asking for food, accustomed to being fed by humans," Leland Anders would later explain to her on his television show dedicated to their experience. "But when you started screaming and running—a perfectly natural reaction, by the way—the wolves saw you as prey. And that's why they attacked. It's unusual for wolves to attack people. But you're lucky that you were together, that you *stuck* together, and that you were able to save each other."

"We always have worked as a team," Elise said proudly during the show. They had always been close, but she felt that now, after the terrible incident, they were closer than ever. Shared tragedy had strengthened them.

At the hospital, all three of them were treated. Between them, they had two hundred and forty-eight stitches. Poor Colin had the most: one hundred and forty-two of them. They had to stich two layers of muscle and the skin in each calf, thigh, and buttock. "I won't be able to sit for weeks," he griped from his hospital bed. Elise and Ally needed stitches on their legs and arms.

"I'm lucky to have such wonderful kids," Elise said in one of many interviews that would come in the days to follow. "They could have turned, running and scared. But they stayed with me, and together, as a family, we were able to drive them off."

Lucky was a strong word, and perhaps the wrong word, Elise sometimes considered. Her injuries ached, and she knew the pain was worse for Colin. Elise was scared to death, traumatized by the attack. There had been talk, in the months before the wolves struck, of getting a family dog, but that wouldn't happen anytime soon. Only time would tell if and when they'd feel brave enough to go for a hike in the woods or a walk in the park again. She didn't even want to step into her back yard, having fallen into the habit of going from house to garage to car to urban destination, seldom coming into contact with outdoor areas that did not come lined with concrete and steel.

But Elise had her family. Her pack kept her going.

Before and After

I interviewed Mr. Johnson several times in the past and found him to be a kind and compassionate man. I'm not sure what caused him to do what he did, but I don't think it had anything to do with the war forty years ago or any kind of hate or disregard for his community. Perhaps he felt misunderstood.

— Amy Shivers, Chillicothe Evening News

Sammy wasn't *about* the war. He had a full and rich life. He didn't talk much about his time over there. It's not like that experience defined him. I mean, it was only a couple years, anyway. Sure, he changed some. He saw some rough shit. Just wasn't who he was.

— Willie Johnson, Sammy Johnson's Father

I asked him about the war, but he didn't like to talk about it.

— Marielle Johnson, Sammy Johnson's Wife

War's the one time in life that they give you medals for breaking the law, for breaking God's law. *Thou shalt not kill.* But here's a medal for doing it anyway. For breaking God's commandment to follow your country's own commands. One nation, *over* God.

— Mike Skaggs, Sammy Johnson's Drinking Buddy

There is no doubt that his war experience influenced him. Such traumatic experiences always have an effect on a person. The question is, then, *how* did it influence him?

— Dr. Minnie Fields, Professor of Psychology, Shawnee State University

I can't say whether the war had an influence on his love of exotic animals. I'm sure a psychologist or sociologist will say that it did. But Sammy worked with me at the Columbus Zoo before he ever shipped off, and he had an infatuation with the tigers and lions and apes back then. It's not like a switch was flipped in Vietnam. But maybe he found his nerve there, to begin buying exotic animals for himself.

— Leland Anders, Celebrity Zookeeper

I was a deputy back then, when Sammy returned. It wasn't just him—a lot of the boys came back a little rambunctious. I mean, he'd get drunk, get in a bar fight, and we'd throw them in the tank to sober up. But these guys just got back from havoc, where they were shooting at people and getting shot at. A bar scuffle seemed tame to them, I'd say.

— Roscoe Roy, Ross County Sheriff

Oh, he was different when he came back. I mean, he was still a good boy. But I think war hardens a boy.

— Sally Johnson, Sammy Johnson's Mother

Hardened by war, influenced by a cat-hoarding grandmother, resistant to authority figures, and turned away by the local zoos that had once employed him, Sammy Johnson was a maverick who did things his way: bought a private zoo full of dangerous animals with complete disregard for his neighbors and the community around him. It was his stubborn disregard and his anger at a system he thought was out to get him that led him to unleash the wild creatures on the community.

— Carrie Mortimer, Editorial, CNEN-TV

When we talked about the war, it always came back to two animal experiences. The time he adopted a little monkey and became friends with it, letting it live with him in his tent, and the time he saw a jungle tiger take down a giant water buffalo. Never talked about any action over there. He always went right to the same two animal stories. And you know what? When other vets were around and they were swapping war stories, his were the ones people always wanted to hear.

— Dennis Waltman, Bartender

Alls I'm saying is anyone who goes to war comes back a changed man. I'm not saying he was a worse man or less of a man. I'm not saying he was crazy or weird or a baby killer or even a killer. Alls I'm saying is that he loved him some hamsters and puppies before, and then he loved him some tigers and bears when he got back. Adorable little puppies licking your face before, vicious, flesh-eating beasts swiping at you after. Did the war change him? Damn straight.

— Joey Wallace, Sammy Johnson's former classmate

So he and two other guys are sitting there in the jungle, and they see this huge water buffalo. Then there's this rustling in the plants, and they look over and see this big cat's eyes staring out. The other guys start to panic, but Sammy tells them to stay calm and stay still. He stays right where he is and watches, and this tiger bursts out of the grass and pounces on this buffalo. The beast lets out this blood-curdling bellow. The thing falls over, and the tiger starts eating the thing—chewing out its guts. One of the guys throws up right then and there. Sammy says, "I want the tiger on my side."

— Mike Skaggs, Sammy Johnson's Drinking Buddy

The Army wouldn't let him bring the monkey back with him. He had to leave it there. I think that got to him. It wasn't long before he had a monkey back home.

— Dennis Waltman, Bartender

What Happened After He Came Back

When Sammy Johnson came back from Vietnam at the age of twenty, he felt like a different man. That is to say, he was a *man*. Before being drafted and trained and shipped off, he was still only a boy with a menagerie of household pets. When he returned, he'd aged two years but matured ten. Most of his pets had either died or been given away to neighbors or good homes found through classified ads. His parents had told him about the animals, one by one, in their letters, had explained to him that it just didn't fit their routine and they didn't have time to feed and clean and care for twenty animals every day, and that he'd just have to get new ones when he returned. (*If* he returned, they never wrote, but he could sense the implication in the ink and paper.)

When he returned to Chillicothe, Sammy moved back in with Mom and Dad. He was surprised when he turned on the television and saw his former co-worker, Leland Anders, with his own television show. Leland had always been a political animal and knew how to navigate public relations; it seemed he met with success at every turn. Sammy learned that Leland, who'd already had a degree in zoology when they'd worked together at the Columbus Zoo, and who'd already gained valuable experience during his internship with a veterinarian, had returned to college for a master of fine arts in film and television. That not only allowed him to perfect his pitch for a television show, it also kept him safely home during the draft. While Sammy served two years in Vietnam, Leland left the zoo and parlayed his occasional television appearances and new expertise in production into his own local half-hour kid's show. The program got syndicated, and Leland became a celebrity with his very own "television zoo." *The Zoo for You* was not physically open to the public. It was a real zoo filled with real animals, but it existed only for Leland's television show. Most people who loved animals loved *The Zoo for You* with Leland Anders and his cast of a thousand animals.

Sammy wasn't a fan. He wished he could say, "I knew him when" and "We used to be friends." Instead Sammy felt as though he'd been one-upped.

All that remained of Sammy's beloved pets were two barn cats (who had fended for themselves in the outdoors) and the beagle. Sammy found work at local farms, stripping tobacco, feeding and cleaning after and caring for farm animals. He shoveled shit at a safari park in Zanesville. He saved up his money.

With help from Uncle Sam, by means of special loans for veterans, he managed to start up a little gun and tackle shop on the outskirts of town. As his business grew, so did his ambitions. Within a few years, his business thrived. Selling used and antique guns gave him the means to pursue his dream.

At auction, Sammy found a great deal on a shabby farm just ten minutes east of Chillicothe's city limits. There, he planted an old double-wide trailer, and sank the bulk of his money into the building of a large warehouse. During the months of construction, he visited the crew daily, watching them erect the wooden frame, the steel walls, the individual cages of iron bar and wire. When finished, the metallic red warehouse sparkled in the sunlight. Sammy longed to fill it with happy residents. He picked up the latest issue of *Animal Trader Monthly*.

He found it difficult to focus as he thumbed through the pages. Yes, he'd seen the tabloid before, years ago. But that was before the war, when he was still a young and naive child, when his vision had been rose-tinted and cheery and somewhat unreal. Now an adult with reality-adjusted lenses, he scanned the variety of exotic animals available for legal purchase.

TIGER CUB—three weeks old, only $500, must show proof of land and cage facilities, 555-1985.

Sammy picked up the phone and answered his first advertisement. When he mentioned he lived on his own farm in Ohio, the sellers didn't require him to prove any sort of property ownership or animal facilities, although Sammy was prepared to do so. Sammy purchased the tiger cub for the requested $500 and picked it up himself, driving from Chillicothe up to Marion to meet his new pet. The seller even threw in the cat carrier for free.

In the truck, Sammy let the tiger cub roam free. The cub explored the bench seat, rubbing against his hip and falling next to him and purring. At home, Sammy let the cub roam inside the trailer. He fed it milk from a bottle and placed balls of soft ground beef in a bowl next to a water dish. The cat sat in his lap and purred as Sammy watched the evening news and television shows, then slept with him at night. Off and on throughout the night the cub purred, loud and gravelly and peacefully. He named the tiger cub Tabby.

$600—BEAR CUBS—three to choose from. Grizzly, two weeks old, great personalities and dispositions. Call today before they're snatched up!

Sammy did. This time, he had to drive all the way to Gary, Indiana, to do the choosing. But when he got there, he fell in love with the two cubs that remained. The mother was there, too. He got to visit the full-grown bear in her cage, got to touch it, pet it, even hug it. "She'll get about this size?" Sammy asked.

The seller sized up the cubs. "About that, give or take a dozen pounds."

"Will it get along with a tiger?"

"Couldn't rightly say. I guess for a few months, while they're still young, they ain't gonna bother one another. But I don't think I'd have a grown bear and tiger in the same room together. Especially not with me in it." The man laughed.

Sammy chuckled along. The truth was, that's exactly what he wanted: to actually live with the animals. He pointed to one of the cubs. "Will you take four hundred for her?"

"Tell you what," the man considered, "let's make it five."

"Four-fifty."

"You got it." And Sammy did get it.

When Sammy brought the grizzly cub home, he let it share the house with him and Tabby. The bear, too, drank milk from a bottle, like a baby, and ate balls of soft ground beef. He let the bear sit in his lap, wrestle with his hands and feet, and sleep with him and the Tabby in his bed. He named the bear Abby.

He knew he should stop himself for the moment, that he should wait and see how it went with these two animals before going in deeper. But he wanted just a couple more for his starter pack. The next advertisement he answered, out of the same circular, offered a lion cub. Located in the Cleveland area, he found a lion owner who had eight lions and bred them for sale. She had four cubs available, all of them from the same litter, about a month old. The parents, in another cage but within view of the cubs, did not seem happy about the separation. Sammy knew that lions were family animals, like people. That's part of the reason he wanted a lion as part of his family.

One lion practically lured him in. "I'll take that one." Sammy bought it at a discount with the assurance that he would likely return in a matter of months for both advice on raising lions and to purchase additional ones.

The lion was a little bigger than the tiger and bear, but only because it was a little older. In time, Sammy knew that the dynamics would change: the bear would weigh as much as 800 pounds, by far the largest of the family. The tiger would likely reach around 500 pounds, and the lion closer to 400. But for now, it seemed easy enough for them all to reside together in one home, to sit together on the couch, playing with one another, purring and hugging and petting. For now, they could all sleep in the same bed.

These first attempts at purchasing exotic animals happened quickly, and without much thought. Within the course of two weeks, Sammy had accumulated these three, and another. From his own neighborhood in Chillicothe, he answered an advertisement for a year-old spider monkey.

Sammy had planned to leave it at that for a while. Yet he couldn't help but pick up the next edition of *Animal Trader Monthly*, just to look. Sure enough, another advertisement caught his attention.

FREE TO GOOD FARM—AMERICAN BUFFALO, FIVE YEARS OLD, FORMER PET, MUST GET RID OF BEFORE MOVING TO CITY.

Sammy couldn't pass up a free animal, and this buffalo would be more like a farm animal than a family member, grazing the field and keeping the land trim. Sammy enjoyed seeing the buffalo out in his pasture, grazing the grass. Cars along Rural Place Road would slow down—or even stop in the middle of the road—to catch a glimpse of the unusual sight.

Sammy laughed as he tried to imagine what the reaction of such drivers would be if they knew what roamed inside his house. Word spread about the buffalo, being out in the open, and soon enough he received a call from Mom.

"Sammy? I heard you got a bison out there on your property."

"That's right, Mom. I got it just a few days ago. He's a beauty. Want to come see him?"

"Sure," Mom said. "Me and Dad were just saying that we'd like to stop in and visit."

"Hey, I'll pick up some burgers, and we'll have a grill-out on Sunday. How's that sound?"

Mom agreed. "We'll bring the baked beans and potato salad."

When his parents arrived, he offered them lounge chairs outside and did not immediately invite them in. Sipping on light beer, the three of them watched the buffalo roam the field. After some time, Sammy lured the buffalo over to the side of the fence with some hay. "Go ahead and pet him," Sammy offered.

"Looks kind of like a cow." Mom reached out and patted the fluffy fur. "Only he feels more like a sheep."

"Can you keep him with the grass and weed from your field alone?" Dad asked. "Or will you need to buy feed?"

"I'll need to bale some hay before winter. And if he does eat it all,

I'll just buy some hay from one of the neighbors. Can probably cut their meadow for free and keep the hay. Win-win."

Construction had begun on his warehouse, where he hoped to one day store his personal zoo of animals. But at the moment, it just looked like a big barn. The empty metal cages at the side of the double-wide, large enough to jail people, drew his parents' attention.

"What are those for?" Dad asked.

"You know I've always wanted to get some animals, right?" Sammy smiled excitedly. "Some exotic animals, like at the zoo?"

"I know you always talked about it," Dad said. "But I thought you grew out of it."

"Nope. I still want to surround myself with animals."

Dad stepped up to the cages and inspected them: frames of strong steel with bars and chain links all around the sides and top. "Serious stuff, here. Guess you're really going to do it."

"Yep. But I don't quite need the cages yet. I will soon, though. Let's go inside."

Mom and Dad followed Sammy into the trailer. When they entered, a screeching sound greeted them.

Mom put her hands over her ears. "What's that noise?"

"That's just Jojo," Sammy said. "My spider monkey. I've got him caged up, because he was getting into the kitchen cabinets."

They placed their glasses on the counter, where Sammy had laid out the raw hamburger meat, already made into patties and ready to grill. He brought the monkey out in the cat carrier that he had gotten with his tiger cub. Sammy offered to open the cage and to let them play with it, but Mom and Dad both declined. Sammy put a finger in to pet Jojo's head, and the monkey held his finger, shaking it in playful greeting. He put the cage down on the kitchen table. It was too early to start cooking the burgers, so Sammy gave Dad and Mom a couple more beers and invited them to the living room.

"Holy shit," Dad said. "What the hell kind of housecat is that?" The tiger cub rubbed against Dad's leg. He already had an adversity to cats, after Grandma's hoarding. But this was no ordinary cat.

"It's a tiger cub, Dad!" Sammy lifted the cat by the scruff of the neck and offered it to him. "Surprise!" Dad backed away, so Sammy cuddled it in his own arms. Tabby began to purr. "He's harmless, Dad."

They spotted the lion cub next. "How many of them do you have?" Concern padded Mom's voice. They weren't exactly frightened, the cats still small enough to be just cats. But Sammy could see in their eyes the fear of what may come.

"Only the two cats. And Abby."

"Who's Abby?" Dad asked.

Sammy called his bear cub so he could introduce them. Mom and Dad took seats in a rocking chair and recliner at one side of the living room. Sammy carried his tiger and fell onto the couch, and the lion and bear jumped up with them. Sammy laughed playfully as he toyed with the three young animals.

"Good thing you got those cages out there," Dad said. "Ain't no way these things can stay in here with you."

"Yes, Sammy." Mom looked anxious. "When are you going to put them out?"

"Oh, don't worry so much. They're just like people."

"People don't rip your guts out when they're playing with you," Dad warned.

"Neither do these guys." Sammy rubbed the lion cub behind the ears, then tickled the belly of the bear. "They're just sweet little cuddly babies. And when they grow up, I'll put them in their houses outside."

"You may want to do it before they grow up," Mom said.

The lion jumped off the sofa and ambled over to Mom. It smelled her legs and rubbed against them, then playfully batted at them. The scratch on her skin grew red, but blood did not flow.

"They may look like cute little animals now that they're babies," Dad said, looking at Mom's leg, "but they can get big and vicious overnight."

"I know, Dad." Sammy said, annoyed at their reaction. The lion had run out of the living room, sensing that it may get in trouble for the matter of the leg. The bear lumbered toward Dad, but he kicked it away and it followed the lion into the kitchen. "Believe me, Dad, I know these guys better than anyone. I've been reading about them and spending time with them all my life. I know all about them. And I know what I'm doing."

"You can't live with them when they get big. Not any more than Grandma could live with all of those cats."

"That was different." Sammy grew impatient. "I'm not getting a hundred of the critters. Now, let's get the burgers on the grill."

They went to the kitchen to find the tiger and bear on the kitchen floor, eating raw ground beef. They had managed to knock the plate to the floor, and ground beef mounds were all about, shards of white and orange glass in them.

Dad frowned. "Know all about how to take care of them, huh?"

Mom put on a cheery smile. "At least we have beans and potatoes."

"Guess I'll order a pizza." Sammy walked toward the phone on the wall.

Dad watched the animals feeding. "You think it's normal for them to eat that meat, with glass in it?"

"Don't worry about them, Dad." Sammy picked up the phone from the kitchen wall to dial the local pizzeria. "They're tough. They have stomachs of steel. They can digest anything."

"That's right," Dad said, watching them devour the meat hungrily. "Even people."

Animal Affection

Marielle frowned into her cup of lukewarm coffee, as though searching for words. "People like to frame things in ways that interest them, or that perhaps reflect their own perceptions. Reporters, psychologists, police, zookeepers, neighbors, friends—they all like to look at Sammy as a 'before and after.' Before the war and after the war. Before his grandma got rid of her cats and after she got rid of her cats. Before he got the animals and after he got the animals. Before his lion attacked my friend—it was really her own fault—and after it attacked. Before he got hit with a gun charge and went to jail and after he served his time." She paused, took a sip of the bitter coffee, lowered the mug to her lap, and then eased into a contemplative smile. "But that's not how I see things. I knew Sammy better than anyone. He wasn't just a 'before and after' sketch."

Marielle straightened her back, placed her mug on the side table, and repositioned herself in her chair. Sammy's favorite: a plush, checkered armchair. The reporter had come up with the idea, to conduct the interview here in the home where she and Sammy lived for years. She felt as though she could sink into the soft, warm upholstery and disappear.

"How do you see things?" the interviewer asked.

As though awakened from a daydream, Marielle quickly looked up to face the reporter. "Sammy Johnson was a lovable, huggable person with a big heart. Big enough to handle the big cats, the bear." A nervous sound, more breath than laughter, fell from her mouth. "Big enough to handle me."

Marielle figured she and Sammy knew each other before they remembered knowing each other. They went to school together from kindergarten through high school graduation, according to the school yearbooks and class photographs, although Marielle didn't actually recall knowing Sammy until they hit fifth grade. She remembered sitting with him at lunch in the school cafeteria. He was a shy boy then, but when she mentioned her family might get a llama, he got excited and started talking about his own animals.

"He would just light up when he talked about his animals," Marielle told the reporter. "In school, and in adulthood, whether he was talking about his dogs and house cats or his bears and big cats, he got excited about his animals."

In high school, she remembered, he became less shy, more outgoing, talking to other guys about the big animals he got to pet and play with when he visited the zoo, talking about how he was going to own a zoo of his own one day and get into the cages with the wild animals anytime he wanted. The other guys were tough on the basketball court and football field, but Sammy one-upped them with talk of being a master of wild beasts.

Sammy was a wild beast himself, but his wildness could be tamed. It took him time to get the courage to move from friendship to courtship, but when prom came along, he asked Marielle to go with him. There, on the dance floor of their school gymnasium, as they swayed hip to hip, their arms around one another, their faces nearly touching, he swooped in like a hawk and snatched that first kiss. A first for each of them. But not a last.

"I wasn't sure, though," she told the reporter. "I was fond of him, and we knew each other pretty well, always talking during lunch and after school, catching movies together on Saturdays. But after that prom, we didn't go on another date like that for a long time."

She was certain he was on the verge of asking her to a formal at the local American Legion. But he got drafted. She saw him off, along with a few of their friends and his parents, at the bus stop. She gave him a parting kiss that morning to rival the one at the prom. Their next kiss wouldn't come until he returned two years later. That post-war kiss was an animalistic kiss, passionate and ravenous.

Now, Marielle remembered how they made love in the woods the day after he returned from Vietnam. A picnic dinner with red wine and cold cuts and bread and cookies, a clearing in the trees, brushing aside the sticks and rocks and leaves and putting down a thick blanket, then a quilt over that, and dining there. Drinking there, love songs crooning on a cassette player, slow dancing amongst the swaying trees. The wind gently brushed them and the trees seemed to be dancing with them and it almost felt like they were back at the prom, only better. They cleared the quilt of the basket and bottle, cleared one another of their clothing, and made love right there in the woods, like animals.

How Marielle loved Sammy. Before then. Then. After then. She never stopped loving Sammy.

Even after that experience, Sammy did not treat her like a steady girl-friend, exactly. Not that he played around, but he didn't call her and take her on dates every weekend the way some guys might. He would call once in a while, maybe every couple weeks. But he kept himself busy, between working and saving for his own place (since he lived with his parents when he returned from the war). As much fun as they had when they were together, he remained somewhat of a loner.

Not long after Sammy got his own place, he invited Marielle over for dinner. He had a nice piece of land, more than ten acres, and he had a double wide put at the end of the long drive from the main road.

"The trailer is temporary," he assured her. "This is just until I get my other buildings taken care of." He showed her his blueprints, his plans for having a giant barn, or "warehouse" as he called it, built on his property. His plans for cages lining the private drive.

"Some people have lion statues at either side of their driveway," Sammy boasted. "I plan to have the real deal."

She giggled, tickled by his excitement. "That's wild."

"Do you mind dating a man who owns lions and tigers and bears?"

"Oh, my!" She laughed, playfully. The truth was, she found it fascinating, the prospect of being able to pet a lion or tiger. "As long as it's not dangerous!"

"Not at all," he promised. "They're just like people, only cuter and not as cunning. Not as quick to stab a person in the back."

That night, after burgers and salad, beer and bourbon, they spent the night together in his new pad. After they'd made love, he showed her the *Animal Trader Monthly* he'd picked up, and she understood the reality of his plans.

As if to prove to her how beautiful exotic animals could be, he took her for Saturday trips to the zoos in Cincinnati and Columbus, took her on day trips to safari parks and smaller farms where you could actually touch the animals. He convinced her that animals and people could live together, could form a family unit. He hadn't proposed to her, or asked her to move in with him. He hadn't even verified that he thought of them as a steady couple. For all she knew at the time, he was just a big-hearted friend who liked to fool around.

"But he was priming me for what was to come," Marielle told the interviewer. "Preparing me for life with the animals."

Some of the things Marielle remembered, she didn't tell the interviewer.

At the interviewer's prompting, Marielle stood and they walked along the property as they continued to talk. The police tape now gone, the hoard of exotic animals buried in a mass grave. So many of her fondest memories were planted in these ten acres.

"Those first few years, after he came back from the war, were so irregular and spontaneous," she told the interviewer as they explored what used to be their happy preserve. "We'd get together for a date, have a great day, then we wouldn't see each other for a week or two. But when we got back together, it seemed like we'd never been apart. He was just so focused on working, saving up for the life he wanted to create for us. Once he got his place and moved out of his parents' house, things really started to move faster for us." Marielle felt like a young woman in love again when she recalled her budding romance with Sammy.

"Where are we going?" she asked when Sammy picked her up for a date after he'd established his own homestead.

"We could go out to a movie or the bar," he teased. "But I'd rather take you home tonight."

"Oh, really?" she asked playfully.

"I want to show you my wild side."

What she saw surprised her. First, even before they pulled into his drive, she could see the buffalo grazing the field, the sun setting beyond the trees and backlighting the large grazer. Then, as they drove along his private drive, she noted the new cages along the sides.

"Are those for the buffalo?" she asked.

He smiled. "No. For the others."

When they went inside, she jumped and yelped when she saw a lion cub, a tiger cub, a caged spider monkey and a bear cub.

"Oh my God," she gasped. "You didn't!"

"Would you like to play with them?" Sammy smiled, all boyhood excitement. The same kind of sparkle in his eyes as he got when he flirted with her.

"Yes," she said. And they spent the next couple of hours playing with the animals. The lion and tiger cubs pounced around like big housecats, batting their heavy paws at one another, the bear cub bouncing around on the floor, rolling between the cats and joining in the fun. Each of the three cubs made their rounds in Sammy's and Marielle's laps, purring, rubbing, playfully batting. They were warm and soft and beautiful.

When Sammy brought the spider monkey out of his cage to meet Marielle, he seemed unsure of her at first. But it took little time for the baby to give her a hug and sit on her leg.

Now, looking at the mound where the animals were buried, Marielle remembered how funny and playful and beautiful and magical the little cubs had been. They bounced around like puppies, had the agility, even as cubs, of cats. She remembered them being heavy for their size, large boned, big heads and paws, and they were warm to hold and purred in a way that no other cat ever could. Especially the lion cub. She fell instantly in love with the lion.

"My beautiful lioness," Sammy had said, watching her as she held the lion cub close to her. "My beautiful lioness has a lion."

"And you," she said, purring herself. "My bear of a man."

"A bear!" he laughed, then growled. And then they made love with the animals all around them.

The morning after, they woke in his bed with the cubs. The screaming monkey served as an alarm clock. As soon as Sammy fed it, the monkey quieted. He got back in bed with her. Yes, she had noticed him gone, but she had remained warm and cozy even after he left her in bed, because he did not leave her in bed alone. The bear and tiger and lion cubs nuzzled against her.

"So, now that you're awake and fully sober on a Sunday morning," he whispered in her ear, "do you think I'm crazy? Do you think you can handle all this?"

"Handle it?" A warm giggle bubbled from her chest. "I think it's great. What other lucky lady in Chillicothe has all this to wake up to?"

"They'll stay in the house until they get too big. Then, they'll go out to their outdoor homes, their cages. But they'll still be our babies. And we can get in the cages with them. Can't all sleep in the bed together when they carry sixteen thousand pounds between them. But we'll still be able to love them."

"Sounds dreamy."

Standing outside with the reporter, Marielle realized now that it was, in part, her acceptance of his desire for exotic animals that gave him the confidence to ask for her hand in marriage. In the days that followed that first night with the animals in their bed, a nervous tension had been broken. He would later reveal his fear that she might high-tail it out of his life when she saw the reality of the situation, the extent of his love for animals. But she shared his love. And in those weeks that followed, they began seeing each other nearly every day. And not more than a month later, he asked her to marry him.

A few months after that, she did.

"He was such a passionate man." Marielle smiled at the reporter. "I loved him."

"But you did leave him, right?"

She frowned. She could tell this reporter wanted something scandalous, something he could sink his teeth into. By now, Marielle had read enough negative ink about Sammy Johnson. Yes, she was still angry at what he did, pissed beyond words that he left her in such a dramatic way without talking with her first.

"Temporarily." She glared at the interviewer. "I needed time to sort things out, after he went to jail." She looked the reporter straight in the eye. "Sometimes he drove me crazy. But usually, he drove me crazy in the best way."

Advertisements Sammy Circled

CHEETAHS AND LEOPARDS, we have litters of cheetahs and leopards available; range from 2 weeks to 4 months; $300 each or buy a set of two for $500.

SIBERIAN TIGER CUB, very rare, two available, five weeks old, only $1,500 each or highest bidder.

BUZZY THE WRESTLING GRIZZLY, available for adoption—playful, full-grown bear known throughout the mid-west for his performances wrestling with volunteer members from the audience, great opportunity to purchase a professionally trained grizzly bear, eight years young, perfect for use in circus or animal act, or great for a private buddy, good around kids and household pets but needs to be caged when not actively engaged, call to make an appointment to interview for adoption and to meet Buzzy to see if you're a good fit for each other.

BLACK PANTHER available, three months, answers to name of Malcolm, very affectionate around people and children, $700 or $1,000 with full-grown cage (suitable for use when panther reaches full size).

BABOONS CHIMPS GORILLAS—all of your primate needs in one location. We specialize in well-trained, young, and hard-to-find primates for use as household pets. There's nothing like looking into the face of a primate—Call today.

REPTILES!! We have CROCS, GATORS, IGUANAS, KOMODO DRAGONS. Clamp your jaws down on a deal.

WOLVES for sale. Pure wolf, not cross bred with dogs. Eight to choose from $300 OBO.

LION CUBS, male and female, two weeks old, adorable, five available, only asking $400 apiece, $700 for two, $1,500 for all five. We'll keep mom and dad but can't afford to keep the whole pride. Please call now. Three females, two males.

Honey Moon

Sammy did not take Marielle on a traditional honeymoon. For one thing, Sammy had too much money tied up in the property, warehouse, and in plans for a house to replace the trailer. For another, who could he find to take care of their unusual family? Owning such creatures was a privilege and a pleasure. But also a tether and an anchor. They just couldn't get away for more than a few days at a time.

After the sensible wedding ceremony on their own property, attended by their family and friends, old teachers, classmates and bar fellows, they enjoyed a reception under a makeshift tent. They stayed put for their wedding night.

"You have to take your new bride somewhere," Dad had insisted. "It just ain't right to stay in your trailer."

"Maybe if you just go on an overnight trip to Windsor, Canada. Or to Sandusky. Or Put-In-Bay?" Mom had been generous with nearby suggestions.

Dad put an arm around Sammy. "Tell you what. I know I said I didn't want anything to do with the beasts. But if you cage the animals up out here, I'll check on them and throw some meat to them. If that'll get you away for a day or two. Just make sure they're locked up nice and tight."

That next week, with their young bear, lion, tiger and monkey secure in the outdoor cages, Sammy took Marielle on a weekend trip. They drove in his Dodge Ram from Chillicothe up through Columbus, Marion, all the way to Sandusky. There, they spent a few hours walking along the windy beach of Lake Erie, and a few more hours at Cedar Point, riding one thrilling roller coaster after another. In the evening, just as the sun began setting, they took the ferry across the lake to Put-in-Bay Island.

"First trip off the mainland?" he asked.

"Guess so." Marielle laughed. The sun made her eyes sparkle.

"Welcome to the wild west, baby."

This "Key West of the North" appeared more middle-aged drunk than young-love intoxicated. But Sammy and Marielle made the best of the destination, ditching their usual lives for a few hours, at least.

"Let's buy cigarettes," Marielle suggested, even though they never smoked. They got a pack of Kools and took them to the bar. It seemed to them that bars, beer, whiskey and cigarettes went hand-in-hand in Put-in-Bay.

They hopped from bar to bar, kissing one another, drinking rum punch and screwdrivers and Alabama Slammers, listening to Caribbean songs in one bar and dueling pianists playing contemporary hits in another.

They visited the "longest bar in the world," which spanned more than one hundred feet, most of it filled with people ordering tropical drinks. Sammy and Marielle lit their cigarettes, drank their margaritas, tipsy as they took it all in.

After a sobering stroll through a grassy park, they hopped back on the ferry and rode across the lake to Sandusky, where they had a motel room waiting for them. They turned on the television and found a wildlife program for background—they missed their family back home—and they tumbled into bed to make clumsy, drunken love, savoring one another's menthol-smoked mouths.

They woke late the next morning with hangovers. Sammy drank a room-temperature can of beer to quench his thirst.

She had one as well, to medicate her headache. "Hair of the dog," she chimed. "Just what the doctor ordered."

It was 10:30, and they'd missed the free continental breakfast they were counting on in the motel's lobby. So they hopped in the pick-up, went to a local mom and pop diner and ordered a late breakfast.

"That was fun," Marielle said over blueberry pancakes and chewy bacon.

"We've only just begun!"

He wouldn't tell her where they were headed. "It's a surprise." Back in the Ram, she rode with her window down, the wind in her hair. Soon, they crossed into Pennsylvania.

When they got to their destination, Sammy parked in a large gravel lot next to a huge warehouse of corrugated metal. He could tell that the unmarked building spooked her a little; she had no clue what they were in for. The license plates of the cars from numerous states dubbed this a national event.

People exited the building with caged animals. Marielle and Sammy went inside, and the overpowering smells and sounds of the interior made everything perfectly clear.

"It's an exotic animal convention!" Sammy bellowed.

"How cool!" Marielle exclaimed. Sammy could tell that the sheer number and variety of animals overwhelmed her. He followed along as she moved from one cage to another, spellbound by the beautiful creatures. And the not-so-beautiful ones.

Marielle cringed at the reptiles and snakes here. Asps. Boa constrictors. Cobras. Anacondas. There were alligators and crocodiles. Geckos, iguanas, armadillos. Even Komodo dragons.

"Look at those things!" Sammy pointed.

"I can't get into the reptiles." Marielle scrunched her face. "They creep me out."

"You're cute when you're creeped." Sammy nudged her in the side and she laughed. "But I know what you mean. You just can't cuddle up with a cold-blooded lizard or snake." He took her hand and led her away from the reptiles. "Over here, this is more like it." Sammy pointed to a fluffy Siberian tiger cub. "You could just reach out and hug that thing to death."

Marielle nearly burst with excitement. Even he couldn't believe the number of animals under one roof. It seemed they were in a concentrated zoo where everything was up for sale. Kangaroos, bison, spiders, insects, birds, tigers, lions, cougars, cheetahs, leopards, panthers, hyenas, primates, rhinos, hippos, aardvarks and all sorts of creatures—some of which they'd never even seen before, not even at a zoo. Like the tree sloth. And the white tiger.

After spending a few hours going through the warehouse, the commotion of people yelling over one another, haggling over prices, the sounds of animals competing for attention and the smells of animals taking care of business, the time came for Sammy and Marielle to leave and make the drive back home. On the way out, Sammy already had a vendor picked out, one he'd talked with when Marielle had made a trip to the bathroom.

"Here we go." Sammy pointed to a lion cub. The vendor, a skinny man in beige clothes and an orange baseball cap, retrieved a cub from the larger cage and handed it to Sammy. The lion cub purred and rubbed her head into his chest. "Do you like her?" he asked Marielle, and he handed it to her.

She took the warm, playful cub into her arms and hugged it. The cub purred deeply, loudly. "I love it," she gushed. Sammy already had a male lion cub growing into adulthood. Now, they would have a female lion in the family.

"We'll take it," Sammy said.

"Do you need a cage or carrier?"

"Nope." Sammy paid in cash. "It'll live in the house with us."

"All right." The vendor took the money but showed some concern. "Be careful."

"I know what I'm doing." Sammy put an arm around Marielle as she played with the lion cub at her breast. "See? Lots of people conceive during their honeymoon. But we don't have to wait nine months. We're already bringing home a baby girl."

Marielle giggled. As they drove home, the cub playing on her lap, falling out of her lap and onto the bench seat between them, rubbing against her hip and hopping back into her lap, Marielle told Sammy what she wanted to name it. "Honey Moon." She tried out the name. "Our honeymoon baby."

As though she already knew her name, Honey Moon responded by sitting in Marielle's lap, stretching up tall, and rubbing the side of her fuzzy face on Marielle's chest. They both purred.

Refined Search

FREE TO GOOD HOME—Adult Black Bear, used to being around people, not trained, will make a good pet, to experienced bear keeper only.

PAIR OF LIONS YOURS FOR FREE—one male, one female, free to good home. The mates have been together 7 years. Had cubs, not able to keep them. We do not want to break up the pair; please call if you have room for both lions.

FULL-GROWN BLACK PANTHER, free to good home. Must prove land ownership. You pick up, only for states where law allows exotic pet ownership. In some states, must show permit. Call if interested.

OUR LOSS = YOUR GAIN: Unable to maintain our three mountain lions due to economic situation. Must give away ASAP. Mother, father, and adult female cub. Prefer to give set to one person, but breakup negotiable. First come, first take.

BEE-BOP THE CHIMP—Birthday Party Chimpanzee retiring because his owner, Bo-Bo the Clown, is quitting the business after 30 years. Well-trained, knows lots of tricks, or good as a house pet. Call to meet the funniest monkey you'll ever see!

KOMODO DRAGON, CROC, AND IGUANA FREE TO GOOD HOME—must take entire lot, not pick and choose. Want the Komodo, take the Croc and Iguana. Animals are free but asking for $200 for the cages, heaters, rocks, etc. More than $800 invested in these setups, and the animals free. Be a dragon keeper; call today.

YES, VIRGINIA, THERE IS A LIGER—*you won't believe your eyes when you see this amazing cat. Half tiger, half lion and more than 1,000 pounds of big cat. Poor eyesight, needs loving care. Be prepared to feed this liger 40 pounds of meat per day. If you have a large enough cage and big enough meat budget, please call today to adopt this biggest of the big cats.*

LIONS, AND TIGERS, AND BEARS, ALL YOURS! I'm getting rid of my entire collection due to pressure from my new in-laws. They're great animals, wonderful pets, but if you have exotic animals you know they're not for everyone. Take one, take all: 3 lions, 2 tigers, 4 bears, also a cheetah and leopard. Believe me, I would give away the in-laws instead if my wife would let me!

How it Continued

"Sammy Johnson didn't go into anything half-assed," Marielle told the interviewer. "When he got into something, he went all the way."

Sammy started his gun and tackle shop with a dozen guns, and besides paying himself a decent salary, he spent most of the profits on inventory. By the end of a year in business, he had more than a hundred guns in the shop. He had just about any kind of bait and tackle a person could want, too.

He began selling other items on the side, out of his store. Cars, for example. He got a small dealership license, and he began stocking his parking lot with classics: a 1962 Austin-Healey, a 1968 Corvette, a 1971 Ford Fairlane, a 1977 Porche, a 1981 Mercedes and a 1983 DeLorean.

The same "all-in" attitude held true when it came to his animals.

In the early days, when it was just Sammy, Marielle, and their two lions, one tiger, one bear and one spider monkey, it had seemed easy enough to keep them all in the house. But as the pets grew, it became obvious that the animals needed to go to their cages permanently. Sammy eased into that permanence, first just caging them during the evenings. It was impossible for the year-old animals to all squeeze into their queen-sized bed at once. They weaned their pets into permanent cage life.

"It isn't a bad life," Sammy insisted when Marielle felt sorry for the animals, alone in their cages. "It's great for them. They never have to worry about where their next meal will come from. They have each other, and you can see that they care for each other, they're family. We're family."

Sammy regularly entered the cages. He didn't get in with every animal every day, but he spent a little bit of one-on-one time with each of his animals in any given week. And he assured Marielle that they appreciated it.

"Sammy could tell they understood," Marielle told the interviewer. "They cherished him being in the cage with them, spending time with them. And they were full of love."

Sammy had designed the cages so that each could open into the next. For the most part, he kept each animal in his or her own cage. But sometimes Sammy would open the door between the male and female lions, and the two of them mated. It wasn't long before they welcomed new lion cubs into the family.

Other family members were welcomed as well, from the outside. When Sammy decided to collect the exotic animals he loved, he didn't monkey around. He continued to read *Animal Trader Monthly*, highlighting advertisements that interested him. And he began to notice a trend. Exotic animal cubs were priced at a premium. Adult animals were far less expensive, and often free.

He was leery of the first few advertisements he came across that offered exotic animals, such as tigers and cougars, free to a good home. But when he answered the advertisements and met with the animal owners, he discovered that what often happened was that piddling pet buyers would lose interest when the animals got larger, more expensive to feed, and more difficult to control. A lot of money could be made with young animals, but the adults could sometimes be hard to give away.

So Sammy began obtaining animals that were rescues, rather than purchases. That's how he justified it to Marielle. She'd become a little concerned, a few years into their marriage, at the growth of their family. She'd told him as much.

"But Marielle, how can we turn our backs on these guys? We're rescuing these animals from poor treatment, malnourishment, even death!"

The gun and tackle shop was doing well, and occasional car sales added a little boost to their books. Once Sammy knew his business was secure and that he had an ample inventory, he took his profits from the business and put it into his private property. Marielle was impressed by his drive, his refusal to kick back and relax in the face of an unrealized goal. He completed the warehouse: a massive compound with room enough to stock a zoo's worth of animals in comfortable pens. He expanded the cages along the private drive, so about halfway between Rural Place Road and his trailer, cages lined the drive on either side; large and roomy dwellings for the animals he most wanted to display to anyone brave enough to visit.

After the warehouse and cages were completed, he had a nicer, sturdier, four-bedroom home built, constructed of wood and vinyl siding, just behind the trailer. With their house built and hooked up to electric and water, they moved in and hauled the empty trailer back in the field to use for storage. He had their front yard (where the trailer had once been) professionally landscaped with a lush turf, complete with a koi pond, flowering fruit trees, and a flower garden.

When the compound was finished, Sammy focused on expanding his animal kingdom. He and Marielle had two prides of lions, each in their own set of interconnected cages. Siberian tigers, Bengal tigers, white tigers and all sorts of mixes. Brown bears, black bears, Grizzlies and Kodiaks. The only common bear Sammy didn't get was a polar bear, which he'd always wanted but knew he couldn't keep without installing a proper pool and cooling system. They cared for mountain lions and cheetahs and leopards, bobcats and coyotes and hyenas, wolves and panthers and even a Komodo dragon. And the primates: macaque, spider monkeys, chimpanzees, baboons, lemurs and others. Marielle forgot what to call some of them.

"Sammy, Sammy, quite contrary, how does your garden grow?" she teased him when he came home with a new animal in the back of the pickup. "A tiger, a bear, a lion right there, and animals caged in a row."

Marielle loved the animals, too—although perhaps not as obsessively as Sammy. She cared for them the way one may love a dog or a cat. Sammy, on the other hand, loved them the way one may love a parent or child.

Or a wife.

Marielle knew without a doubt that Sammy loved her. Of his faithfulness, she had no doubts. But he spent so much time with the animals that it sometimes became difficult for her not to get a little envious of them.

"I know that sounds crazy," she told the interviewer, "but sometimes

I was jealous of the animals. I adored them, especially the lions and tigers. But Sammy spent so much time with them that sometimes I'd wish I could be one of the animals. Sometimes he'd be out there feeding them and talking with them, getting in their cages and cuddling with them, and he wouldn't get back until late at night, after I'd already fallen asleep. I wanted him to rattle *my* cage more often. I know Sammy loved me from the bottom of his heart, but I think he loved the animals even more. From a place deeper than the bottom of his heart."

Marielle recognized that Sammy had a big heart. But their family of animals was growing bigger than even a bottomless heart could handle. Looking back, Marielle couldn't pinpoint the moment Sammy went overboard, the specific animal that rendered the collection too big for them to manage. But she knew it had grown too big for *her* to live with any longer. It saddened her to think that too much of a good thing had become a terrible reality. In the end, the animals were killed by what she understood must have been a confused and conflicted act of love.

As a Matter of Fact

Authorities have confirmed that Sammy Johnson, the keeper of the animals now roaming the area, is dead—and may have been attacked by one of his pets. Residents of Chillicothe and vicinity, as far north as Columbus and south as Portsmouth, are advised to stay indoors. Dangerous animals remain on the loose.

— Amy Shivers, Chillicothe Evening News

SHOCKING DEVELOPMENT IN THE "CHILLICOTHE CARNAGE" STORY—the private zookeeper who released dozens of dangerous animals into the streets of Chillicothe, Ohio, is not only dead; reports indicate that he may have been mauled by one of his own animals. Sources on the scene say that a tiger was found feeding on the body of Sammy Johnson, the owner of the wild zoo. Dozens of man-eating animals remain on the prowl in central Ohio, and authorities continue to hunt them down.

— Carrie Mortimer, CNEN-TV

We advise all people to remain inside tonight. That will prevent additional loss of life. Watch or listen to local broadcasts tomorrow morning before venturing out to work or school. In the event that these animals are still on the loose in the morning, we're advising people to call in and stay home, and we encourage all employers to implement a liberal leave policy for the day. People's lives may depend on it.

— Roscoe Roy, Ross County Sheriff

It does appear that Mr. Johnson was attacked by one of his animals. That may or may not be the cause of death. We're waiting for an autopsy before we say for sure.

— Chuck Ellison, Deputy, Ross County Sheriff's Department

In order to understand why the animals were released, it is important to try to understand the man who released them. And since he left no note or diary—at least none authorities have mentioned—it is only possible to speculate. In this ongoing series, I will delve deep into the thoughts and opinions of those who knew him best: his wife, parents, friends, neighbors.

— Blake Hartle, *Cleveland Plain Dealer*

As far as we know, approximately thirty-two animals have already been killed. As many as forty-one may still be at large. Three individuals—people—are confirmed dead, including the owner of the animals. And at least four others have been injured. That's what we know at this time.

— Roscoe Roy, Ross County Sheriff

A cat story? Dammit, Blake, get me something juicy—the bastard's war experience, his getting fired from the zoo, the gun charges, why the crazy ass had all these wild animals running around. Granny's cats! You think that sells newspapers when lions and bears are ripping people apart in the city? Dig me up some meat!

— Blake Hartle's Voicemail, Message from Editor Simon Myers

Dude had some rough times with them animals, sure enough. I'm not saying he fought with them all the time. Alls I'm saying is I seen the scars. Showed them off when he was drunk. Across the chest, on his arms, down his right side. I'm not saying he couldn't handle them. But they handled him all right.

— Joey Wallace, Sammy Johnson's former classmate

Who was Sammy Johnson, to those who knew him best? What does his estranged wife think? What do his parents and friends believe prompted this act? Answer those questions, and you'll be as close to the truth of the situation as you're going to get.

— Blake Hartle, *Cleveland Plain Dealer*

Threatening the free press with imprisonment and tampering with our ability to cover the event: that's the *truth* of this situation. The number of animals local authorities are inhumanely slaughtering while we're not allowed to watch: that's the truth.

— Carrie Mortimer, CNEN-TV

The truth? The *reason* is what we're after. People in Chillicothe want to know: why did their friend and neighbor release these animals? Why did he sacrifice himself and those around him? Why did he send the animals he loved to their deaths?

— Amy Shivers, Chillicothe Evening News

The truth is, we just want to keep everyone safe. That is my number one goal, and the Sheriff's number one priority.

— Mark Vernon, Mayor of Chillicothe

The truth is just another way of framing a lie. You know?

— Mike Skaggs, Sammy Johnson's Drinking Buddy

Dragon Slayer

If you'd asked Guy Stanborough yesterday, he'd have told you dragons existed only in fairy tales. But today, he shot one in his own back yard.

Guy never dwelled on fantasy. He considered himself a no-nonsense, shoot-from-the-hip kind of guy. He'd bagged a gator once, when he'd lived in Louisiana. He'd seen a number of reptiles, from crocs and gators to the little pests that darted all over the streets and sidewalks in Orlando.

When he'd taken his own son and daughter to Orlando to dip them in and out of theme parks a day at a time, he remembered them being frightened by the little green and brown lizards running all around, scurrying over their feet, in the parking lots and even in the hallways of their cheap motel.

"Daddy, it's going to bite me, get it away!" they'd cried. He remembered squashing a couple of the lizards under his boot, like he might a big spider or roach. Scraped 'em off his boot on the curb, and thought nothing of it.

But for all the lizards and snakes, gators and crocs and reptiles he'd seen in his life, he'd never seen one like this. This doozy spanned a good eight feet and it stood up on four muscular legs, a good foot and a half high. This lizard was a bad ass. Guy could see it when he spotted the thing creeping into his back lawn. He didn't want to imagine what kind of damage a monster like that could do.

He walked out to the patio for a closer look. That's when he noticed the woman screaming and the boy crying. It was the Parker lady down the way, screaming for help, a little boy, about eight, crying and bleeding, a neighbor trying to calm them both while another neighbor cried into the cell phone to the police.

Guy had never seen a lizard this big before in real life, though he'd read about oddities such as this before. For some reason, he'd thought these guys were extinct, lizards this big, gone the way of dinosaurs. He seemed to remember seeing a giant stuffed lizard like this once at a roadside attraction out west. They called it some kind of dragon.

"Help him," the mother cried over her whimpering son.

"Get it," one of the neighbors yelled in Guy's direction. The dragon was well inside the parameters of his yard, so Guy wouldn't have to answer to the authorities if he killed something he may not otherwise be allowed to hunt. A real threat to the community, this thing had already hurt a boy. It scurried along his property. He went inside and got his hunting rifle.

A dragon, he thought and laughed. His kids had watched so many movies and cartoons about dragons, good and bad. He remembered an invisible dragon the old drunk sang about in that musical, and that song stuck in his head now as he walked back outside and aimed his rifle. How did it go? "A dragon, a dragon, I swear I shot a dragon?" Even Eddie Murphy played a dragon in one cartoon and got hitched to a dragon in another.

This real-life dragon burst into a sprint in Guy's direction. It looked determined and enraged, as though it knew its rival had come to fight. Guy shot the reptile. There, in the middle of his yard, it slumped and died. Guy held his rifle in one hand and walked out to inspect the lizard. He nudged it with his boot. The lizard had shed life like a spent skin.

The police arrived, only to find that their job had been done for them. Medics came, too, and treated the boy on the spot. His hand had been bitten, but no major damage done. He wouldn't lose a finger or anything. They wouldn't even have to take him to the hospital.

"Just leave the body where it is," the police ordered. "It's one of the animals that escaped from the Johnson place. We'll come back for it after we get the others."

"Know what it is?" Guy asked.

"A Komodo dragon," the policeman said.

Guy chuckled. "Guess that makes me a dragon slayer."

The policeman smirked. "Guess so."

The boy and his mother were back inside. Marge, from two houses down, looked at the dead reptile. "What the hell is it?" she asked.

"A dragon," Guy called back.

She snorted. "Didn't know there was any such thing."

"Yup." Guy Stanborough stood tall. "I'm a dragon slayer."

Pride

The dense, narrow forest provides sanctuary now, but this place is not a safe location for a home, not even temporarily. The pride does not take time to rest or relax, as they would like. They could go another sunset, maybe two, without food if needed. Food will not come to them from Master, as it always has. Master has fallen and become prey to Tiger. Neither Master nor his woman nor his helper will feed them. It is doubtful any human will feed them as Master did. Most men carry the exploding sticks and want to kill them.

The pride must travel, must put distance between them and the old home. Alpha determines to find a safe place where they will be hunters, not hunted.

Night falls and a full moon rises. The light of the moon gives prey an advantage; the lions have the best vision under cover of dark. The lions are powerful and fast and skilled, despite their lack of practice. Instinct guides them as they supplement their travel with hunt.

They number five. One kill should be enough to nourish them all for now. Two males, three females. The oldest female lion is the first to twitch at the sound and smell beyond the trees. No houses or cages, just a trail of dirt and rock. On the trail, a woman walks. The lion looks, listens, smells. The lion senses no cubs, no man, no companions. This woman appears alone, making her an easy kill.

Alpha's purr begins to rumble into what will become a roar if she does not stop him; the female lion shows her teeth and hisses at him, before he even has time to open his mouth. He understands what is at stake, and he submits to her warning. The female detects no changes in the human's pace or chemistry—she has not heard clumsy Alpha. The lioness creeps closer to the edge of the woods, carefully inching toward the path, waiting for the human to cross into her line.

The lioness crouches and springs out of the woods. She lands with heavy paws on the woman's back and chest, digs in with her claws, and immediately bites the woman's neck, cutting off the wind before she even has the opportunity to yell. The human struggles, her body flinching beneath the lion's weight. The struggle ceases. Claws still securely inside the woman's flesh, the lion drags her kill off the path, into the woods, secluded in the shadows. She begins to feed, but her mate roars and runs her away. After Alpha eats, she resumes her meal. Each lion gets a chance to eat until little is left of the human but bone, hair and rags.

They could eat more, but they continue their journey. They seek safety. They move within the woods, crossing over from one patch of forest to another, across vast black surfaces with yellow markings, dodging the motorized metal shells of man along the way. They encounter more of man's mark than they do natural habitat. Vehicles and large structures and hardened paths of black and white and yellow. They find cover in the narrow forest. They move north, tasting in the air the vast expanse of land that waits for them in that direction. The land unsettled by man, full of meat and field and stream.

They have licked the blood from their fur, from their mouths, and they move on, freshly invigorated by not only the nourishment, but also the excitement of the kill. The food provided by Master was easier to come by, more plentiful, perhaps better. But this fresh meat, hunted down and caught and killed, has an especially delightful flavor. The conquering lioness purrs, particularly pleased. The instinct to hunt and kill and feed comes nearly as boldly as the instinct to move north.

Rain and Pain

There were memories lodged in the corners of Ketchum's mind that he'd rather not bring to light. He'd served as a marine in two wars. Did time in Iraq, then in Afghanistan. He'd killed men. People he'd known as friends had fallen at his side. Ketchum had seen terrible things. But he'd never experienced anything quite like this.

His watch read just past midnight, and already they'd shot down more than three dozen exotic animals. He'd personally shot bears, wolves, lions, cougars, tigers and leopards in those first several hours. Truth was, in some ways he'd rather be shooting people than these animals. At least people at war understood they were at war. These creatures were noble, just to look at them, and innocent. They didn't ask to be put in this situation. They were draftees, so to speak.

But Ketchum was quick to remind himself that innocence was relative. The animals were designed to kill and eat. If he didn't have a gun, and if he didn't shoot the animals, no doubt these animals would be eating people. Ketchum knew that not one of the animals would think twice about eating his own guts out as he screamed for them to stop. Innocent? Not exactly. Just doing what God designed them to do.

"Oh, shit." Chuck extended his hand to catch the droplets. "Just what we need."

The rain began as a light drizzle, barely noticeable under the canopy of trees. They were in the woods, at the edge where the trees met the grass and the grass met Route 23. They hunted a tiger.

"The rain will make him harder to track," Jackson said.

"Maybe we should get back to the car," Chuck suggested. "Now that the tiger and animals have the advantage."

"I don't think so." Ketchum spit out tobacco juice. "It's just a little water. And we're dealing with animals that are used to living in cages. Maybe *we* have the advantage."

"Who has the advantage really just comes down to who takes who by surprise," Jackson said. The animal expert looked nervous. Ketchum could see the rifle shaking in his hands. Or maybe Jackson was just cold, with the onset of the rain. Now it poured.

"Then we better keep a careful watch." Ketchum looked attentively about them. "Besides, we're halfway to the rendezvous point by now. If we keep going, we'll meet up with Roscoe sooner than we'd be able to get back to the vehicle."

The rain grew heavier, pounding down through the branches. Ketchum imagined this must have been what it was like for Sammy Johnson in the jungles of Vietnam.

A snap echoed, a rustle from deep within the woods where the only thing they could see was darkness.

"What's that?" Chuck asked. They all aimed their guns.

Ketchum looked through the night vision goggles. "A deer," he said. Everyone sighed. "Just a deer."

It wasn't until a moment after everyone let down their guard that Ketchum realized...maybe they shouldn't have. He heard it before he saw it—a growl and the sound of branches breaking and leaves crunching, a body falling and bone cracking. They all looked back and saw the eyes reflecting. But the eyes were not looking at them; they were focused on the deer. The deer was on the ground, a tiger ripping at its flesh.

Jackson—animal activist though he may be—was the first to fire toward the shadows. Chuck and Ketchum fired, too. It angered the tiger, and the large cat ran in their direction. They could see it clearer now that it had come closer, rain soaking its fur, falling onto its face. They fired again, and it fell, just like the deer behind it. The deer seemed a needless kill, the meat uneaten.

"That's one more." The way Ketchum saw it, the tiger was a needless kill, too.

"Yup," Chuck agreed. None of them seemed very happy about their progress.

They heard another crackling in the woods. It came from in front of them. Startled, they raised their weapons. Ketchum peered through the goggles. "It's Roscoe." They all sighed.

"That you, Chuck?" Roscoe asked.

"Yup," Chuck called back.

The men came together. Roscoe greeted them "Leland and me got us a bobcat back a ways. Sounds like you got something, too."

Regret burdened Jackson's voice. "A Bengal."

Leland sighed. "It's a shame." The rain poured down on Leland's leather fedora so hard that the heavy brim drooped, adding to his sad appearance. Leland put a hand on Jackson's back, water splashing off and hitting Ketchum in the face. "A necessary shame."

Chuck and Roscoe nodded, their heads hanging like the water-heavy tree limbs all around them.

"Guess so." Jackson looked Leland in the eye.

Ketchum pushed through the two animal experts. "Don't make me cry. We've got us more cat to kill." But the truth was, the scene even penetrated Ketchum's hard shell.

The rain splattered loudly on and around them. Ketchum spoke, just to get everyone's minds off of the tiger and bobcat and all the other kills. "I remember a kid in Afghanistan."

"Here we go, another war story," Chuck cracked. But Ketchum knew Chuck didn't mean it.

"This kid had an animal, did he?" Jackson asked.

"No, it ain't an animal story. Got enough of those here." Ketchum spoke only loud enough for the guys to hear, in a hushed voice. He remained focused on their surroundings, alert to any animals. "So, anyway, while I was over there, I used to go to a local market where I knew a kid I'd buy nuts and fruits from. Freshly shelled almonds, walnuts, pistachios and sun-dried apricots and dates. Got my fill of military food at camp. But, you know, that got old. Besides, I liked trying out the local favorites when I was overseas, and getting face to face with local people—the people we were there to protect." Ketchum felt a little silly now. Truth was, he only went there because they sent him. He only joined because he didn't know what else to do.

"Anyway, this kid who sold me the fruit and nut mixes..." Ketchum spit.

"What was his name?" Leland asked.

"I never got the kid's name. Would you guys shut up and let me tell the story?"

"Well, hurry up and tell it," Roscoe said.

"The boy was probably about fifteen, sixteen years old. His parents owned the business, I guess, whether they farmed the food themselves or bought it from a local wholesaler, whether they owned the stall where they sold their goods or rented it or just occupied it. I don't really know how the system worked. I just bought the damn snacks from the kid."

The rain continued to patter against their hats and shoulders, their guns and noses. As Ketchum talked in his calm voice, they all watched cautiously for signs of animals. They knew a tiger and cheetah still waited for them in here, at least—a tiger and cheetah had been spotted and called in by residents in the area, in addition to the tiger and bobcat they already shot. Ketchum's muted story served as their background music, but their eyes remained alert as they looked in all directions for their prey.

"So one day, there's a battle, and I'm there in the thick of it, and who do I see facing me down with a machine gun at his side?"

"The kid," Roscoe guessed.

"The kid," Ketchum confirmed. "The look on his face—I could see it clear as day—when he saw me, it was just confusion and shock. He was about to kill me, I know it—if I had been any other guy, he would have shot me dead right then and there. But I guess he felt like he knew me, so he turned and starting shooting at other guys. But these guys were my buddies and my brothers, and I couldn't let him do it. So I did what I had to do. I took him out."

"That's raw," Chuck said.

More raw than Chuck could understand. Ketchum had felt the boy's eyes on him, had known that if he'd looked into the boy's eyes again, he would have had to let the boy go. Let him go to kill his friends and brothers. Ketchum didn't just take out the boy. He took out the boy's dumbfounded stare. Watched numbly as the boy's face exploded in blood, one pleading eye blown away, the other left lifeless. The boy fell onto the dusty ground, blood oozing from where his eye had been and clumping the sand beneath him.

"I felt like I betrayed the kid. But that's plain stupid, because he was just some kid who sold nuts and fruits, not a friend or anything. But he spared my life, and I didn't spare his."

"He was killing your allies," Jackson said. "You were just doing what you had to."

Ketchum stopped walking and looked Jackson square in the eye. "Exactly."

Jackson took a step back from Ketchum's intense stare and nodded. Ketchum looked at Leland. Leland turned his gaze into the dark of the rainy forest. Ketchum shook the rain off his cap and moved forward.

With the help of night vision binoculars, Leland picked up the trail of the cheetah. The tracks left in the mud were now paw-shaped puddles, trampled grass and leaves and sticks. They followed the trail, and before long, they found the cheetah deeper in the woods—although these woods were not deep, cut away by freeways and housing developments. They found the cheetah crouching under the cover of trees. It didn't attack them, perhaps thinking it could go undetected, or hoping it would be left alone. Or, more likely, waiting for the right moment to catch one of them off guard and pounce.

Ketchum could see the cheetah's eyes; they pleaded for mercy. Chuck and Roscoe opened fire. Blood exploded on the cheetah's neck, shoulder and back, between his right eye and ear. From where Ketchum stood, he could see what was left of the cheetah's remaining eye, lifeless. Ketchum and Roscoe and Jackson and Chuck and Leland stood over the dead cheetah. The rain washed blood off its coat and onto the muddy leaves.

The others cursed the rain, but Ketchum didn't mind it. He wished it would stop, but knew that it could be far worse. Ketchum remembered being in the desert, in the scorching heat of the yellow sun, the dry sand, always thirsty, praying against all odds for just a little bit of rain, rain that would never come. He remembered thinking, then, that he wished he could trade Afghanistan for Vietnam, trade the dry, harsh desert for the lush green jungle. It didn't occur to him—during the war—to wish for trading war for peace. He just wanted to trade one set of surroundings for another. Even now, Ketchum realized he would never really know what it was like in Vietnam, not the way Sammy Johnson did, not the way countless others did during that long and drawn-out conflict. But he imagined now, as they trudged through the muddy ground in the trees under the heavy rain, that maybe *this* was *something* like Vietnam. Maybe this was how it was, to be at war surrounded by water and leaf, tree and mud. And he realized that it was not better. It was different, and that was all. War was war. And however you looked at it, wherever you stood—in desert sand or muddy jungle—war was bullshit.

"Bagged us a cheetah," Ketchum said with gusto. He brought himself back to the moment. "Add that to the running tally. What's next, Siberian tiger?"

Ketchum talked tough in front of the guys—just who he was. But when he looked into the face of the dead cheetah and saw the one remaining eye, he remembered the boy's eyes. That look of raw shock, of betrayal, the look that asked, *Why are you shooting me when I spared you?* A look he didn't even think was real, not one that he saw with his own eyes, anyway. But he couldn't be sure. *Is it something I saw for a split second, or just something imagined that I'll remember for years? Does it make a difference?*

The dispatcher came over the Sheriff's radio. "Roscoe?"

"What is it, Delores?"

"Lions spotted in the city, north side. And a woman reported missing, no body found."

"Send Tom and Toby."

"They're already downtown with Morris on another call. Some giant cat—weren't sure whether it was a tiger or a lion."

"All right." Roscoe looked at the men. "Jackson, you think you'll be able to find the other tiger?"

"Not sure, but I can keep trying."

"Good." Roscoe nodded. "How you doing, Ketchum?"

"Just dandy." Ketchum cracked a smile. "Ready to shoot me a Siberian."

"All right." Roscoe put a hand on Ketchum's wet shoulder. "You two stay here and see if you can track down the Siberian. Leland, Chuck, why don't we go look for those lions."

They agreed. Roscoe, Leland and Chuck wished Ketchum and Jackson luck and headed forward in the direction of the car. Tom and Toby and Morris must have been downtown by now, hunting the urban jungle for a giant cat. It wasn't long after they split up that Jackson found the remains of a monkey in the muddy brush. Nearby, the imprint of a cat where it had rested in the leaves and dirt, feeding. Then, paw prints.

"At least it already ate," Ketchum said.

"That's something," Jackson admitted. "But not enough to rest easy on. A Siberian tiger is the largest cat in the wild. It can eat a lot of meat. That chimp was just an appetizer."

"Good to know." Ketchum made light of the fear that held them together. The leaves made it slippery in the wet mud underfoot. Ketchum wondered whether hunting the Siberian in his natural habitat might be more fitting. To snowshoe through the white terrain in search of the orange-and-black-striped prey.

Ketchum suspected the climate would have its own miseries. Numb fingers and toes. That terrible feeling of cold flesh against metal. Shivers in the frigid air. Rain or shine, sand or mud, snow or clear skies, there seemed no such thing as perfect weather for war.

In the darkness ahead, they heard a rustling of leaves, a deep growl. Eyes reflected the moonlight back to them. They found the tiger. There was no denying the cat's eyes, boring into him, asking for mercy. The tiger remained in the brush, crouched in a defensive position. The tiger looked confused, unsure, as though all it really wanted was to go home. Ketchum and Jackson readied their assault rifles. Swallowing the gut-wrenching sensation, Ketchum aimed right into the boy's pleading eyes and fired.

In Hindsight

I remember he used to bring that bear to the bar. Funniest thing. They even advertised it: Thursday night is Bear Night! Have a Beer with a Bear! People would come and eat and drink just to see Sammy sitting there at the bar with his bear. The bear would drink an ounce or so of beer out of a saucer. People would come and pet it. Funniest thing you ever saw.

— Mike Skaggs, Sammy Johnson's Drinking Buddy

As many as fifteen thousand exotic big cats are estimated to be privately owned in the United States.

— Leland Anders, Celebrity Zookeeper

I went to the place once to interview Sammy Johnson and saw some of the caged animals along the sides of the drive. I just backed out and left. I mean, I didn't want to end up being lunch, you know?

— Amy Shivers, Chillicothe Evening News

It's estimated that more tigers live in captivity in the United States than live in the wild all around the world. Chew on that for a moment.

— Leland Anders, Celebrity Zookeeper

There are no universal registration requirements, so it's just an estimate. It's impossible to know for sure how many tigers there are.

— Jackson Withers, Animal Protection Agency

Why *should* there be laws to register pets? Why do people need to pry into our home and check on our animals?

— Marielle Johnson, Sammy Johnson's Wife

Thirty states allow predatory pets. Nine require a license or permit. When it comes to animal regulation, Ohio is like the wild west.

— Jackson Withers, Animal Protection Agency

I have called for a moratorium on the buying and selling of exotic animals. We're not rushing into a law or restriction—we don't want to step on anyone's rights. And we think such legislation belongs at the statewide level. But we also have to look out for the welfare of our citizens. Maybe if we'd had stricter rules, this tragedy would not have happened.

— Mark Vernon, Mayor of Chillicothe

Maybe? Am I missing something?

— Mitch Henderson, Sammy Johnson's Neighbor

If I had to describe Sammy's relationship to the animals, one word comes to mind: love. Sammy really loved those animals.

— Morris Jones, Animal Caretaker

The excuse always seems to be one of two things: conservation or education. People buy these animals thinking they're doing good. Well, they simply are not. It usually boils down to selfishness. The need to take charge of majesty.

— Jackson Withers, Animal Protection Agency

There's no doubt that ego's involved. There must be a great sense of power to stand as master over such a massive beast. But there was undoubtedly affection as well. Just like in a human relationship. Sometimes it's hard to tell where ego ends and where love begins. It's seldom *only* one and not the other.

— Dr. Minnie Fields, Professor of Psychology, Shawnee State University

"They won't hurt me," he used to say. "If one of my animals ever hurts me, it's my own fault for not asserting myself strongly enough, my fault for not impressing them with my intentions, or not understanding their mood or intentions." Guess it was his fault.

— Bobbie Anne Thompson, Sammy Johnson's Neighbor

It's a miracle that the kids are all right. They were sitting right here in the garage, playing with that monkey for hours, half the day. Didn't know it until I got home from work. Come to find out, that chimp could have ripped them apart. Could've killed all of them. But it just played along with them, like it was another child. God was watching over them.

— Milly Saunders, Chillicothe Mother of Two

Any time you take a wild animal and put it in a cage, it becomes an ethical issue. Believe me, I know. I've grappled with that issue many times.

— Leland Anders, Celebrity Zookeeper

This tragedy should be a lesson to anyone considering an exotic pet. Keep your love of wild animals in your heart—not in your home.

— Jackson Withers, Animal Protection Agency

Night Sounds

Jan had become accustomed to the sounds of the city at night, having lived in Chillicothe all her life: the ongoing chirps of crossing lights and the passing cars at all hours. She knew the scuffling of riff-raff along the streets in late hours, the hum of occasional drug deals or pimp negotiations going down under shadow. She was used to seeing police lights, hearing traffic continuing its ongoing circle. But she'd never heard *this* before.

A strange noise, like something out of a bad dream—a dream that involves carnivals and aliens, things creepy and otherworldly. A barking, a laughing, a moaning, a squeaking, a rambling hum all at once. She couldn't pinpoint any one distinct sound in the collection of sounds. The strangeness reminded her of clowns and dogs and laughing and yipping.

Jan looked out the window, but couldn't see what made the noise. She called the police, but she had trouble explaining her emergency.

"There's a weird noise coming from outside. I can't say what it is. It's just got me spooked."

She gave her urban location and expected them to dismiss her as a crank caller. But she was not dismissed at all.

"We've had other calls," the woman on the line said. "We think there's a wild animal on the loose. Stay indoors, ma'am, and let us know if you see anything."

"I see something now!" Jan screamed into the phone, because at that moment she did see something. A whole pack of the animals. "They're dogs," she said. "Or wolves. Or something like that. About eight of them, running around like crazy. Right down Main Street."

"Someone's on the way, ma'am. Stay inside."

They weren't dogs, exactly, and weren't really wolves, either. Jan wasn't sure what they were. Maybe hyenas? They laughed and barked. This sounded different, a collective clatter, like a host of animals acting as one.

"Coyotes," Jan heard someone else call out, someone out on the sidewalk, running for shelter. Then, from the safety of her window, she spotted three men, charging toward the coyotes in the street. Two of them in police uniforms, one of them in a flannel shirt and jeans. They all sported rifles. They opened fire on the strays.

She couldn't believe she was seeing this right in the middle of downtown Chillicothe. *Wild animals daring to roam the city streets!*

"We've had other calls," the woman on the line had said.

Jan looked out and swore she could see something moving, more than one thing, ducking beneath the cover of some trees off in the distance. They looked like lions. The police didn't seem to notice, and she wondered whether she should pick up the phone and call 911 again. She considered opening her window and yelling out to the police, but she didn't want to distract them—and she feared bringing the attention of a wild animal to her open window. She decided to go back to the phone. Then she spotted a tiger in a parking lot, crouched between cars and waiting. She wanted to call out to the hunters, but couldn't move. Even in the safety of her apartment, she feared the city's wild animals. Jan stood and watched, paralyzed.

Parked Cars

Tiger hears the coyotes, is annoyed by the barking and squealing and yipping. Even the laughter of the hyenas and the howling of the wolves are no match for this maddening racket. A meal, perhaps, but not an easy one—this pack of coyotes, running as one through the black streets. Better to target less bothersome prey.

Gun bursts hit the air and Tiger's ears twitch. The coyotes are down—killed without the men even coming near them. Such is the power of man. These men must be killed if they challenge him. Better to avoid them altogether.

Tiger finds a hard, black, lifeless field littered with husks of metal and plastic and rubber, cold and silent and dead in the night. Tiger moves to the forest of metal and rubber and hides between two of the boxy frames.

The men inspect their kills, sound off to one another in what sounds like a scuffle of authority and ownership. But they do not feed. They leave the coyotes where they have fallen and walk on. The men are coming near.

In the distance, Tiger smells and sees the pride of lions from home, also here in the city. The lions duck off into the trees at the edge of this urban setting, reentering a more natural habitat. Tiger wants to go there, too. But the territory is already taken, and to go up against five lions is unthinkable. He must find another hunting ground. For now, it is here.

Tiger stares at the fallen coyotes. If the men leave, he will eat their kill. But the men are coming nearer, and Tiger fears he may have no choice but to attack them. One smells of sulfur, another of roasted bean, another stinks of salt and oil. The rain pours and he can see that it makes the men uncomfortable and cold. The rain does not faze Tiger. The rain invigorates him.

The men don't seem to notice his presence, but they continue to stride in his direction. It appears inevitable. Either attack, or be attacked. Ducked behind the metal husk, he does not see them at the moment, but he can hear their steps coming closer, can smell their salty sweat and oily flesh beneath the rain. They are too close for him to keep hiding. He takes his advantage now.

Tiger jumps up on top of the vehicle next to him. He stands tall upon the roof of the metal shell, growling and showing his giant teeth and the size of his bite. The men fall back, startled. But they collect themselves and aim their guns at him. Tiger leaps down upon the man closest to him. He shreds the man's outer layers and flesh with the batting of his clawed front paws. The sulfur man falls back with the tiger on top of him, red blood oozing from the slick, blue coat and washing quickly onto the black ground beneath them. The rain pours. Tiger opens his jaws, and he strikes the neck, between this man's head and shoulders. He tastes the warm blood as he steals the man's breath. But before he can enjoy a shred of flesh, Tiger hears the explosions of the other two men's guns and feels the sting of the projectile in his head. He falls onto the man and, for a moment, he stares into the man's eyes. But he can feel life draining away, and he can only look into those eyes for so long before his own vision blurs. He can no longer feel the man beneath him, can no longer feel the strength of his own body. He hears the men chattering anxiously above him. He goes limp, into a mass of release. Still vaguely aware of the man pinned beneath him, Tiger dies.

Dead of Night

Roscoe found it a fitting term. *The dead of night.* The phrase had meaning to him now in a way it never had before. This night had been full of death. The night itself was coming to an end, but the killing was not done. In fact, what he had feared most was dawning now: the sunrise, a weekday morning with exotic beasts still on the prowl. He looked at his watch. Nearly five o'clock, and early risers were already on the road, starting their morning commute.

Chuck glanced at his watch. "My shift's over." He forced a laugh. "Twelve hours in. Can I go home now?"

Roscoe cracked a smile. "You're more rested than any of us. You were ready to work the night shift. Rest of us worked day shifts first."

"Ready? I wasn't ready for this."

Roscoe looked around. The streets and sidewalks remained empty. "I hope everyone has the good sense to watch the morning news."

"No one in their right mind would leave their homes this morning for something as unimportant as work or school," Chuck said.

"Not the best sound bite." Leland smirked.

"You know what I mean."

Roscoe, Chuck, and Leland walked carefully through the streets of downtown Chillicothe as though navigating a war zone. Each of them carried an assault rifle and they each had backup weapons on their person. They went from vehicle to vehicle, from dumpster to building edge to bus stop shelter, keeping an eye out for the exotic animals while trying to stay out of an animal's view.

If the count Morris had given them was correct, Roscoe figured they still had five lions, two leopards, a bear, a panther, and a tiger on the loose.

And the lion-tiger mix. Things were bad, but they could get worse.

Dead of night? Roscoe thought but didn't dare say. *What might be worse is the dead of day.*

"Of course, we don't want any of these animals to hurt anyone." Rain pelted Leland's leather fedora as he spoke. "But let's look at the bright side. During the day, we have the advantage. These are all nocturnal predators, most alert at night. Now, it's our time. We have a better chance of finding them during the day."

Having tracked them for hours, Leland seemed confident that the lions had come out of the woods and into the city, but once they got into the streets of Chillicothe, it was hard to keep their trail. No tracks or disturbed foliage highlighted their path in the city streets. Now, they more or less explored the streets in general areas where sightings had been reported with hopes of coming across the pride of lions.

"Officer down," Toby called over the radio.

"Who is it?" Roscoe asked.

"Tom," Toby called back. "Didn't know what hit him."

"Well," Roscoe huffed, "what hit him?"

"Tiger," Toby said.

"Medics are on their way," Delores responded.

Roscoe was impressed that Delores was still awake. In some ways, she had the most difficult job, staffing the phones, dispatching, keeping track of who was where. Roscoe and the hunting party were out and awake; you couldn't easily fall asleep in the rain with the wild animals lurking about. But for Delores, sitting at a desk, it would be easy enough to drift into sleep, Roscoe imagined. Then again, you didn't get mauled to death nodding off at a desk.

Soon enough, Roscoe, Leland and Chuck reached the other hunters in the city. They were easy enough to find, with the ambulance there, lights flashing, white-coats clamoring about. Toby and Morris paced in the parking lot scattered with cars. They'd shot the tiger. It looked like another of the cars, laid out in a parking space, between the lines. The medics closed Tom's eyes and covered his face.

"Damn it, anyway." Roscoe removed his hat and shook his head. Chuck did the same.

"He was already gone when they arrived," Morris said. "That tiger really did a number on him. Only took him a minute."

"A tiger can take down an animal three times his size in less than a minute." Leland removed his fedora and held it over his heart. "Once struck, Tom didn't have a chance."

"We'd better stay alert." Roscoe put his hat back on. "We've got to find the animals before they discover the morning commute."

They didn't wait for the medics to drive off with Tom's body. They had no time to mourn now, so they moved on as a team of five.

"It's anyone's guess where they are," Leland admitted. "But I'd say they're either somewhere in the city where they can find cover—like in a parking lot or junkyard or a park with lots of trees—or they've gone back into the woods at another side of the city, along the freeway or somewhere."

"Surely someone will spot them and call 911," Morris said. "Five lions prowling the city?"

"They can be stealthy." Leland gripped his fedora in his left hand, rifle in his right. "They can find places to blend in."

Roscoe looked at the sunrise. "Now that it's getting light out, we need to get a copter in the air." They'd decided earlier that having a helicopter with a spotlight chopping through the rainy night would cause more disruption than good, frightening the animals and scaring people awake to come out and look to see what the ruckus was about. A recipe for disaster.

The rain continued to fall even as the sun lit the morning. They walked with their rifles down at their sides, not wanting to startle the people beginning to appear on the street. Buses were en route, despite warnings from the police. Bicycles and cars and trucks. Business was business, and it would not stop for threat of a few deaths. School buses, at least, were not in service as schools had closed. But people who apparently had not heard the news or heeded the warnings—or who considered their business more important than their safety—now walked along sidewalks, into and out of buildings.

Ketchum came over the radio, startling them. "We got the Siberian tiger, and another cougar. Now Jackson and me are hunting a bear. Spotted near Main Street, headed downtown, so we may meet up with you soon."

"Copy that," Roscoe said.

Roscoe, Chuck, Leland, Morris and Toby continued slowly from one block to the next, looking in every direction for any detection of animal. The lions and the ligress, in particular, had been spotted a few times in the Chillicothe's historic city center. Roscoe hoped they'd find the cats before the cats spotted them.

Delores came back on the radio. "Roscoe?"

"What is it?"

"The Mayor. He says he wants you downtown, at the courthouse, for a press conference in about an hour."

Roscoe huffed. "Tell him I'm already downtown. Saving people's lives."

"He insists. Said the people need to hear from their Sheriff."

"Bullshit!"

"Press conference is scheduled for eight." Delores paused. "Want me to try to stall him a little longer?"

Roscoe felt a gentle hand rest on his tensed shoulder. Leland looked sympathetically at him. "The Mayor has a point. You might save even more lives letting people know the situation than you're able to save out here. You can only reach one animal at a time. But you can reach thousands of viewers and listeners at once."

Chuck sucked in and wiped his nose. "They've got talking heads for that."

Leland turned to Chuck. "It'll mean more coming from the person in charge than a stuffed suit."

Roscoe blew out a discouraged breath. "Oh, all right. I'll do it." He looked at Leland. "But you'll do it with me. People trust you more than anyone when it comes to animals."

"That's fine," Leland said. "We can expect some backlash about these animals being killed. I can try to..."

"There it is," Toby blurted out.

Revealing itself from around the corner of a building as though crossing the intersection like any other vehicle, the gangly ligress walked into their view. It stood not more than twenty feet away, half a block from them, and when it saw them, it seemed to hone in on Morris. It stepped brazenly on the asphalt in their direction.

Roscoe stared in awe. It looked like something out of a storybook, bigger than he'd imagined it. He looked around to see the same astonished expression on each of the men's faces, save one. Visibly upset, Morris pinched his temples with his thumb and index finger.

The ligress broke into a trot in their direction.

Traffic Report

This is your eye in the sky, the WCHL Traffic Copter. If you're just now tuning in for the first time today, here's a word of advice: stay home. You heard me right, folks: authorities have advised everyone in the Chillicothe area to remain indoors today and to stay off the roads. If you're already driving to work, go back home. It's a zoo out there—literally.

Lions and bears, wild cats and wolves have all escaped from a local animal reserve here in Chillicothe. If you leave your house today, you're walking into a danger zone. It's best to stay indoors.

For those of you braving the commute, be advised that bears have been spotted along Main Street headed into the downtown area. Already this morning, four reports have come in of bears attacking cars at stoplights. No windows have been broken or injuries reported, but there have been some frightened passengers and some dinged up vehicles.

A pride of lions—that's a whole family of them— is reportedly traveling together. I haven't been able to spot them from up here, but authorities believe they were in the city early this morning and may be headed north outside of Chillicothe. They could still be in the downtown area, so stay alert.

Also, leopards and panthers and other wild cats are on the loose that have not been found since their escape yesterday afternoon. I'm telling you folks, it's the day to call in. If you can stay home, you'd better do it.

Right now, I'm looking at a major traffic jam entering downtown Chillicothe on Main Street, and the cause is a bear that keeps banging into bottlenecked cars. Police are aware of the bear and are said to be on their way.

Oh, my! I'm seeing police respond now! The police—two of them, racing up the shoulder, jumping out of the car and...yes, they have opened fire. The bear—yes, yes, it's down. It looks like the bear's dead, right in the middle of Main Street. Wow.

Folks, the bear is down, but lions and other wild cats remain on the loose, so today is the day to avoid the roads. Do not leave your house if you don't have to. All state, federal and local government have implemented liberal leave for the day—you will not be denied leave—and schools are closed throughout Chillicothe and the surrounding areas. Businesses and employers have been asked by police to approve requests to take the day off, and everyone is encouraged to stay home.

If you're just tuning in, folks, a bear has been shot and killed by police on Main Street only moments ago, and that's causing a major backup. Other wild animals are on the loose and may possibly be in downtown Chillicothe and the surrounding area. I'm your WCHL eye in the sky, looking today not only for traffic conditions, but for the animal conditions in Chillicothe. Stay indoors, and stay safe.

Sympathy Pains

Morris stared down his favorite animal. It was as though he could sense its presence before it peeked its head around the corner of the building and came into the intersection, turning to see him standing there with the rest of the Sheriff's team. Morris considered the cat a marvel. Graceful? No. Beautiful? Not exactly. But as affectionate as it was huge.

Morris's headache, which he'd thought had faded, now throbbed worse than before. He tried to massage it away with his monkey-bitten finger and thumb, but that only reminded him that they hurt, too. He registered the quiet panic welling in the men around him, in Roscoe and Chuck, Leland and Toby. *Am I the only one who can see she's not approaching to attack? She's greeting us. She's scared and wants to go home.*

A cat like a liger or ligress had no *real* home. No place for it in the wild, because it did not come from the wild. It was not a creature of nature, but a creature of human intervention. And Morris had been instrumental in this particular liger's design.

"Let me have a go at it," Morris had asked Sammy years ago. "I'm here with the cats all the time anyway, I know them almost as well as you do."

"I'm not sure." Sammy had shown an uncharacteristic reluctance. "I don't mind cross breeding within species. Mixing the tigers and such. But a tiger and a lion?"

"No harm in it," Morris had assured Sammy. "Just let me mate them, and we'll keep the liger separate from the others. I'll take responsibility for it."

Morris had raised her from a cub, called her by the name she was: Ligress. He took Ligress out and fed her milk from a bottle, played with her every time he came to feed the animals and clean out their cages.

Secretly, he gave Ligress the best cuts when they got proper meat. When they used road kill, he'd give the freshest and least damaged carcass to his baby. Often, he would let Ligress out of her cage, leading her by a heavy chain, and he'd walk her, play with her. Even when full-grown, he'd romp around the property with the thousand-pound cat, nearly twice the weight of a full-grown tiger or lion. On all fours, she stood head and shoulders above Morris.

She's just a big baby.

Now, Morris watched the men raise their guns. Ligress wobbled toward them, her clumsy feet unsure on the hard asphalt street. Ligress came to Morris for help, approached her trusted caretaker for food and security and care. But Morris knew what the other men saw. They saw a thousand pounds of massive cat, twelve feet of muscle, heavy paws with large claws, an enormous head with a jaw and canines to match.

"She won't hurt us," Morris said. "She's gentle. Just a big, fluffy oaf."

Toby glanced at Morris, but quickly returned his attention to the cat. "I don't see how anything looks like that could be gentle."

An SUV came from around the other corner and turned toward the giant cat, not seeing it until it had already turned. Ligress looked back at the noisy vehicle. The SUV skidded on its breaks and tried to turn, spinning around and driving back through a red light in the other direction. The SUV hit a pickup truck. But the drivers and passengers did not get out of their vehicles. Morris could make out their terror-stricken faces staring out their windows at Ligress.

In the distance, people came to the dented vehicles to see if they could help, but they caught sight of Ligress and darted away. The cat, confused, let out a growl. Morris understood it as a plea for help.

"Calm down, Ligress," Morris called in a gentle voice.

Ligress looked away from the crash and back to her caretaker. She bounced into a clumsy gallop and headed his way. Having shaken their stunned gazes, sobered by the car accident and the pedestrians in the distance, Roscoe and Toby and Chuck and Leland opened fire on the cat, careful not to miss, should any stray fire go beyond the creature to the people in the distance.

"No!" Morris yelled. But trigger fingers had tightened. Ligress stumbled, heavy paws tripping over one another, and came toppling down. Morris grimaced at the crunching sound her face made when it hit the pavement. Ligress let out a sad growl that sounded more like a whimper.

Morris approached her, crouched down next to Ligress, and laid a hand on her warm, sand-tinted fur.

Leland placed a hand on Morris's shoulder. "We had no options."

"She wouldn't have hurt anyone," Morris said in a matter-of-fact tone.

"No way to know that for sure," Leland said. "Big cats are unpredictable. No matter how well you think you know them, you never know when they're going to do something unexpected. Especially when out of their usual environment, a place like this."

Morris wanted to argue. Instead, he rubbed Ligress's head. His own headache throbbed with newfound intensity. *Sympathy pains?*

"We still have a pride of lions, a panther, a tiger, and some leopards out and about," Roscoe reminded. "Now's no time to rest."

"Or mourn," Chuck added.

"Besides," Leland said, lifting his hand from Morris's shoulder and looking at his watch, "I think we have an appointment to keep with the Mayor."

Pressed

Sheriff Roscoe Roy

At approximately four-thirty yesterday afternoon, we responded to calls along Rural Place Road, reporting that exotic animals had been sighted and were attacking horses and livestock. We arrived on the scene at the property of Mr. Sammy Johnson and discovered that approximately fifty-four exotic animals had been set loose, including tigers, bears, cougars, wolves, panthers and lions.

We have been working under counsel of Jackson Withers of the Animal Protection Agency, and animal expert Leland Anders. We had already lost one officer at the time that we made the difficult decision to euthanize the dangerous animals. Even these animal experts agreed, given the situation, we had no other choice. But what we need to focus on now isn't the dead animals—it's the living ones, out on the loose.

As of this time, we estimate that we have euthanized approximately forty-five of the animals. We believe there are as many as ten or eleven animals still at large, and these animals include a pride of lions, a tiger, a panther and two leopards. The animals pose a serious threat to anyone who encounters them. We strongly advise all people remain inside at this time. We believe we will be able to track the remaining animals down this morning. If we don't spend too much time here.

I'll take questions in a moment. First, here's Leland Anders.

Leland Anders

Hello. I regret to say that I have been witness to the atrocities that have taken place yesterday afternoon, last night and early this morning. And

I must admit that it's a horrible, sad thing. One of the worst moments in my life, as a person who loves animals, as someone who has dedicated his life to the care and preservation and understanding of these beautiful creatures...it is a terrible, terrible day.

Having said that, I fully support the actions that Sheriff Roy and his team have taken. They've had to make hard decisions. But they were necessary decisions.

When this ordeal is over, I will personally fight to bring stricter laws limiting the private ownership of dangerous, exotic animals. But right now, the Sheriff's job—with my help—must be to get the remaining threats off the streets before we suffer additional human casualties.

Jackson Withers

Um, yes, if I may...I'd just like to back up what they both said. None of us are pleased to report that these innocent animals have been put down. But I think most would agree—most people, anyway—that the sanctity of human life comes before that of animal life. Even endangered species. I assure you that we're eliminating the threat and euthanizing the animals in the most humane way we can.

Sheriff Roscoe Roy

We can take a few questions now. Then we really need to get back to work. We have teams of officers and experts tracking the animals now, but we should really be out there with them.

Carrie Mortimer

Sheriff, the scene at the Johnson compound is horrific. Words can't describe the terrible carnage there, seeing all of these slaughtered animals laid out, dead. Why weren't more measures taken to try to capture the animals?

Jackson Withers

Can I take that? Yes, we actually did try to tranquilize, but it was unsuccessful. You have to understand that to tranquilize an animal is not a cookie cutter thing. The amount of medicine must be exactly right, and you don't know unless you know the exact weight of the animal. Too little medicine has no effect; too much will kill the animal. And you have to hit them in just the right place. And even if all goes well, it takes several minutes for the drug to take effect, so you've got an angry tiger thrashing around, and you're dead before the tranq even takes effect. We just couldn't do it.

Carrie Mortimer

Couldn't you have lured some of them back in their cages?

Sheriff Roscoe Roy

That wasn't an option. The cages were *cut* open, so they could not be recaged. We had to eliminate the threat.

Leland Anders

The Sheriff's Department did what it had to do. When you have dangerous animals like these—nocturnal predators—and it's nighttime, and they're near large populations of people, you don't have the luxury of trying to humanely trap them or bring them in. Human life is at stake. There would have been a massacre.

Carrie Mortimer

I believe there *was* a massacre.

Sheriff Roscoe Roy

Is there another question, please?

Blake Hartle

What can you tell us about Sammy Johnson? Did he take his own life or did the animals kill him? Is it true that one of the animals was feeding on him when you arrived? And do you have theories as to why he released the animals?

Sheriff Roscoe Roy

Mr. Johnson was dead when we arrived on the scene. We're waiting for the official autopsy results. But it does appear that Mr. Johnson took his own life and one of the tigers then attacked the body after he was deceased. At this time we're not working on any theories as to why he did what he did. Our main concern is getting these dangerous animals off the streets. Next? Yes, Amy?

Amy Shivers

Sheriff, how are you and your team tracking the animals and do you have a general idea of where they may be right now?

Sheriff Roscoe Roy

Mr. Anders and Mr. Withers have been essential to helping us track down the animals. We're also working off leads from people calling in. So if anyone spots an animal—a lion, tiger, bear, leopard, cougar or anything that seems out of the ordinary—please report it. You can call the Ross County Sheriff's office direct, or the Chillicothe Police, or dial 911. We also have helicopters on the lookout, although the animals are good at blending into their environments, both in the city and in the woods—they can hide themselves well. So it's the eyewitness reports that'll help us most.

Amy Shivers

Where do you think the remaining animals are right now? What's the possible range?

Leland Anders

I would suspect they're still in the Chillicothe area, although the *possible* range is larger than we'd like to think. They could have roamed as far south as Portsmouth, or as far north as Columbus.

Sheriff Roscoe Roy

We're working closely with authorities in the nearby cities and counties.

For now, we continue to advise all citizens to remain indoors and watch out for animals.

Blake Hartle

Were you aware of the private zoo Sammy Johnson kept? Why do you think he released the animals, knowing that it would be certain death for them? What was going through his mind?

Sheriff Roscoe Roy

Yes, we knew about the animals, but he wasn't breaking any laws. I'm not prepared to speculate on what was going through his mind. Not right now, anyway. That's not my priority.

What Was Going Through His Mind

Since childhood, Sammy wanted to be the best and biggest at everything he tackled. His classmates asked their parents for dogs and cats. Sammy asked his for an entire zoo of little creatures. As an adult, he still needed to be the biggest and the best. He lit up when he showed off, whether regarding his rare guns, rare cars, or rare animals.

So what was going through his mind, toward the end, was: "When I go, I'm going to go big."

Other ideas had come to Sammy. He'd thought about getting into his 1968 Corvette and driving it on the wrong side of the road down Main or Paint, maybe waiting for a public bus to come along to maximize the attention. He'd considered jumping into his 1983 DeLorean and racing through downtown, mowing through a city park during a busy afternoon, maybe colliding right into a historic building. There was always the option of gathering some guns and going on a shooting spree. Those would be ways to ensure national coverage of his demise.

But Sammy's animals defined him. He had to do something big that included his family.

Before those final days—the days that came after gun charges and arrest, after love lost, freedom taken, after the stability he'd spent a lifetime establishing began to tremble—he'd been known for his big love.

Even bigger than his ego was his capacity to offer affection to those he cared about. Sammy had a big heart, a happy soul, and he adored his animals and his wife.

"My lioness with a lioness," he used to call Marielle.

"My bear with a bear," she would say back.

He had big plans, back then, just a few years before everything fell apart. Sammy and Marielle already had the biggest family in Chillicothe—perhaps the biggest family in Ohio.

"Maybe even the biggest in the world," he'd convinced Marielle. "Other zoos and preserves aren't families, like we are. We live *with* our animals, love them. That's different than just taking care of them. We know them all by name and hug every one of them like our own children."

"Yes," Marielle had agreed. "But don't you think the family is getting just a little bit *too* big?"

"How can you have too many soulmates?"

When you can no longer afford to feed them, Marielle had answered—not verbally, but with that certain glint in her eyes. She'd dismissed his notion in that way her facial expressions and body language had a tendency to do. Tightening of the eyes, crinkling of the nose, sinking of the sides of her mouth, a slump in her posture. Sammy knew how to read unspoken language, in animals and in people.

And Sammy knew that Marielle was right. The animals were getting to be more than they could afford or physically handle.

Early in their marriage, she had left her job as a secretary to come work for him at the gun and tackle shop. The business was still running, a few years before everything changed. But the store wasn't doing as well as it had been during better times. Sales were down, fewer people purchased collectable guns and war memorabilia, and the tackle side of things never had generated much income.

Sammy had planned on an early retirement anyway. Planned on selling off the business so they could focus their autumn years on each other and their extended family. Running the shop, they didn't really have enough time to take care of the animals properly, so they'd hired Morris to help: to scout for roadkill, clean out the cages, feed them. When they sold the shop and had more time, Sammy figured they'd still keep Morris on for a few hours a week, but Sammy and Marielle would have much more time to spend with the animals themselves.

"If I need to," Sammy said, "I can sell off the cars, too. Just keep a few of them. To use."

But Sammy detected Marielle was no longer excited about their large family. That although she still loved Sammy, she'd grown resentful of the animals. Her fear of them had begun to outweigh her love of them.

Sammy knew, in those days before everything changed, that he was entering a new chapter in life, a chapter that required going smaller instead of bigger. That he needed to sell off instead of stock up. To minimize instead of maximize. Let go instead of accumulate.

A penny-stock day-trader had once told him at the bar that the concept of continuous growth was unsustainable. That the buyers and sellers of stocks wanted to see growth every quarter of every year. "But things can't grow forever," the broker had insisted. "Only so much exists in the world, and balance is law. An ebb and flow."

What was going through Sammy's mind, then, was that this truth transferred to his own life. That it wasn't sustainable for him to continue getting bigger.

Eventually he needed to scale back, let go. To continue living, he needed to become less.

Sammy could agree—although he never verbally did—to stop buying more animals, to stop rescuing animals being given away. And he could sell off the business, the guns, the cars. But he couldn't bring himself to give away his animals. They were more than pets. He provided his animals with more than meat and land. He and Marielle provided the family with love and affection.

Sammy decided he'd rather set them free—let them have a fighting chance—than give them away for someone else to abuse. He'd rather set them free than to imprison them in a life without the kind of love and care that only he could provide.

That's what was going through Sammy's mind.

Horseback

Dustin prepared the horses for another day of riding. The sun had barely risen, but he'd already put in a few hours. Earlier, he'd made breakfast—eaten three eggs, bacon, toast, and gravy—and brewed a pot of coffee to fill his Thermos. He went to the stables, loaded the horses into the trailer, and hit the road from his home farm in South Shore, Kentucky, to his job across the river at Shawnee State Forest in Ohio.

Once at the state park, he went to the riding stables, set the horses out in their individual stalls, made sure they had plenty to eat, and turned the sign on the post from "closed" to "open." Then he kicked back in the wooden rocking chair, crossed his boots on the split-rail fence, and drank the last of his coffee from the plastic thermos cup.

It was just after seven when his first customers of the morning came along. He set his coffee cup on the wooden side table and approached the family of four: man, woman, teenaged girl, little boy.

"Howdy." Dustin tipped his cap.

"Morning." The father of the family looked about forty, clean cut, business part in his hair. Looked like a talking head on the news, only he wore a flannel shirt and blue jeans. The woman looked about the same age, maybe a little younger, with wavy blonde hair and makeup that made her look too done up for a camping vacation. The girl giggled, already petting the horses tied up to the split-rail fence, talking to them in a syrupy voice that he imagined she once used on her dolls, or might use on a man in a few more years. And the little boy stood behind his sister, looking at the horses like they were some kind of wild animals, not quite sure about them. Dustin smiled.

Beyond his initial "Howdy," Dustin didn't say much, just stood there and waited for the man to talk. The man was reading the sign and the sign pretty much said all they needed to know.

> *Horseback Riding: 45 minutes, $50*
> *1 customer per horse, Must be 6 years or older*
> *Your guide today is two-time national rodeo champion*
> *Dustin Coomer*
> *Tips Appreciated*

Dustin looked down at the dirt and turned over a rock with the toe of his boot. He waited for the tourist to say something. Finally, the man opened his mouth.

"So, you're open?"

"Yup."

"We'd like to ride, I think." The dad mentioned it as though he hadn't been sure half a minute before, as though they hadn't come all the way out here knowing that they wanted to ride.

Dustin looked at the man from beneath the brim of his cap. "All right."

"Can my son ride with me?"

"Nope. Only one person per horse, like the sign says."

"But he's little, and kind of uneasy about riding a horse."

"How old is he?"

"Seven."

"Well, then, he's plenty mature enough to ride his own horse."

"Do you want to give it a try?" the dad asked. The boy shook his head and backed away.

"Ain't nothing to it," Dustin said. "When I was your age, I was riding and roping cattle. You can ride. We can put your horse between your mom and dad."

"It's safe, isn't it?" the mom asked.

Dustin chuckled. "Ma'am, riding a horse is a lot safer than riding a car."

"No, I mean out here, with all the animals."

"Ain't no animals gonna hurt you," Dustin assured. "Safer here than a city."

"All right then," the father finally committed. "Four."

"That'll be two hundred."

The dad had it counted out and folded up in his pocket already, like he'd already known the price, had already seen the sign by the park entrance or looked it up on the computer. Dustin sized up the four of them and selected the best horse for each.

"I want this one." the teenage girl stood before the big black stallion.

"That one's mine." Dustin gave his favorite a playful swat. "That's Romeo. You'll get Smokey. He's more suited to your pretty little frame."

He walked over to the father. "Daddy, you get Charger. Mommy, you can ride on Buttercup. And son, you get the best horse of all. You get to ride Wild One."

The boy didn't look thrilled. Dustin was tempted to tease the boy a little but decided against it. Better not to lose two customers since the mom would probably sit out with the boy, wouldn't think to let her baby out of her sight unsupervised for an hour. Dustin needed the money.

A few minutes later, they all sat in their saddles (with a bit of help) and began riding the trail up into the treed hills.

The dad took in a deep breath of fresh morning air. "It's beautiful country out here."

So, this one's going to be a talker. "Yup," Dustin agreed. "Between the rivers and the mountains and the woods, it don't get much better."

"We're from Cincinnati."

"Camping?"

"That was the plan. But we decided to get a hotel."

"Guess that's more comfortable." Dustin smirked. These city slickers probably couldn't figure out how to pitch the flimsy tent they bought at their local mall.

Dustin led the horses. They were not tethered, but they all knew the path and only deviated once in a while to grab a mouthful of grass or weed. The horses climbed the path of dirt and gravel up the hill, up the side of the mountain, the trees all around them. If not for the gravel, the path would've been too muddy to navigate—for tourists—and he'd have closed down for the day. It had rained all night, but the sun shone bright now. He looked behind him to make sure everyone was in line. The dad followed Dustin, then the girl, the boy, and the mom.

The dad asked, "So, you were in the rodeo?"

"Yup." Dustin wrote it on the sign to impress people, to let them know he wasn't just a stable buck. He used to be a living legend. He'd been somebody before starting his own business. He'd had status before trading it in for security. "Kentucky State Champion three times, rode the circuit about eight years, two-time National Champion."

The dad's nod bounced with his horse. "Guess there aren't very many older rodeo stars still working," the guy said. Dustin took this as a way of asking why he'd quit the rodeo instead of making a life out of it. Dustin was accustomed to such questions.

"Broke my legs twice, pelvis once. After I broke my pelvis, I had to take it easy. I can still ride, love to ride. But I can't do the tricky stuff no more. You don't see very many daredevils out there much more than thirty."

"What did you do? In the rodeo, I mean."

"Oh, a little of this and that. I roped steer, rode bulls, did some bull fighting. It was a bull that broke my pelvis."

"Wow," the dad said.

"Wow's right," Dustin said over his shoulder. "Two thousand pounds of rodeo bull crashed down right on top of me. I'm lucky to be alive."

Dustin made light of it, but truth be told, when it happened, he didn't think he would live through the ordeal. Riding the bull, fully expecting to be thrown but not expecting the bull to fall over with him still riding, not expecting it to crush him beneath its flexing muscle and kicking legs. Dustin was used to the bucking, but it was unusual for a bull to fall over. During those seconds, as the hide-brown ground came toward him, as he still straddled the muscular bull, Dustin counted himself as good as dead. When the bull finally stood and Dustin was still conscious, he found that he couldn't stand up himself. He couldn't move or feel his legs or anything from the waist down. He'd expected the bull to come back for him, to trample him, and lifted himself to his arms, trying to drag his useless body off to the side. He knew he didn't have the strength or time to make it, that the bull would be on him before he could cover two feet of dusty distance. But the rodeo clowns got to the angry bull first, some of them distracting the bull, others pulling Dustin out of harm's way. His doctor told him the same thing he'd told him after past injuries: that he should hang up his rodeo hat. This time, Dustin decided to listen.

His own dad hadn't listened. His dad was a rodeo star, too, and had taken Dustin with him on the circuit as far back as Dustin could remember, back when he was four or five. By the time Dustin turned six, he was riding alongside his dad. By the time he reached ten, he worked in the rodeo himself, in solo acts without his dad. When Dustin was fifteen, his dad got killed by a bull.

Now a dad himself, Dustin had a boy of twelve in school. He didn't want such a risky life for his son. That's why Dustin opened his own business, taking tourists out for rides. He'd conned himself into appreciating the beauty of a slow trot across the forested mountains instead of longing for the thrill of cowboy stunts. When he started, he enjoyed the peace and quiet of Shawnee State Forest, the beauty of the mountain paths, river views. Truth was, sometimes he longed for a little more excitement.

"Ask him about the animals," Dustin heard the mother saying to her husband. The husband cleared his throat.

"So, how about those animals?"

Dustin looked around them for evidence. "Oh, we see some deer out here pretty often. Squirrels and bunnies and chipmunks. Once in a while you might see a bear or fox. Wolf or coyote."

"No, I mean Chillicothe."

Dustin swatted at a fly on his neck. "Chillicothe?"

"Haven't you heard? It's all over the news."

"I ain't seen the news since yesterday morning."

"Oh my God, he doesn't know." The woman's nervous voice grew higher in pitch. "We need to go back to the car."

"Don't worry," the dad assured her. Then he addressed Dustin. "Some crazy guy let loose a bunch of wild animals in Chillicothe. Just last night, around five o'clock."

For the love of God. Dustin sighed and took a look around them. The new park ranger, in charge of notifying recreation vendors, always seemed to forget about him and his operation, forgetting to tell him about things like early closings and severe weather conditions. But there'd never been news like this to share before.

"They couldn't have made it this far, right?" The woman's voice didn't sound so sure. "It's safe out here, right?"

"Don't worry, ma'am," Dustin comforted. "There ain't never been any animal attacks out here." But Dustin was a little worried at this news and considered cutting the ride short as he tried to do the math in his head. Lions...tigers...leopards...panthers. He didn't really know his wild animals that well, but based on what he did know, he figured some of them *could* travel from Chillicothe to this area in twelve, thirteen hours. Perhaps paranoia was playing tricks on him, but he began to consider it likely. Shawnee State Forest seemed a welcoming place for such an animal to hide. Away from the city, lots of open space, trees and brush. "Just to be on the safe side," Dustin suggested casually, "let's go ahead and mosey on back."

He heard the woman worrying aloud as he turned his horse around and passed them all. "Oh, it's *not* safe, is it? You think they're out here?" His horse now stood next to the woman instead of the man.

"Everyone just pull on one side of the reigns and turn your horse around. We'll just mosey on back, nice and easy. Ain't nothing to worry about. Nice and peaceful out here."

Dustin wished he could have turned the whole train around, so the man rode at his back instead of the woman. She sounded worried even when she wasn't making a noise. But he didn't say anything to upset anyone. He tried to ride casual, looking about him for signs of unusual life. He convinced himself he was just being paranoid—just another ten minutes and they'd be back to the stalls. No predator in its right mind would come to these parts to attack people when there was an abundance of wild animals. "Almost back," he assured the family.

Shawnee State Forest was quiet. Songbirds chirped in the distance. He heard two deer scurrying out of the woods, crossing the trail behind them, then leaping back into the trees on the other side, down toward the river.

Then, he heard the snarl, the feline growl, heard the leaves and tree branches rustle, then not rustle, as though the animal had left the surface. Dustin looked behind him and saw beyond the terrorized faces of the woman, the teenaged girl, the little boy. Their father had fallen off his horse—or rather, had been knocked off by a large, spotted wildcat.

"Help him, help him, help him!" the woman screamed.

"Dad!" His daughter cried out in a shrill voice that Dustin hoped would drive off the cat.

"Kill it," the boy cried. "Just kill it!"

The dad flopped his arms beneath the leopard, apparently hoping to hit it, but not focused enough to aim as the cat sat on top of him. The leopard looked up at the screaming people around it and growled. The horses all broke into a frightened gallop—fortunately in the direction they were headed, along the path.

"Stay on the horses," Dustin yelled to the family as he jumped off his. "They'll head back to the stable." Dustin ran to help the pinned man. The guy grasped around him with one hand, as though for a stick or rock to hit the cat, while his other hand was beating the leopard in the skull with the palm of his hand to no avail. The cat had a grip on the man's shoulder and was clamped down. He opened his jaw every few seconds, then clamped down again, as though to get a better grip, or to cause more punctures, more damage, perhaps seeking out a main artery for a quick kill. Dustin saw a large branch on the ground near the path. He took it and beat the cat across the head with the blunt branch. The leopard backed off just a bit, just enough for the man to scoot back, crawling crab-style on his hands and feet out from under the cat and off the path. Dustin beat the leopard on the back and across the face, but the wildcat didn't back down. Dustin tried ramming the blunt end of the branch into the leopard's face, which seemed a little more effective than swinging. Dustin stepped slowly back, putting distance between him and the cat. Then Dustin charged, ramming the leopard in the face again. The leopard swept up the tree in a flash, regaining its strength on a high branch about the same size as the one Dustin held in his grip.

Dustin kept the branch close to him and his eye on the leopard, but he walked over to the man. "Can you get up?"

"I dunno," the stunned man said, as though he didn't even know what he was saying. Dustin helped him find his feet. The city slicker had lost a lot of blood; he looked as pale as a dead man.

"Let's walk back." Dustin dropped the branch and draped the man's arm around his neck, pulling his limp body along.

"Tell...Karen...that I...love her...tell the...kids that ..."

"Enough of that." Dustin didn't have patience for dramatics. He was scared for this man's life and his own. Dustin looked back every few steps, knowing that the leopard was fast and could be on their backs without a second's warning.

Dustin could see the stable ahead, just a hundred feet away, and he could see that the woman had locked herself and the kids in their car. She screeched into the phone, undoubtedly to the police. Dustin wondered whether this tragedy would get him shut down. Would blame fall to him, or to the nut in Chillicothe who let these animals out? He wondered whether he'd have to give up the business and sell the horses and find another way to make a living and support his wife and boy. He wondered whether he'd live to do it.

Instead of looking at the stable and wondering, he realized he needed to look behind him. When he turned to look, he saw the leopard drop out of the tree. It sprinted in their direction. Dustin saw it looking at him and the other man, sizing them up, determining the easier meat. The leopard leaped—seemed too far away to have begun his leap—and then flew toward them. He almost looked like he was going to soar over them. As though he had rudders to control his altitude, the leopard adjusted his path as he came down on them. The leopard targeted the weaker, injured man. The dad fell to the ground with a scream, and the cat snarled and clamped his jaw around the man's shoulder while standing on his back.

Dustin pulled out his hunting knife. He jabbed the cat in the shoulder and it flinched, turned to face him, then dug his claws into the lifeless body beside him. The leopard turned away from Dustin and proceeded to drag the body toward a tree, as though it planned to pull the corpse into the safety of the branches. Dustin wasn't sure whether the man was dead or alive, but he knew he didn't want this cat to go free. He stabbed it again with his knife, in and out of its right front upper leg, then he stabbed it in its face. The cat let out a snarl and batted a paw at Dustin. Dustin jumped on the leopard, wrestling it away from the still body, and sliced the blade of his knife across the cat's throat. After a few moments of struggling, of avoiding the cat's sharp claws and large canines, the cat went limp.

Just like the man.

The woman and the kids were crying, hyperventilating, not believing what just happened before their eyes.

Dustin knew what it was like to lose a father to an animal. "I'm so sorry, ma'am. I tried to..."

The woman screamed at him. "You should have stopped it! You should have told us it wasn't safe!"

"Mommy, is Daddy gonna be all right?" the little boy asked.

"I killed the leopard," Dustin offered. But, of course, no one gave a damn about that.

"Can't believe you didn't stop it!"

"Mom." The daughter wrapped herself around her mother.

"Is Daddy gonna be all right?" the boy asked again. Dustin wanted to pick up the boy, but he knew it wasn't his place.

The ambulance arrived from Southern Ohio Medical Center, and the Portsmouth police came minutes later. By the time police arrived, asking Dustin to relay the story, the medics had already put the man into the back of the ambulance and rushed away. One of the police drove the family to the hospital—the wife was in no condition to drive—and Dustin figured that he'd end up delivering their vehicle to their hotel or a shopping center or something, because he knew it would be too traumatic for the woman to come here again. Dustin took the officers to the leopard.

"Get Chillicothe on the horn," said one of the officers—Heaker, according to his metallic tag. "Let Roscoe know we got one of the leopards."

"What else is out here?" Dustin asked.

"We're not certain." Officer Heaker looked him in the eye. "But they've got animal experts tracking them. Said there could be two leopards and a tiger coming in our direction."

"That don't sound good." Dustin looked at the dead leopard.

"We got the good end of the stick." Heaker looked around them, into the woods. "They think a black panther and a whole pride of lions are headed up to Columbus. And Chillicothe's just crawling with wild beasts."

"Hard to imagine." Dustin lifted his cap and wiped the sweat from his forehead.

"Yeah, don't I know it. I'd get my horses barned up if I was you. And stay inside with your family, if you got one."

"Yep," Dustin said. "Be a good idea to close shop for a few days, I reckon."

As Dustin prepared the horses for the ride back across the river, he thought of his son. He decided to pick him up early from school. He couldn't help but thank God it was the other father, and not his son's father. Not a nice thought, but an honest one. It's how he felt.

Dustin reveled in the thrill of the hunt just like he had the excitement of the rodeo, but knew he had to take care of his son and wife, to make sure they were safe and secure at home. When he made the decision to walk away from the dangers of animals, he didn't expect the danger to follow him here. He was anxious to pick up his son and get home to South Shore. And he thanked God they weren't visiting his in-laws in Columbus.

Notes on Columbus

Columbus, Ohio, is average-town USA. That makes us a popular place for focus-group testing. You want to see how America will react to an item or a product or an idea, you bring it to Columbus. New York and Los Angeles are extreme cities. You want *mainstream* America, welcome to Columbus.

— Dimitri Silverstein, Business Marketing Consultant

Best place in the country to raise a family.

— *Business Week*, 2009

Number 1 up-and-coming tech city in the nation.

— *Forbes Magazine*, 2008

Some may call Columbus the "biggest small town in America" and "Cowtown." But I'll tell you what. Columbus is the largest city in Ohio, and the sixteenth largest city in the entire United States. We've got the world's largest private research and development foundation and the nation's largest college campus. We're more than small-town cows.

— Everett Scott, Ohio Tourism Center

Seventh best place to do business in the nation.

— *MarketWatch*, 2008

One of the top 10 best big cities in the country.

> — *Relocate America*, 2010

Today we're pleased to highlight the public library in Columbus, Ohio—by many measures, the most successful in the nation. According to *American Libraries Magazine*, the Columbus Metropolitan Library was ranked number one in 1999, 2005, and 2008, and it's been in the top four every year since rankings began in 1999. In 2010, *Library Journal* named it *Library of the Year*. It's been one of the best libraries in the world since opening in 1873.

> — *Writeful: A Weblog for Readers and Writers*

Eighth best big city in the country to live in.

> — *CNN Money*, 2006

Columbus was founded in 1812 and became the state capitol in 1816. Before that, the capitols were Chillicothe, then Zanesville, then Chillicothe again. The meeting of the Scioto and Olentangy rivers made Columbus a perfect location, because most shipping was done by river back then.

> — Dr. Charles Humphries, History Professor, Ohio State
> University

The Columbus Zoo is one of the best in the nation, and in the world. If not *the* best. In 2009 it was ranked as the best zoo in the United States.

> — Leland Anders, Celebrity Zookeeper

You can cite all these stats, best place to live, best library and zoo, best place in the country for families and gays. But here's the stat I like:

Sperling's called Columbus the second most manly city in America. You got guys like me to thank for that.

> — Mickey Ketchum, Chillicothe Resident, originally from
>   Columbus

Columbus is a town in which almost anything is likely to happen, and in which almost everything has.

> — James Thurber, Author, Humorist

Breakfast

The lions have traveled through the rainy night, and they are more invigorated than tired. They rest now, in the light of morning, under the shelter of trees. They have more or less followed man's back road, Alpha realizes as he scans the area, peeking out from the trees to see the vehicles rushing in both directions. It is not coincidence. They *must* follow man's road because the forest bends to its whim. The trees and wildlife are simply remainders man has not yet cut away.

Alpha recognizes familiar food on the side of the black road: animals hit by vehicles and left partially mutilated. The scent of the kill has brought Alpha back to the forest's edge, to peek out and see the road. The alluring smell of meat proves more powerful than the offending scent of man, of exhaust from fast-moving metal shells or smoke from enormous shelters. As Alpha makes his way casually out of tree cover, into the tall grass, then into the open patch of cut grass, vehicles begin to slow and swerve and speed up—an irrational mix of different behaviors—in response to his presence. Alpha picks up the small deer with his mouth and drags it away from man's road. Back into the tall grass, into the woods. He feeds on the carcass.

Once Alpha's had his fill, he allows the others to eat. They've eaten one human and one deer, since leaving home. They take a moment to rest. Sun shines through the glistening trees. They sleep on the moist ground. Then they continue north.

The trees gradually thin as they smell more of man's work in the path ahead: buildings, cement, chemicals, sulfur. The noise is unmistakably man's mechanical symphony: cars, buses, buildings, factories, electronics, chattering. But the city ahead is full of meat. If they can choose the right paths and go unseen by the herds of people, they can cross through the city, feed, and continue north where vaster patches of wooded land and grassy pastures await.

The key to eventually finding the right place to live is to continue going in the same direction. To not deviate from the path. So the lions continue north, into the city.

New Mascot

After talking with Officer Heaker, Dustin loaded up his horses and high-tailed it out of Shawnee State Forest. He crossed the bridge back to South Shore, Kentucky, stabled his horses, and told his wife he was going to pick up Kasey early.

"Make sure you stay inside, no matter what," he insisted. "Wild animals are on the prowl. Stay locked inside."

Seemed like a normal day out and about. Nothing out of the ordinary. And for most people, that was true. It wasn't likely a tiger or leopard would swim across the river. But the possibility remained. Some breeds of tiger were good swimmers. He'd once heard about a waterborne tiger jumping out of the water and swiping a fisherman from a boat in India.

Dustin picked up his son, brought him home, and they had an early lunch together in the safety of their locked house. He told them what had happened at the horse trail that morning. His wife and son appeared both excited and horrified at his unexpected adventure.

Dustin felt antsy. "I can't fight the notion I should do something."

"Just stay home with us," his wife said. "We'll make some kettle corn and play some board games. Maybe watch a movie."

"Oh, I'm all for that," Dustin said. "But it's morning yet. I owe it to that guy and his family. To help find the other animals and make sure they don't hurt no one else."

He desperately wanted to stay home with his wife and son. But the desire to take action was too strong for him to ignore. Before he knew it, he was crossing the bridge back from South Shore to Portsmouth.

Cruising Portsmouth in his pickup, Dustin tuned his radio into the police activity. He'd been a radio hobbyist off and on for some time, but he hadn't really tuned in for years. With the gun-show Colt M1911 he bought at the Scioto County Fairgrounds a few years back sitting in his passenger seat, Dustin drove slowly down Gay Street. Then along the floodwall. Up into the Boneyfiddle District and along Chillicothe Street. He looked in the alleys between historic buildings and new builds, on the sidewalks and streets. He drove along Third Street, and around the campus of Shawnee State University.

Where Southern Hospitality Begins. He chuckled at the Portsmouth motto. Hospitality wasn't what any animal he came across would find here.

As Dustin scouted for animals, he took in Portsmouth as it appeared now, and as it had been before. Ten, maybe twenty years ago, this had been a different place. Second Street was still a street, not a sidewalk. The university had taken over the area, nearly taken over the city. The institution used to be a rinky-dink branch of Ohio University. Shawnee State had grown, with new buildings everywhere. Every time he drove up this way, seemed a new building had shot up like a mushroom.

College students filled the spaces between buildings. SSU had a good number of older students, guys like himself, people who had already tried at one career and were starting over. *Non-traditional students*, they called them. Sometimes Dustin thought about going to college, maybe getting a degree in animals, veterinary studies, zoology, something like that. It just seemed to him like a lot of work and money without much promise of a job at the end of the road. So he always came back to thinking that he was better off doing what already did: running his own business, being his own boss, and being around the horses and land he loved.

He heard a scream and understood it wasn't that of a fun-loving college kid goofing off—this was a worried sound, a terrorized noise, and it swelled into a chorus of startled voices. He stopped his truck in the middle of Third Street, just in front of the campus apartments, and jumped out with his Colt in hand. He spotted the leopard. It looked just like the one he'd encountered in the forest earlier that morning.

There was a girl on her back in front of the University Center, her books scattered all about and blood splashed on the open pages. But the leopard hadn't killed her. The commotion of the swelling crowd had driven it back and it stepped unsurely away from what should have been an easy kill. The leopard darted toward Massie Hall, running across the green, past the white lion statue, and toward the cement square. Dustin wanted to open fire, to shoot the animal, but he was reluctant here in the open courtyard. A student could get into his line of fire. He didn't want another person's life on his hands.

Dustin followed the leopard. Most students were backing away from it, yelling and screaming, and the only reason the leopard hadn't followed instinct and chased these running baits was because when the leopard approached one person, ten others started throwing sticks and rocks, books and paper cups of hot coffee. The leopard, confused, searched for a place with fewer people.

Dustin followed the leopard from the plaza in front of Massie Hall to the Clark Memorial Library across the way. Fewer students roamed here, making Dustin feel more confident about doing what he must. The leopard was headed for the library's glass cylinder, through which Dustin imagined the cat must have spotted the spiral staircase, the hanging sculptures within it seeming to hover in mid-air. The leopard must have wanted to climb that staircase, unaware of the transparent wall in the way. Dustin aimed and fired.

Police sirens erupted and before he knew it they had arrived. Dustin recognized them: the same two who had come out to Shawnee State Forest. That earlier call had prepared them: they now arrived with assault rifles. They opened fire on the cat, which still stood, stunned. Dustin was convinced he'd already killed the cat, that it was dead when the police arrived. But he had no way of knowing. The officers both hit their marks, and the leopard tumbled into the mud of the weeded crater circling the library's glass tower.

Students collected in a ring around them. Medics arrived over in the plaza, and the girl who'd been attacked now rested in the back of the ambulance, talking, moving, very much alive.

"Hey, we should make that our new mascot!" a boy yelled. "Out with the bears, in with the leopards!"

These kids annoyed Dustin. They treated the leopard like the hero. Even after he and the police had come to their rescue, it was as though they were the bad guys on campus, just by association. These kids knew the cops as the ones who pulled them over drunk, who issued speeding tickets and tried to break up good times and fights. Never mind that they just saved the kids' hides.

Officer Heaker recognized Dustin. "You again."

"Yep." Dustin tipped his cap. "Couldn't rest knowing it was out here."

Heaker eyed the Colt. "You got a license for that?"

"In my glove box."

"Ordinarily we'd take you into custody for opening fire on campus, but we've got a tiger to catch." Heaker shot him a serious expression. "You'd better put that thing away and get back home."

"But I can help," Dustin insisted. "Done killed two of 'em."

"Last thing we need is vigilantes shooting in the streets. Get on home and rest. You've done your share."

Dustin nodded, knowing that his stubbornness would only get him in trouble. As he turned from the policemen, he heard Heaker's partner speak.

"We got a lead on the tiger. It's down on Front Street, by the floodwall."

Dustin darted across campus to his truck; it still idled in the middle of the road. He jumped in and closed the door. He removed his cap long enough to wipe the sweat from his brow. His feet were sweaty within his leather boots and he wished he'd put on his sneakers instead. He pressed his steel toe down on the accelerator and rushed toward the Portsmouth floodwall.

Inside-Outing

When Delores told the team—now in Columbus—where the most recent sighting had been, Ketchum could barely believe the location. He knew the garden well, although he'd never been in person: the Columbus Topiary Garden in Deaf School Park.

Visiting a place in person was not the same as seeing it in photographs. After her visit years ago, Ketchum's wife had brought back a monthly calendar. Each month featured a photograph of some detail from the garden. The calendar included an image, on the back page, of the French painting that inspired it: "A Sunday Afternoon on the Island of La Grande Jatte" by Georges Seurat.

Ketchum wasn't into art, and certainly knew little of French Impressionism. But he was familiar with this painting because there had been a number of times when the timeworn calendar was the only bathroom reading material within reach.

The entire painting, full of people walking in the park and lounging and boating, came to life in this garden with bushes and wire. The original painting hung in the Art Institute of Chicago; he knew that because his wife had visited Chicago once on a church trip and had seen the pointillism up close. She came back saying it looked better from far away.

Ketchum had made a life in Chillicothe with his wife, but he was born and raised in Columbus. He lived most of his childhood right on the edge of German Village, near Shriller Park. He knew Columbus fairly well, probably better than anyone else on the Sheriff's team. But he'd never set foot in this garden.

"Careful," Chuck warned. "It could be anywhere."

"Tell us something we don't already know," Ketchum sassed back.

"Should stand out like a sore thumb," Morris said. "A black spot in all this green."

"Like another blotch of paint on the canvas." Ketchum spit out his tobacco.

Morris gave Ketchum a funny look.

"Never mind," Ketchum said. He pulled out his pouch of tobacco and placed a new pinch into his mouth.

Maybe he was going crazy, lack of sleep, a full seventeen hours of hunting and killing animals. Stress be damned, weird thoughts were creeping into his mind—the sort of thinking that sometimes came in the dark hours of the morning just before waking up, thoughts from the dreamscape between being asleep and being awake. He adjusted the wad in his mouth and spit. The situation with the animals was kind of like this painting and park, this inside-outing of things. A painting of a park had become a park of a painting. The zoo that would normally be caged now roamed in the city, caging people in their own homes. *Inside out.*

"Over here," Morris called. Ketchum heard it, too. A man screaming, "Holy shit!"

"Sir, back away quietly," Chuck instructed. "Nice and easy."

The man's nerves visibly rattled, he did as instructed, his jittering legs taking small steps back, his wide eyes glued to the panther. Ketchum and the others watched as the panther sprang from the tall grass at the edge of the park's pond, tall cattails swaying, and darted across the picturesque landscape.

The panther hid behind bushes shaped like a man and a woman strolling beneath a parasol and peered out from between the figures. Ketchum, Morris and Chuck slowly approached. The black cat was beautiful, and when you looked it in the eye, the creature appeared more frightened than fierce.

Morris whispered to the cat as they inched closer, "Don't worry, Lady. Don't worry." The three men put themselves between the panther and the pedestrian.

Lady snarled and opened her mouth to reveal a large set of canines.

But it crouched back as though considering retreat rather than attack.

"That's a good girl," Morris was saying, a quiver in his voice. Morris had his gun aimed, but didn't fire. He had a clear shot, but he wouldn't take it.

"What'cha waiting for?" Chuck asked.

"Look at her." Morris lowered his gun. "She doesn't want to hurt anyone. She just wants to go home. Maybe we can..."

Ketchum did what the others debated. He shot the panther in the head, and it snarled, lunged and fell. "Sorry Morris," Ketchum said. "You know as well as I, there's no place for these animals. Their home died when Sammy did."

"This feels less like protecting the innocent and more like killing it," Morris said.

"Panther down," Chuck reported over the radio. "Got a location on them lions?"

Ketchum listened as he looked down at the kill. Both the panther's eyes remained intact and open, as though looking up at Ketchum and identifying him as guilty.

"Negative," Delores replied. "Someone thought they spotted something at the Thurber House, but Roscoe went there and didn't find anything. Could be the lions were there and left, or maybe someone saw one of the dog statues and thought it was an animal. South side of Columbus was the last reported sighting."

"We should head downtown," Chuck said. "Not only is it a central location, so we'll be close to wherever they're spotted next, but the Scioto River runs right through downtown. Won't they be looking for water?"

Morris nodded. "The lions may be attracted to the river. They should be thirsty, unless they found some pools of water along the way."

Ketchum considered the black panther's stillness. The panther rested, eyes glaring, sprawled out directly in the path of the topiary couple like a rug. Just one more dot on the canvas of this bloody mission.

Blocked

Tiger has traveled far. He longs for lake or stream or river. He has tasted rain water from leaves and puddles. But he wants to lap from a larger body. He thirsts for living water, moving water. Tiger smells the river, but cannot reach it.

The scent of rushing river water is unmistakable. The sound of flowing water, just as clear. Tiger left the seclusion and safety of the forest to reach this river. He stealthily maneuvered through the people and their settlement, through the great shelters and moving metal shells.

The river's scent has brought him here, but he cannot get to the flowing water. A massive wall blocks his way. The river lies just beyond it. The wall is too tall for him to jump over, so he strolls along its side in hopes of finding an opening.

Colorful dyes paint this wall and the colors change. They are flat scenes, images of things man has made or done, and they are boxed into sections of the wall. Tiger can see them, but his binocular vision tells him these flat collages of color are not real. One scene that nearly tricks Tiger is an image of the river that he knows waits beyond the wall, like an opening. But it is not a passageway, not even a window. He can smell the solid cement.

Tiger is tired and thirsty. He wants the old ways back. The ways of Master. Since he was a cub, Tiger has depended on Master.

When Master cut open the side of his cage, Tiger was confused. He stepped out with his front paw, then stepped back in. Out with two paws, back in. Halfway out, back in again. Tiger stayed inside because he didn't know where to go. He felt secure within his home.

Then, he heard Master's stick explode, smelled the sulfur and the blood, the release of excrement and urine. He could smell Master's death. And chicken.

After some delay, Tiger left his cage. Not to escape, but to check on Master. To help him, play with him, wake him. But even Tiger couldn't wake a dead man. Master was lifeless, blood coming from his head, chicken parts all over his body, as though to entice Tiger, as though inviting Tiger to partake. And Tiger understood that this was Master's last gift to him, the last meal Master would provide.

Confused, Tiger bit Master's head, cracking the skull between his jaws and sucking out the fluid. Perhaps Master had simply lost the will to live. But the scent of chicken innards left no doubt: Master was the meal of the evening. He intended this. The warm, rich fluid from Master's head was delicious.

When other men came, Tiger continued eating. Master and Tiger were tucked away in one of the horse stalls, so the men did not see him at first. By now, many of the animals had left their cages, but none of them—not even the lions or other tigers—challenged him to Master's meat. Some of them appeared more intent on leaving. Others remained in their cages or in the compound, waiting to be fed. Others went out and found their own food. Prey and predator ambled about. Horse and bear. And man.

As Tiger ate Master, a group of men entered the compound together. They closed the doors of the cages, but were unable to close the openings Master had cut on the other sides. Tiger crouched into the corner of the stall so the men would not see him. Something happened to the men; their scents changed in an instant, from curious timidity to raw terror. A leopard attacked one of them. Then, the men exploded their fire sticks and the scent of fire and sulfur filled the compound. Animals began falling dead. The ones that didn't get hurt or couldn't hide attacked, and the men retreated.

It was dark at that time. The men gathered outside like an antsy herd considering fight or flight. Tiger understood that they would come back with more force. Men were gods. They would win. But he didn't want to leave Master's side. He took another bite of flesh and innards.

The wrath of the men came fully into the barn before the men even stepped foot inside, their fire sticks exploding. Tiger's brothers and sisters of all sorts fell dead without a chance. Tiger continued to hide in the stall.

When the loud noises and flashes of fire ceased, the men came inside and chattered. Assuming the men to be occupied with each other, expecting them to be feeding on their prey, Tiger decided to slink out the back of the barn, leaving the remains of Master in the stall. The men in the barn looked as shocked to see Tiger as he was to see them staring back at him. Tiger bolted, making his escape out the back door of the barn. One of the men fired, and the metal wall of the barn sparked beside him. Tiger slipped into darkness, under cover of tall grass, then into the wooded land.

He had eaten a monkey, another of Master's animals. Between the monkey and Master, Tiger had eaten enough to begin his journey. He headed south. The lions had made their way north, and Tiger preferred solitude.

Now, Tiger finds himself at the end of the road, blocked by this wall of dyes, images that obstruct the true vision of river and mountainside and tree—of the land he may soon call home.

Tiger hears a human scream: a woman has spotted him. She squawks from the sky, from a wood platform attached to a building above him. She looks down at him and shrieks. Tiger has no way to reach her or silence her. So he quickens his pace and trots along the hard black ground, searching the wall for an opening to the river.

Another person crosses Tiger's path. This man spots Tiger, yells and runs into an alleyway. Tiger's tail involuntarily flicks and instinct takes over. A fleeing animal is food, and this one appears to be an easy kill. Fat, weak. Tiger charges after the man, into the alleyway. He jumps and lands on the man's back, pushing him to the hard black ground. The man smells of waste and sweat. Other people roam about, but they do not challenge Tiger. Instead, they scatter like a herd of frightened antelope. The people know that to fight is hopeless. The man beneath him yells and kicks and thrashes, but Tiger cuts his air supply with pressure to the neck and the man goes limp. Tiger uses his long canines to shred flesh from the carcass.

But only for a moment. The people who fled have not run completely out of view, but remain nearby, muttering, talking, hiding behind vehicles, chattering into small bits of metal and plastic. Tiger hears the wailing sounds that came to the compound before the shooting began, and soon the blinding lights flash in the distance. Tiger knows man's fire sticks will follow these lights and sirens, so he flees the ally, returns to the wall, and quickens his pace. He resumes his hunt for access to the river, his search for escape from man's habitat.

Tiger will swim across the river and enter the forest—he can smell it—on the hills of the other side. He will drink, then he will find sanctuary in the woods along the tree-coated mountains beyond the river's far shore.

In front of him, he can see a place where no wall blocks the way. In the distance, an unnatural bridge stretches over the river, connecting the land on either side. It appears to be a man-made bridge, and man's motorized beasts cross over it in both directions. If Tiger can get to that place, can get past this wall and under that bridge, he can make it to the river. He can drink, swim, escape.

Behind him, the screaming, flashing vehicle follows. One of the men hangs out of the side and fires his metallic stick. Tiger's back leg stings, but he does not stop. He picks up his pace.

In front of him, he sees another man—on foot. The man stands in his way, his natural hair under a covering with a bill on the front. His upper covering smells of sweat and body odor, like Master's. This man's feet are encased in leathery bull carcass. The man holds a small fragment of metal in his hands, and he points it at Tiger. The man, seeming to realize that he does not have the power to stop Tiger, moves out of the way, begins to run off to the side, toward the buildings and away from the picture wall. Enraged, Tiger no longer seeks water or river or opening in the wall—he hones in on the man, this moving target who has fired into his chest and hurt him. Tiger veers to the right and runs after the man, tackles him, secures his claws into the man's soft, striped top, into the tender flesh beneath. He bites down on the man's wet neck and makes a kill.

Before Tiger can eat, before he looks around him to determine whether feeding is even an option, the two men arrive in their wailing, flashing vehicle. They throw open the sides of the metal beast and jump out. They have smooth fur the color of water at night, except for their fleshy faces. The sunlight glistens off little metal shields upon their breasts. Their odor is strong, as though their fur does not allow their sweat to penetrate. One of the men discharges his fire stick and Tiger feels the sting.

"You got him, Heaker?" one of them says.

"He's down," the other says.

"He did a number on the horse man," the first says.

"Dammit! I told the bastard to take his Colt and go home."

These sounds mean nothing to Tiger. He has been around people—the Master and his mate and their worker—for his entire life, but never picked up the language of their sounds, only the language of their movements and tones and smells. The master and his mate and their helper used to coo at Tiger, sing to him, talk in playful tones that soothed him.

Tiger can see the bridge in the distance, can see the river beneath it, can see that place where no dyed wall blocks him from the river. He can smell the fresh water and the green forest in the distance, still wet from the evening's rainfall. It is so close. But it is out of reach.

There are nearer noises filling his ears. These are not soothing sounds—they agitate him. The rat-a-tat voices shooting out of men's mouths, the high-pitched sounds of the beast they came in, it all hurts. They come closer to Tiger, their long fire sticks still pointed at him. They make more chattering noise, and their odor grows stronger the closer they get, stronger even than the smell of the dead man beneath him. Tiger gets up and stumbles toward the wall and the water beyond it. He takes only two steps, then the fire stick sounds again, and it knocks him to the hard, black surface. Tiger closes his eyes and imagines swimming in the cool, cool river. He drifts away.

First Time

It should have been a warning, Marielle Johnson realizes now. She and Sammy should have paid attention. It happened years ago, back when Sammy still wanted to open a public zoo and safari park. The message was clear as day: *these animals are dangerous.*

Marielle's friends were over for dinner and drinks. Sammy had gone to Dennis's bar for drinks with Mike and Calvin. After a simple dinner of pasta and salad, Marielle and her two girlfriends talked. They had finished eating, but red wine and conversation continued to flow.

She'd just uncorked the third bottle and poured the glasses when their conversation moved from movies and television to actors they considered deliciously wild. Their talk turned then to the wild members of her own family.

"I don't know how you can live with those things in your front yard," Elaine had said. "I'd be scared to death one of them would break loose and skin me in the night."

"They're lovable," Marielle had assured them. "They eat meat, just like we do. But they wouldn't attack us any more than you would kill and cook a house pet."

"I've seen those things at the zoo, and on TV." Lucy laughed. "I don't care what you say, I wouldn't want them living on my property."

"What do I have to do to convince you that they're adorable?" Marielle asked, laughing. "Let's go visit them now."

The ladies seemed a little uneasy, but the warmth of the wine and the courage that came with it made them perhaps a little braver than they'd otherwise have been. Crystal stems in hand, the three women left the house and walked to the outdoor cages lining the drive.

Perhaps Sammy had forgotten to feed them that day. Maybe he had planned to feed them when he got back from the bar. But the cats seemed a little friskier than usual. One of the tigers roared.

"The roar of a meat-eating tiger is like nothing you've ever heard," Elaine would later say in a newspaper interview. "It's not the roar of a circus animal or zoo animal. It's the sound of a man-killer."

Marielle looked at the hungry tiger and soothed it. "Be nice, Simba. You're a good girl." She balanced her wine glass on the ground, put her arms in the cage and rubbed her hands behind Simba's ears. The tiger began to purr.

Elaine and Lucy watched with wide-eyed amazement. Marielle giggled. "They respond to a soothing voice, just like a house cat or dog. And they can sense when you're upset, worried, concerned. These cats can pick up your mood, and they act accordingly."

"So they have their own personalities?" Elaine seemed to warm up to the possibility that these were not simply one-track-minded killing machines.

"Yes!" Marielle looked at the ladies as she continued to pet Simba. "So if I was upset, they would respond by lowering their heads, putting their paws down, looking away from me—to show they don't want to bother or challenge me. Especially if I was in the cage with them."

"In the cage?" Lucy asked. "You actually go in there with them?"

"Sometimes," Marielle admitted. "Sammy goes in a lot more than I do."

Lucy shook her head. "That's crazy."

Marielle took her hands out of the cage and retrieved her wine. "Go ahead," she offered. "Pet Simba."

"No way," Lucy said, keeping her distance.

"Is it safe?" Elaine asked.

"Absolutely," Marielle assured with perhaps too much certainty.

Elaine held her glass of red wine in one hand and reached in to pet Simba with the other. She rubbed the tiger on the top of the head, found the soft spot behind the ear and massaged. The tiger purred. "Wow,"

Elaine said. "You're just like a big house cat, aren't you?"

"See?" Marielle laughed. "She's just a big ball of love."

Elaine, with her arm still in the cage petting the tiger, turned and looked at Marielle and laughed. With her other arm, she lifted her wine flute to her mouth and took a drink of the blood red wine. A little dribbled off her lip and onto her white shirt. She began to pull her hand away from the cat to wipe the wine droplet from her blouse, but as she pulled her hand away, Simba pawed at it, snagging Elaine's arm with her claws.

Elaine dropped her wine flute and it shattered on the gravel. She screamed as Simba dug her claws deep into her forearm and pulled her against the bars of the cage. Simba pulled with such force, she seemed to want to pull Elaine through the bars, into the cage with her.

Lucy backed away, screaming. Marielle didn't know what had gotten into her cat. She tossed the red wine from her glass into Simba's face. The tiger flinched, but did not let go. Marielle grabbed a nearby crook that Sammy kept hanging near the cages—the one he used in the unlikely event of aggression—and she used the straight end of the stick to butt the tiger's face, hitting its nose and eyes. Simba released Elaine's arm and moved back out of the crook's reach.

Elaine, hyperventilating, pulled her arm out of the cage and stared at it. But in her stunned state, she did not immediately back away from the cage. Before any of the ladies had noticed, the tiger had come back to the edge of the cage, cringed down at the bottom, and batted its paw under the door. Simba snatched Elaine's leg. The claw shredded through the blue jeans and into her flesh, knocking Elaine off her feet. Simba then proceeded to drag Elaine underneath the door—the opening where Sammy usually slid their food. In a painful tug-of-war, Marielle pulled Elaine's arms and Simba—her claws securely fastened deep in flesh and muscle—pulled on Elaine's leg. Holding Elaine as best she could with one arm, Marielle used her free hand to retrieve the crook and rammed it into the cage, hitting the tiger on the shoulder, then in the face—the nose and eyes and mouth. The ram to the mouth caused Simba to gag. She loosened her claws and, with Lucy's help, Marielle managed to pull Elaine fully out of the cage and out of the tiger's reach.

Lucy called 911 and the medics arrived within ten minutes. Fortunately, Elaine was all right. She needed stitches in her forearm and lower leg, but no life-threatening damage had been done.

But damage had been done to Sammy's dream of opening a zoo, and to Marielle's confidence that their family was safe. The incident was life-threatening to Simba.

Elaine decided not to press charges. But she insisted that the offending animal be put down. And the authorities agreed.

After that, Marielle never got in the cages with the animals again. She still loved them, absolutely. But she no longer trusted them. Trying to read their emotions and motives could be like playing a deadly game of chess. She preferred not to play with the stakes so high. Sammy, on the other hand, still got in the cages with them daily.

That should have been the first sign, Marielle realizes now that she has lost her man, her animals, her family. The first things she lost, all those years ago, were her friends, Elaine and Lucy. They said they didn't blame her, but Marielle knew they did. Hadn't she promised them that the animals wouldn't hurt them?

Had Marielle heeded the warning Simba gave then—had she seen the foreshadowing then instead of noticing it now—maybe things would have turned out differently.

Now, in the midst of the tragedy, Marielle stands on the land she's known as home for decades with the animals she's known as her family for nearly as long. The carcasses are all around her. The ones gunned down here, on site, and the ones that had been hauled here from all around Chillicothe, Portsmouth and Columbus. They would all be buried here, where they lived, all united in a mass grave. If legal, she'd have considered throwing Sammy's body in the same mass grave, just throwing one more wild, misunderstood animal corpse on the heap.

Cruelest Animal

Some people talk to animals. Not many listen though. That's the problem.

— A.A. Milne

If a man aspires to a righteous life, his first act of abstinence is from injury to animals.

— Leo Tolstoy

Never, never be afraid to do what's right, especially if the well-being of a person or animal is at stake.

— Dr. Martin Luther King, Jr.

People speak sometimes about the "bestial" cruelty of man, but that is terribly unjust and offensive to beasts, no animal could ever be so cruel as a man, so artfully, so artistically cruel.

— Fyodor Dostoevsky

Animals don't hate, and we're supposed to be better than them.

— Elvis Presley

May all that have life be delivered from suffering.

— Gautama Buddha

We are lonesome animals.

— John Steinbeck

The greatness of a nation and its moral progress can be judged by the way its animals are treated.

— Mohandas Gandhi

If there only was a tiger to devour him!

— Herman Hesse

Every dog must have his day.

— Jonathan Swift

Man is the cruelest animal.

— Friedrich Nietzsche

Scioto Mile

The female lion follows her mate—Alpha—through the landscape at the edge of the city. Alpha's brother and two other females make up the rest of the pride, or what remains of it. They have traveled together through the night. They have eaten a human and a deer, one hunted and killed, the other found dead along the side of man's black path. A far cry from what each lion needs per day. But they will eat soon enough. She will lead the hunt, once Alpha slows to rest. They have followed man's black path, beneath the seclusion of the trees beside it, until coming to the line that separates the forest from man's urban jungle.

She lingers, unsure. Dangerous ground awaits in man's unnatural habitat. Alpha is braver than she, perhaps, or less cautious. He leads the pride out of the trees.

She does not growl, but lets out a low, gravelly bark, like the pelting of stones against a hide. She asks Alpha to reconsider. To remain in the woods for now, until nightfall, at least. But Alpha is in charge, and he lets out a roar of dominance. None of the pride challenges him. After a moment of sitting and resting at the edge of the wooded land, Alpha walks out from the protection of the trees, onto the smooth, rock-like ground beneath the open sky and before the towering structures inhabited by men.

The dominant female, Alpha's favorite, grows increasingly uneasy. It would be safer to rest by day in the woods and perhaps scoot across man's urban landscape under cover of night. She knows they could survive some days and nights within the woods where they are. She has the instinct to hunt deer and fox and dog and whatever animals they may find here. They could bide their time hunting smaller animals, like rabbits and gophers, for sport and practice and snacking. She does not trust this urban landscape, and knows that humans can prove deceivingly powerful for their small, weak appearances. But Alpha, with his need to assert his aggression and a seeming belief that they must move with urgency, leads the pride forward, from the hill down into the city. A body of water awaits them in the distance. A river.

The sun blazes high in the sky; it is nearly midday. People appear everywhere, walking on the streets. She sees people through the windows of buildings, outside, eating meat and vegetation. The five lions do their best to remain in the shadows of buildings and potted trees growing out of the stone-hard surfaces. People see them and they run or jump for cover, scream and make the strange noises that humans make.

For the most part, the people scatter as the lions come near. No human challenges their dominance. But the lions will not rest here, will not mark this as their territory. Instead, they will pass through to the river. Perhaps they will feed here.

Between the pride and the river, she sees an unexpected oasis of green grass and silver trees and water trickling from the sky and cascading from the ground. She can see that this is where Alpha is leading them, out of a curiosity to inspect this airborne water and the silver trees from which it sprays.

As they come nearer to the oasis, they discover young man-cubs running about in the water. The smooth-stone ground is wet, but it holds none of the falling water. Growing from this stony ground are silver trees, wet, glistening in the sun. The thin trees look like birches, only thinner and metallic, almost as though encrusted in ice—only there's no ice and no cold, and they reflect a metallic gleam. Like the silver of man's creations—motorized shells and building and fire sticks. The silver trees have no leaves, but spiral branches circle the treetops like crowns, dispersing water.

Water spouts directly from the hardened ground as well, like a waterfall in reverse. The pride steps into the water, into the forest of silver trees. The man-cubs scream and run from the lions. The lions have little interest in these minuscule morsels. They are intrigued by the silver water trees, this mist that can be felt but not found. It wets them, but they cannot drink or swallow. They can drink from the water that sprays from the rocky ground, but the mist enveloping the trees cannot be consumed; only its essence can be felt. Man-cubs and their parents begin screaming and scampering about, fleeing their pride. No one has challenged them or has come with fire sticks or cages. Far off in the distance, the female lead sees a man-made bridge of metal and stone. The tall fortresses of man's urban jungle tower high in the sky, and their lights of red and blue and white reflect off of the water.

An intense noise—distortion and plucking of string and blowing of horn—comes from a platform at the far edge of the open green. In the green, masses of people sit on patches of cloth, or stand in the grass, some of them making movement in time with the sounds being made by the platform people and their instruments. The people in the open field appear to be focused on those on the platform. Spectators. Just as she and the others might sit and watch with interest should another male come to challenge Alpha for dominance over the pride.

It was not her plan, but when the female lead sees the green field next to the trees and notices the large crowd of people there, she decides it is time to hunt. Time to eat. She sounds off so that the other lions pay attention to her lead. She signals them to take their positions with her language of barks and purring growls, wrinkling of nose and showing of teeth, movement of ears, flicker of tail and flex of whiskers, facial expression and head movement. These people are abundant and distracted. The time has come.

They hunt together, as a team. Even after a lifetime of captivity, they know, by instinct, their talents and their places.

Alpha does not participate in this hunt. He rolls around in the silver-tree mist with his mouth open and tail flicking. He bats his heavy paws on the base of the silver trees. He feigns disinterest in the hunt as he trots in the water, although he'll undoubtedly make sure he is the first to eat once the hunt is over.

The dominant female lets out a roar for all animals near and far to hear. The sound is deep and loud and carries farther than any of them can see, above the noises of the platform, beyond the grassy green and the silver forest, beyond the river and the bridge, into the natural forest from which they have come.

Her roar can be felt as well as heard. It begins between her ribs, where she can feel her muscles work like bellows, pushing air forward at a speed twice as fast as she can run. The air rushes over massive vocal folds, vibrating, and it resounds in the cavity between the roof of her mouth and the back of her throat, the cabinet that really gives her roar its power, intensifying the sound, strengthening it, resounding it, and then pitching it out into the air beyond her body.

At her signal, the other two female lions dart toward the crowd. The people have been warned by her battle cry and they are now looking, but they have no chance against the pride's teamwork. As the two flushers run toward the crowd—which itself has scattered into every direction, swarming around like a herd of any other sort of wild animal—the dominant female scans the people for the best option. The weakest, the injured, the meatiest. Not necessarily the easiest kill, but the most meat for the least risk. Within seconds, she has decided. She sprints.

The noise from the platform has ceased, and the only sound now is that of the people screaming. The dominant female darts into the green, running faster than the other lions, passing them, and jumping onto the back of a large male human. She extracts her claws and rips into the flesh and muscle of the man's back and shoulder. Four razor-sharp claws facing forward and one inverted, they hook in and will not come out no matter how strong the human's kick or buck or fight. But this human barely bothers to fight. Within seconds, she and the two flushers are on the man, and she has taken the man's neck in her mouth and pressed down on his windpipe, blocking air, taking life.

Alpha has stepped out of the silver forest and he shakes the water off his fur. He breaks into a trot, roaring every bit as loud as the female did a moment before. He chases the other lions off and begins to feed on the large human.

The other male lion must have seen, before Alpha exited the silvery trees, the inevitable. Before the ladies even downed the human, Alpha's brother could see there would not be enough for all of them to be full. Watching the people running about slowly and clumsily, he also can see that man is an easy kill when not protected by cage or armed with fire stick. So he has charged his own man, has made his own kill. He feeds on another man.

The dominant female realizes little meat will remain once the males eat. With such an ample supply available, she makes the decision to strike again and signals the other two females. The crowd is not as full as it was, most of the humans already off the open green and spilled into their territory—the city streets and buildings and cars. So this kill won't be as easy as the last two. But before she and the other females can initiate the attack, the men who attacked Master's home come toward them with their fire sticks and begin a counterattack. The lions know they are no match for these weapons that killed so much of the family back home. The lions retreat. They do not wait for Alpha's signal to lead them into retreat. Alpha is the closest to the attacking men, and their first target. He does not move now. Alpha slumps lifelessly over the man she and the flushers took down.

She won't submit to dominance challenges now. In normal times, Alpha's brother would take over, but the dominant female does not have time for games of society. She is in survival mode, and they have to flee these men with guns. She, being the fastest among them, leads the other lions out of the green, out of the silver-treed waters, back onto the lifeless, hard surface of man's preference. The river visible far below, she feels trapped, corralled between a fence and a line of black, metal benches and swings. Eventually, she finds an opening to her right, and she leads the lions back onto the black streets where they can hide between buildings and vehicles. They run along man's black road, empty now, the people evacuated. They run, looking for a sanctuary. Looking for a place away from man.

After Attacks

Slaughter whores! Are guns your answer to everything? You should have let them go free and live in the woods. Whoever's responsible for these killings should be arrested.

> — Call to Ross County Sheriff's Department

We were faced with a difficult decision, and we had to make it quick. Night was falling. Human lives were in danger.

> — Roscoe Roy, Ross County Sheriff

Each one of them animals had the potential to take a person down. We took them down first.

> — Chuck Ellison, Deputy, Ross County Sheriff's Department

We will do everything we can to lobby for change in the law so that this sort of thing never happens again.

> — Mark Vernon, Mayor of Chillicothe

Callers are outraged at the inhumane slaughter of these five dozen animals by the Ross County Sheriff's Department in Chillicothe, Ohio.

> — Carrie Mortimer, CNEN-TV

Last thing I need is for someone else to try to make me feel bad for something I already feel miserable about.

> — Morris Jones, Animal Caretaker

The people whose lives we saved are the same people calling in to give us hell.

— Mickey Ketchum, Deputy, Ross County Sheriff's Department

Just weeks before the one-year anniversary of the Chillicothe animal slaughter, the Ohio Legislature has passed laws limiting and regulating the ownership of exotic animals statewide.

— Amy Shivers, Chillicothe Evening News

Why did he do it? I deal in facts, not speculation. What do I think? That Sammy Johnson wanted to make news. But society has a short memory. Colleagues at cocktail parties ask me, "What's this series about?" When I tell them, they say, "Oh, yeah, I think I remember that. Or something like that." They vaguely remember pictures of the corpses. "A shame, really," they say, "those poor animals," and then on to the next topic. Did Sammy leave a mark? Sure. Will the world remember Sammy Johnson? It's already forgotten him.

— Blake Hartle, Investigative Reporter, *Cleveland Plain Dealer*

I hated Sheriff Roy's decision. But I fully support it.

— Leland Anders, Celebrity Zookeeper

Atrium

Jackson Withers had always despised Leland Anders. The smug way the celebrity made a showcase of animals. Turned them into clowns and stupid pet tricks. The way he seemed to cultivate fame more than education, riches more than preservation. Leland got on television with his interviews and his own nature program, dog food commercials and zoo endorsements, and he used the animals to his advantage. The "animal kingdom capitalist" even had animal treats and lunchboxes and pet toys with his picture on them, had his own line of animal print T-shirts and stuffed animals with his signature on the soles of their paws. As Jackson saw it, Leland was more interested in helping himself than helping animals.

Now, as he stood shoulder-to-shoulder with Leland, Jackson realized that maybe he had been a little too hard on the guy. Working with him through the night and into the noonday sun under such intense circumstances cast Leland in a new light. Leland had shed sincere tears and showed an honest sense of loss at the animals that they'd killed. And even under these most difficult of circumstances, he'd helped the authorities hunt them down for the good of the people, without giving a thought to how damaging it could be to his reputation among animal advocates or his fans. Because, as terrible as killing the majestic creatures was, letting them wreak havoc on a city—or two or three cities—would not only mean massive loss of human life, it would mean a backlash against preservation efforts, a vilification of the animals themselves. That was something Jackson and Leland both wanted to avoid. Were rare animals who were on the verge of extinction more important than a few human lives? In the larger scheme of things and given human overpopulation, yes, they were. And Jackson believed that Leland probably felt the same way, although he would never say so publicly, just as a politician might not admit that he inhaled. They had to eliminate the danger of these rampaging animals, not only because of what the animals may do to people, but because of what angry masses of people may do to animals.

In their work together, Jackson and Leland had bonded. Come to think of it, Jackson realized that if *his* love for animals had dropped opportunities into his lap the way Leland's had, he'd have taken to them like a lion to warm meat.

After the press conference, Jackson had gone with Roscoe, Leland and Toby to join the others in Columbus. They took two vehicles: Roscoe and Leland in one, Toby and Jackson in the other. Of course, as always, Leland Anders got top billing, riding with the head honcho. But that was fine. They were all on the same team. Maybe he could even get Leland to help him out at the Animal Protection Agency a little more after working through this ordeal together. An endorsement or donation. Maybe some air time on his show.

By the time they got to Columbus, the rest of the Sheriff's team (Ketchum, Chuck and Morris) had already hunted down and destroyed the black panther. Reports had come in that the leopards and tiger were killed in Portsmouth. Other than some monkeys, the only animals left to find and eliminate were a pride of five lions. The lions had been spotted as recently as half an hour ago in the outskirts of Columbus.

"But we have to use caution," Leland had said in his theatrical, after-school-program voice. "Lions work as a team, and that makes five lions together as dangerous as ten alone."

Ordinarily, Jackson might have sassily asked Leland to show the math, to explain how he'd come up with such an out-of-the-fedora calculation. But everyone knew what he meant: *Be alert, because a pride of lions is more dangerous than its individual parts.*

Some unverified sightings and false alerts had been called in. The helicopter hadn't been able to get a positive visual on the pride. So, with no decent leads, the four of them in their two cars drove to the downtown Columbus area.

After dealing with the black panther in the topiary garden, Ketchum, Chuck and Morris had cruised down to the Bicentennial Park area and the Scioto Mile, a riverside mile of parks and paths, walkways and bicycle trails, interactive fountains and a concert green.

"The lions will probably be interested in the river, in finding a reliable body of water," Jackson said over the radio.

"That's exactly what Leland just said," Roscoe's voice sounded.

Of course, Leland said it first, Jackson thought.

"We're on the same page, Jackson," Leland radioed, as though he could read Jackson's thoughts as clearly as a lion's intentions.

"Ketchum, Chuck, and Morris are at the river front," Roscoe said. "We'll wrap around and come in on the north side of town. Comb the area until we come together in the middle."

They'd been working with Columbus police, and patrols were on the lookout. Between the city and the suburbs, they had a lot of ground to cover. Much of the Columbus force was focusing on the parks and wooded areas in the suburbs.

Now, Roscoe, Leland, Toby, and Jackson cruised the Short North area in their two cruisers. It was half past eleven, a full nineteen hours since Sammy had released the animals. People who hadn't heeded the warnings now took their lunch breaks, walking from office to restaurant, eating bagged sandwiches, speed walking along the sidewalks.

The city known for its Americana centricity was as busy as Jackson imagined it must always be: people walking on the streets, cars driving in both directions along High Street. He supposed the busy lives of business people just couldn't be put on hold, even with risk of death by lion.

Later, Jackson would feel as though he knew two versions of that noontime ordeal. One limited to the events as he saw them, as they transpired before him. The other, a fuller version of how things transpired around them enriched with things he would learn in the hours and days that followed. These things filled in the gaps and, in time, seemed to be as much a part of his memory as his own first-hand experience.

For example, Jackson wouldn't know, until later, that as they cruised in the north part of downtown Columbus, a lunchtime concert blared in Bicentennial Park. He wouldn't know until later that workers were eating their lunches in the green and dancing to the live music of a local band, or that young children were playing in the interactive fountains, water spraying from the ground and from silver poles with silver spiral tops. He wouldn't know, until eyewitness reports were recorded after the attacks, that children and mothers and fathers and nannies went screaming and running and snatching up and fleeing.

Although he would be filled in on all the details later, Jackson could not hear the sounds, as they happened, of people talking or music playing through large speakers. But even from the other side of the city, more than a mile away, he could hear the unmistakable growl of a lion, breaking 110 decibels—louder than any rock concert, louder than anything else in the city. Jackson heard it, and the others heard it. They knew what the sound was a full half-minute before a call came over the radio.

"The lions are in Bicentennial Park! In the concert green!"

On went the flashing lights, on went the sirens. Their cruisers sped forward. Just a minute later, Chuck came on the radio: "Civilian down! Ketchum got one of the lions, male. The alpha, we think—it was feeding. Lions left the park along the Scioto. We're in pursuit, headed north."

Jackson listened over the police cruiser radio as the chase progressed. The lions came out of the Scioto Mile at Battelle Riverfront Park. He'd forgotten about the park, but now he remembered it. He'd visited the park as a child when his family was in Columbus for business. He remembered a story in statues that involved a boy named Pickaweekwee, his hound, an owl, unicorn and lion. "The secret of the lion is courage," an inscription had said. Leland remembered the bronze statue of the proud lion sitting at the edge of a fountain.

"They're on Broad Street now," Jackson heard over the radio. "Almost got hit by a truck! They've turned left on High Street!"

High Street was the main street across town, the street Jackson himself now cruised upon with Toby, driving into the heart of downtown Columbus from the north.

"Let's go on foot," Roscoe said, knowing they might cross the lions soon. They used their cars as a barricade to block traffic as well as they could. They got out, Roscoe, Leland, Toby and Jackson. Assault rifles ready, they proceed along High Street at a jog, waiting for the lions to come into view. Skyscrapers of cement and glass and granite surrounded them. Although they could not see them, Jackson knew that Ketchum, Chuck and Morris were chasing after the lions, coming from the south in their direction along the same street.

Minutes later, they all came together, within sight of one another—the pack of lions between them. They remained on High Street, on the grid between Spring Street and Nationwide Boulevard, standing at the mid-point where Walnut connects to High. Jackson stopped in his tracks, as did Roscoe, Toby and Leland.

Jackson stared in disbelief as he watched the lions come in their direction, right between the Federal Building and the Nationwide Plaza. Ketchum, Chuck and Morris, behind the lions, were not using their weapons, not wanting to stop and let the lions escape their sight. Roscoe and Toby aimed.

"Wait!" Jackson cried. The policemen heeded Jackson's warning, realizing their risk of overshooting the lions and hitting one another. Toby fired a warning shot into the air.

Between their groups of men, the female lion—who appeared to be leading the pack—stopped. Jackson understood: the lions heard and smelled and saw the gunfire in front of them and knew it was on their tails as well. The lead lion twitched her tail and looked for an alternative.

That alternative, Jackson realized, called to the lions in sounds and smells the way a neon sign calls man into the shadows of a nightclub or the comfort of a restaurant. There, between Spring Street and Nationwide Boulevard, between the Federal Building and the Nationwide Plaza, the park and courtyard system surrounding the red granite complex must have seemed an oasis: birds chirping in the forest of planted trees; tall grasses and bushes waving in the light wind; rushing waterfalls and flowing streams along the intermixed network of fountains.

The lions turned aside and darted up into the brush of the building-front plaza. They nearly concealed themselves behind the planted grasses and bushes and trees. The hunters trailed them. Jackson, Leland, Roscoe and Toby followed directly up the ramp after the lions. Further south on the block, Ketchum, Chuck and Morris shot up the steps to the top of the brick courtyard. They all came to the same place, right next to the Nationwide building. People who had been eating their packed lunches along the wooden benches and granite ledges fled in a panic.

There, encased behind a wall of glass several stories tall, beckoned an indoor oasis. Within the building, a tropical atrium of trees and bushes, flowers and pools, streams and fountains called to the lions. Jackson understood that this must have looked like a perfect enclosure for them. A home. Jackson imagined that the lions had finally come to understand why people spent their days and nights enclosed in buildings of their own design—imagining them to be filled with trees and flowers and plants and vegetation and pools with springs of bubbling water just like this one.

The lions bounded from the courtyard's warm brick floor onto a large granite box filled with yellow-green grass. A wide-reaching tree stood at the center of this grassy field. Jackson figured the tall vegetation would have been the perfect camouflage for lions had they not been followed here. But this large rectangular planter was only a stepping stone for the lions now.

Jackson watched the female lion leap toward the atrium. The other lions watched their female lead for just a few seconds before following her, vaulting toward the clear wall separating them from the sanctity of the jungle.

It was beautiful, but tragic. Jackson watched the female lion crash against the thick, clear wall—watched her paws stop in what appeared to be midair, then her face crash, left side in, almost facing them, into the surface, followed by her shoulders. The rest of her body could go no further, so it curved into itself and landed sideways, flat into the transparent wall. Her stunned body slid limply down the wall of thick glass as the others, who had followed her, slammed into the same wall. By the time the third of the four lions hit the atrium wall, Ketchum, Morris, Chuck, Toby and Roscoe all stood well within range. Jackson and Leland did, too, but they did not fire, could not fire, mesmerized by the spectacle of the pride's last dash.

The secret of the lion is courage, Jackson remembered from the statue.

As the third lion—the male—slid down the glass, Ketchum's fire and Roscoe's fire hit it, and killed it, and blood spurted out of its head and shoulder and smeared down the glass. Chuck and then Toby and Ketchum and then Roscoe fired at the fourth lion just before it slammed against the glass in a bloody heap and bounced off.

What Jackson did not notice, but would hear about later, was the terror breaking out inside the soundproof atrium as people eating their lunches and enjoying the peaceful indoor garden in the middle of the city looked up to see lions lunging for them. How the people flinched as the lions smacked against the windows with such hard and loud thuds that they feared the impact would shatter the glass and allow the great cats in. How they saw the lions break out in blood, watched their injuries splatter the windows. How people lost their lunches and their consciousness and their sanity, caged inside the windowed atrium with bloody lions trying to break in.

Outside, two lions struggled to stand back up from where they had fallen on the brick plaza. Jackson watched—he was stunned himself—as the lions tried to walk, barely able to stay on their feet. Jackson knew he should shoot, should put the lions out of their misery and end this bloody twenty hours, thereby closing the darkest ordeal of his life. But he just couldn't bring himself to shoot these injured creatures.

Ketchum and Chuck did the job for him. The stumbling lions jerked, whimpered, and fell. Jackson stood before the pile of lion and blood, dropped his rifle, and cried.

Roscoe sighed, the weight of a lion seeming to fall from him. "Couldn't have happened any other way but worse."

Jackson couldn't hold back his tears. Leland put an arm around Jackson. "It had to be done. It's over now."

Jackson sighed. Once again, Leland Anders, celebrity zookeeper, knew exactly what to say.

Deranged Man Unleashes Terror; Authorities Respond With Violence

Dan Charles

We've been following the story about exotic animals on the loose in central Ohio. Now we turn to Carrie Mortimer for the latest. Carrie.

Carrie Mortimer

Thanks Dan. It's been a terrible time for residents of central Ohio since around 4:30 yesterday afternoon. This shocking event has left at least six people and five dozen animals dead.

Yesterday evening, Sammy Johnson, a lifetime resident of Chillicothe, took his life after releasing his private zoo of exotic animals into the community.

A team assembled by the Sheriff in Chillicothe shot most of the animals point blank on the Johnson property before they had a chance to leave. The Sherriff's cadre then hunted down and killed the others.

People around the world—and right here in Chillicothe—are outraged that a person could be allowed to own these dangerous killing machines, and at authorities who slaughtered them. Here are a few I had the opportunity to speak with.

Bobbie Anne Thompson

It was terrible. I looked out my kitchen window and saw a tiger attacking my horses. We always knew that he had these wild animals. But we didn't know he had so many.

Mitch Henderson

It's not the first time his animals got free. I've seen his bears and lions and tigers out before. Killed my dog, few years back. This time was different. I'm glad the Sherriff's team arrived when they did.

Carrie Mortimer

But not everybody feels that way. A number of animal activists have called this atrocity the worst act against rare animals in recent history. Among the dozens of animals shot down and murdered were Bengal and Siberian tigers, two prides of lions, cheetahs, leopards, wolves, monkeys, bobcats, bears and cougars.

Jackson Withers

When I arrived on the scene and saw what was going on, saw all of these beautiful animals dead, I wanted to cry. Just terrible.

Carrie Mortimer

Some blame the lax laws that allowed Sammy Johnson to accumulate such a large collection of dangerous beasts, some blame Mr. Johnson himself, but some blame the Sheriff's department and are calling for Sheriff Roscoe Roy's resignation. There's even talk of bringing animal cruelty charges against the members of the hunting party that slew these animals.

Leland Anders

It was an awful sight to see all of these animals put down. But it had to be done. If these animals weren't destroyed, there would have been carnage in central Ohio.

Carrie Mortimer

Carnage? Just look at these troubling images of animal carcasses on the

Johnson estate. It looks to this reporter as though there *was* carnage in central Ohio. Carrie Mortimer, CNEN-TV, reporting. Dan.

Dan Charles

A fascinating story, Carrie. And, after the break: will the Cincinnati Reds get clear weather for tomorrow's game? Sports and weather, after these messages.

Breathe

Zachery Adams

After two days on edge, residents of Chillicothe and the surrounding area can finally breathe easy, knowing that the streets and parks are safe again. Local authorities have eliminated the threat of dangerous, exotic animals. Our own Amy Shivers has more. Amy.

Amy Shivers

Thank you, Zachery. That's right, residents of Chillicothe can finally breathe easy; the outdoors are once again safe. It is confirmed that Chillicothe resident Sammy Johnson committed suicide, but not until after he released his entire zoo of exotic animals. The event has left many—even those who knew him best—wondering why he would do such a thing, not only to his neighbors and friends, but to the animals he devoted his life to.

Marielle Johnson

Sammy was such a gentle, loving man.

Amy Shivers

Sammy Johnson's wife, Marielle Johnson.

Marielle Johnson

He loved the animals; they were our family. I can't imagine why he did such a thing. I know he wouldn't have wanted them harmed. He must have thought he was somehow helping them. I don't know.

Amy Shivers

No one knows for sure why Mr. Johnson released the animals, but the Chillicothe Police Department responded quickly with a big-game hunt across central Ohio. Some have criticized the maneuver as cruelty to animals. But most residents are grateful that authorities acted as swiftly and decisively as they did.

Sheriff Roscoe Roy

As of this time, all of the animals have been accounted for, except two or three monkeys and a chimpanzee. We believe these animals were eaten by some of the lions, tigers, bears, cougars or other animals on the premises.

Amy Shivers

Neighbors of Johnson and his animals lived in constant fear that something like this might happen one day.

Mitch Henderson

This isn't the first time the animals have been out. But I guess it'll be the last.

Amy Shivers

Authorities are still on the lookout for the monkeys and chimpanzee that may be on the loose, but they're confident these animals do not pose a threat. It's been a difficult twenty-four hours in central Ohio, but citizens can finally rest easy. Zachery.

Zachery Adams

Disturbing story, Amy. We'll take a look at the victims of this ordeal, after this.

Sammy Johnson and the Animal Massacre of Central Ohio

by Blake Hartle, Part of a continuing series for the *Cleveland Plain Dealer*

CHILLICOTHE—Animal experts, psychologists, neighbors, family and friends continue to debate the motivation of this exotic animal owner. It seems likely that we won't soon—if ever—know *why* Sammy Johnson did what he did. But it is clear *what* he did.

Dr. Minnie Fields, professor of psychology at Shawnee State University, was on campus when students were being attacked by one of Johnson's escaped leopards. Dr. Fields stated, "Understanding exactly what happened can help us ensure it never happens again."

Sammy Johnson, owner of about five dozen exotic animals in Chillicothe, unleashed his dangerous pets—lions, tigers, bears, panthers, mountain lions and cougars—on central Ohio, resulting in the deaths of each of his animals as well as six people. Johnson's own demise brings the human death toll to seven, although his was an apparent suicide before allowing his animals to feed on him.

Johnson had been collecting exotic animals all his life. As a child, he showed an early interest in animals.

"He always did love animals," his mother, Sally Johnson, said. He would accumulate stray cats and dogs before she began purchasing mice and hamsters and other household pets for him.

After returning from a tour in Vietnam, where it's said he befriended a monkey and observed a wild tiger at close range, Johnson began purchasing and keeping bears, tigers, lions, monkeys and other exotic animals. Prior to his tour abroad, he worked at the Columbus Zoo briefly and reportedly was let go because he entered the animal enclosures after several warnings to stop.

Johnson's life work and passion was collecting the exotic animals. But he reportedly collected other things as well. Guns, for example. Even after selling his gun and tackle store, which he ran for more than 20 years, he kept a number of his prize collectables. These unregistered collectors' items got him charged, tried and convicted to a year in prison.

Johnson served nine months of his 12-month sentence and was paroled for good behavior. The charge was for two guns that did not have serial numbers. He claimed they lacked serial numbers because of their antique status and that they did not have serial numbers when manufactured. Authorities say that the weapons should have been registered and issued numbers at the time of purchase, but never were.

Part of the condition of his release was that he submit to house arrest for six months. When he returned home, he discovered that his wife was not there. In her place was a "Dear John" letter stating that she had decided to separate from him after nearly 30 years of marriage.

That letter (along with all other letters, personal papers and records) was not recovered. The papers were likely burned in the bonfire, the remains of which were found when authorities arrived to find Johnson dead and the animals released.

Records show that Johnson had recently been investigated by the government not only for his unregistered gun and animal ownership, but also regarding his taxes. He was audited by the IRS just a year before and owed more than $140,000 in back taxes. Liens had been placed on his property. His bank account had been garnished. He was broke and alone with only his animals and the expenses they entailed.

"He went off to jail a proud man with everything going for him," said Morris Jones, the person who cared for his animals while Johnson was imprisoned. "He came back with no wife, no money and the prospect of no freedom and no property."

Even Morris Jones, who arguably knew the animals better than anyone except the Johnsons themselves, claims not to understand why Sammy Johnson released them to certain death. "He probably thought he was doing them a favor," Jones speculated. Jones was a member of the Sheriff's hunting party that killed the released animals, giving him the unlikely dual roles of animal caretaker and killer.

When the Sheriff's office responded to reports from neighbors of animals on the loose, they arrived to find lions, tigers, bears and wolves already stalking and attacking people and horses on neighboring properties. When authorities came to the Johnson estate, they were shocked to find all of the animals not only with opened cages, but with openings cut into the cages so they could not be sealed back in. That evening, night and the next day, it was to be a fight to the death.

The first of Johnson's animals killed were the ones on the neighboring properties. Then, the Sheriff's department went to work on the animals at the Johnson farm. After they entered the warehouse containing the cut-open cages, they noticed the body of Sammy Johnson in a stall, being eaten by a tiger. In addition to the animals in and around the warehouse, a pride of lions hovered in the distant field. The authorities shot all of the animals they could on site.

More than half of the animals were dead within the first hour or so. "But nearly half the animals had escaped and needed to be hunted down," said Sheriff Roscoe Roy. The Sheriff's department called in animal experts: Jackson Withers of the Animal Protection Agency and Leland Anders, zookeeper and star of the syndicated animal show, *The Zoo for You*. With their help, as well as a great deal of assistance from callers reporting sightings, the Sheriff's team tracked down and killed these animals.

The exotic animals were found and killed as far south as Portsmouth and as far north as the state capital of Columbus. In Portsmouth, two leopards were killed, one in the Shawnee State Forest, and another on the Shawnee State University campus. A tiger was killed near the floodwall along the Scioto River in Portsmouth. Two men were killed, one by the leopard at the Shawnee State Forest, and another by the tiger along the

Portsmouth floodwall on Front Street.

A lion just north of Chillicothe killed an 84-year-old woman, but the remains were not discovered until days after the event.

In Columbus, a panther was killed in a topiary garden, and a pride of five lions attacked lunchtime concertgoers in Bicentennial Park, part of the Scioto Mile along the river. The lions killed two men before fleeing. One lion was killed at the scene, and the other four were intercepted along High Street and killed in the heart of the downtown area between the John W. Bricker Federal Building and Nationwide complex. The entire ordeal, from the time authorities responded to the first call to the elimination of the last remaining lions, spanned approximately 20 hours.

When the calls for assistance ceased at the Sheriff's office in Chillicothe, other calls began. Criticism has come from around the world, including death threats and calls for the Sheriff's resignation. But most experts—including animal rights activists—agree that the department did the right thing, given the potential risk to human life. It was essential to the safety of the communities within range for the team to exterminate the dangerous animals.

"Those animals had been caged up so long, they were antsy and ready to hunt," said Leland Anders. "The most readily available meat around was that of people—and the easiest kills, had they been left alone to hunt on their own terms, would have been innocent children and the elderly."

"We didn't have a guide book on what to do," said Jackson Withers of the Animal Protection Agency. "Nothing like this has ever happened before, not anywhere in the world. So we had to work our way through it and figure out what to do as we went along."

PETA has called for an immediate ban on exotic animal ownership in Ohio, which it calls the "wild west of exotic animal ownership." There are virtually no regulations in the state regarding exotic animals, which makes it legal for a man like Sammy Johnson to accumulate such a horde. The Sheriff, the Mayor of Chillicothe, PETA, Leland Anders and Jackson Withers are among many calling upon the Ohio lawmakers to pass legislation that will ban, limit or regulate the ownership of exotic animals in the state.

People across Ohio, the nation and the world continue to speculate about Sammy Johnson's decision to release his arsenal of animals.

"We may never know *why* he did it," said Dr. Fields. "What we do know is *what* happened and we can put that information to use to make sure it never happens again."

###

Why it Happened

Sammy walked through his warehouse, peeking into the cages, gazing at his loved ones. He knew each by name and vividly remembered every family member's adoption. Each animal looked back at him the way a friend or child might. He'd reared many of them from infancy, taking in two- and three-week-old cubs, cradling them in his arms, feeding them milk from bottles, playing with them, coddling them. When they got bigger, he regularly put that mutual love to the test by sharing their spaces, being with them, showing them he trusted them and that he would provide for them.

The animals took Sammy to a place of serenity. Playing with his animals brought him back to his eleventh birthday party, when Mom and Dad gave him that hole-punched, barking box. Every time he opened the door to a cage and walked in to spend time with the tigers or lions, Sammy felt the way he did when he opened that box to see a beagle's wagging tail, to feel its lapping tongue. To Sammy's mind, the only thing bigger than his animal family was the warm feeling that welled inside him when he was with them.

But he didn't pretend his big heart made him a good guy. *Nobody's perfect. Especially me.* Loving Marielle and animals didn't make him a good person. *Everybody has the capacity to love. Love in itself does not make a man good or bad, decent or indecent.*

Looking at his large collection of war paraphernalia, especially the Nazi medals and helmets and guns, Sammy considered the example of the ultimate bad guy. *Hitler loved his dogs, loved his family, loved his country. But nobody would argue that love made him a good guy.* Sammy wasn't a philosopher, but he did think about such things from time to time. He thought about things a lot after Marielle left him alone with the animals. Sammy figured that everyone had a battle going on inside them, a war between ego and love. For Hitler, ego was bigger than love and his ego drove him. Sometimes Sammy figured that's how it was for all great men, good and bad and everywhere in between. Sammy wasn't bad like Hitler or good like Leland Anders. He was somewhere in the middle. Just a man. But he figured his ego was bigger than his love, when left unchecked. His ego drove him to aim higher, to go bigger. Because of his ego, Sammy did not know where to stop.

Sammy sat on a crate in the lions' cage. Alpha approached Sammy, gave a lazy welcome roar, and sat down in front of his master. Sammy took the lion's mane in his hands, gripped the dry hair firmly, and slowly turned the massive head back and forth before easing into a massage of the skin beneath the fur. Sammy smiled and Alpha offered up a lion's yawn.

Sammy wasn't filled with hate. Sure, there were things that left a bad flavor in his mouth, like all those who'd wronged him. He didn't like that his parents hadn't been supportive of his animals. He'd been screwed by the government when they sent him as a child to fight in a war he didn't understand. Authorities really got under his skin, and he couldn't abide cops trying to give him tickets or jail time for trivial things like not wearing a seat belt or not having a government number etched on an antique. Even Marielle had turned on him. He didn't hate her—he hated that she'd left him. It seemed, in the end, that only his animals really knew how to be loyal.

He frowned playfully at Alpha. "And that's just because you're locked up and don't have any choice."

Sammy collected grievances just like he collected everything else. He knew he was a compulsive collector. He didn't just dabble—he dove in. That's why people came from miles around. His guns, for example. He didn't just have guns for sale, but rare collectables: Civil War muzzleloaders, Revolutionary War muskets, World War I and II rifles, Soviet and Nazi pieces. And to accent this unusual collection, he segued into war and military paraphernalia: medals and ribbons and uniforms and medallions and banners and flags and helmets. He didn't merely service the people of Chillicothe and central Ohio. Collectors came from around the nation and world to browse his unique pieces.

Two more of the five lions in the cage moseyed over to sit with Sammy and Alpha. Sammy patted each on the head in turn, then looked back into Alpha's eyes. "Anyone can collect art or toys or trains. It takes a lion of a man to collect the things that most sissies are afraid of."

When profits from rare guns and war paraphernalia allowed, he expanded his business to cars. When he decided to start his small car dealership as a hobby and as a supplement to his income, he didn't follow a proper business model and buy cars the average person would want to buy. He only bothered with the ones worth having: the best classic car collection in the county. And he enjoyed the reputation every bit as much as he enjoyed the cars.

The lioness rubbed against his leg with the side of her head and neck and he rubbed her back. She fell into a warm, soothing rest against him and began to purr. He looked down at the lioness, who displayed complete trust. All of the lions did. His entire family. "I wouldn't have things any other way."

Things could have turned out differently, had he listened to his parents and society and done things normally. But that wasn't who he was. "I was anything but normal," he said to his lions with a laugh. Settling into a job and having a dog and a cat just wouldn't have been natural.

For all the grief it caused, Sammy was pleased that he'd done things his way. It was only natural that he upped the ante on his animal collection when he came back from the war, moved out of his parents' home, and started a home of his own. When he could finally live by his own rules on his own turf. He'd always been fascinated with exotic animals and wanted to have a collection to rival any other private zoo. Even the television zoo Leland Anders had put together didn't compare to his.

Sammy reached his arms out to pet the two lionesses at once. "You're a far cry better than anything Leland ever put together."

Sure, Sammy loved the animals. But it was more than that, he admitted—if only to himself. Sammy got a thrill out of owning big and powerful animals, a high from dominating the king of beasts. And nothing pleased Sammy more than having other people ask him about his animals. The awe they paid him, the admiration, even if they sometimes saw him as a bit off-kilter. He loved the way people regarded him as a master of wild animals that no one else could tame.

"It's my ego that got me into trouble," he confided to Alpha, who still sat proudly in front of him, eyes half-closed as though about to sleep. Sometimes Sammy felt an uncontrollable need to challenge the law, to do things his way because he thought he could. It was as though he almost *asked* the cops to come and slap his hand so he could laugh at them as they tried, but failed, to break him. Like daring someone to punch you in your tightened abdomen. He ruffled Alpha's mane. "Or letting out a roar that tells everyone you're boss."

When he sold the gun and tackle shop to spend more time with his animals, Sammy kept some of his favorite pieces for himself: about thirty guns. Two of the guns, which police discovered during an investigation, did not have serial numbers.

"They don't need serial numbers." He thought he could tell the law what the law was when it came to his guns. "They didn't have serial numbers back when they made these. It's like giving a no-seat-belt ticket when you're in a car from the fifties that doesn't have a seat belt."

But he knew that he should have registered the guns with the authorities. He just didn't want to, because he thought he could get away with it. Just like the time he was issued twelve tickets in one day for not wearing his seat belt because he stubbornly told the officer, "You might as well follow me, since I don't plan to buckle up." Officer Ellison did follow him, stopping him every five minutes to issue him another no-seat-belt ticket. Sammy didn't care. His ego was too big to wrap a seat belt around.

They'd never been able to charge him on the animals, because there weren't any laws preventing his ownership. But they got him on the gun technicalities. And the charge stuck. Sentenced to a year in prison, he went to Chillicothe Correctional Facility, where his neighbor, Mitch Henderson, had once worked.

Alpha slumped down on his side, like a rug before Sammy's feet. He let out a big yawn, his mouth opening wide enough for Sammy to put his head inside. "Yeah, I know what it's like to sit in a cage, I guess." He was only in prison for nine months. He could see in the faces of some of his drinking buddies at the bar and neighbors who had stopped by that they thought jail time had changed him. "Jail time didn't change me none. *She did*."

What had changed him, the way he figured it, was an upset in the balance between ego and love. "Life's always been a constant struggle between ego and love, ain't it?" Alpha's eyes were closed, so he looked at the other three lions around him. The fifth lion was asleep in a far corner of the cage. "You've got to balance the two."

When Sammy got out of jail and found that Marielle had left him, his life fell out of balance; his ego took over.

It wasn't jail time that changed Sammy. He'd done fine in jail. Good behavior for the most part, other than sassing the guards when they got smart with him. He didn't mind sitting in a cage like an animal all day. It was the loss of that counterweight. The loss of Marielle.

Marielle was his biggest casualty, but a hailstorm of problems had pelted him since getting out of jail. He was confined to his property, under house arrest for six months—thus he'd lost his freedom for the first time since getting out of the military. His guns were confiscated by the government. The government had placed liens on his property because of the back taxes he owed. "Guess they'll be auctioning it all off soon, kicking us out of here." He rubbed the lioness, who was still leaning against him, her warm body hot against his leg, her tan fur coarse and slick. "We'll have to figure something out."

The lioness stood and walked out of his reach. She went to the corner of the cage and curled up to sleep. Sammy watched Alpha's chest rise and fall with his deep, dozing breaths. Two other lionesses were awake and with him, one on each side. He put a hand on each lioness's neck and massaged. They purred.

Sammy sensed the world turning on him. Gun charges, jail time, back taxes, liens on the property, house arrest, the possibility of having his land taken away and auctioned off. There was no one around but his animals. No reason to fight the tear that began to pool in his eye. "At the time when I need her most, she bails." For the first time in his post-war adult life, he felt as though he'd lost control of his circumstances.

Sammy still had full control of his mind, if not his situation. If the government took his land, they would take his animals. If the government took his animals, they would probably put them down—or worse, give them to some shit like Jackson Withers to "rescue." And if they were going to do that, Sammy figured he might as well give his family a fighting chance. And make the news in the process. He and his animals would go out with a bang.

The letter Sammy found on the kitchen table when he arrived home from jail explained things by not explaining them. *I still love you, but I feel like I need a break from everything. Living away from you for these past nine months has reminded me that I can exist as an individual, that I'm a bigger person when I'm alone than I am when I'm with you,* she'd written. *I love you, but you are so overpowering that I feel smaller when I'm near you. When I'm a part of us, I'm just a part of you. I want to be me.*

"What the hell does that mean, anyway?" he'd asked Jack Daniels and Jim Beam a hundred times over. He never found an answer. Except that maybe by trying to be the biggest and the best, he hadn't left enough room for the most important person in his life to be much of anything for herself.

Sammy rubbed the lovely fur coats of his lions. One of them noticed the salty stream on his face and licked his tears. The rough, sandpapery tongue felt good against his face. Sammy smiled. "Ego and love." He sniffed. "That's always been the recipe." With the love of his wife no longer taking up any space, ego had room to balloon.

With Sammy in prison, Morris had taken care of the animals by himself after Marielle left. Morris had fed them and cleaned their cages. But Sammy didn't feel they had been treated like family so much as like farm animals while he was away. Now, they felt more like pets than children.

He looked behind him, over one shoulder, then the other. A lion slept in each back corner of the cage. Alpha still slept at his feet and the two lionesses purred at his sides. "I'm backed into a corner," he whispered. With the love of his life gone, he had only his ego to guide him. If he was going to live without his wife and if they threatened to tax away his income and savings, if they wouldn't let him have his guns and if he couldn't afford the money and time to be master of his family, maybe it was time to go.

"That's it." He let go of the lions and rubbed his face dry. "That's just the thing."

The thought began as a sort of manly pout, the sort of thing one may grunt over a drink to someone in hopes that they'll talk you out of it and validate your worth. But no one was around but himself and his animals.

He stood and walked away from the lions. He opened the door, stepped outside the cage, and closed and locked it behind him. The more Sammy thought it over, the more he realized that he didn't want to live a life in which he couldn't have his animals, his wife, his land, his guns, his freedom. And once he'd decided he was going to end it, he decided to do it his way—and to do it big.

If he was going to kill himself, he wanted to do it in a way that would make headline news around the world. A paragraph in the *Chillicothe Gazette* obituary section wouldn't suffice. He wanted coverage on the evening and the morning news, from Columbus to New York to Los Angeles, from London to Tokyo.

The less people understood, the longer they would talk and the bigger mark he would leave. So he burned any evidence that may offer clues. He burned the letter from his wife, burned the taxes and the audit letters and parole papers and court paperwork and letters from his family and friends and all of their personal papers. He burned everything, and then set his plan into motion. Investigators and reporters would uncover some of the details. But that would just keep the story alive.

He talked to his animals, some of them sleeping, others watching him, pacing to and fro at the front of their dwellings. His animals wanted free? "I'll set you free." His wife wanted rid of him? "She'll be rid of me for good." The authorities wanted to take everything from him? "I'll take it away before they have the opportunity." Society didn't approve of his animal ownership? "To hell with them all. I'll unleash my animals on society. See if they approve of that."

Some of his animals, he figured, would make it to the woods and live in the wild, or what little wild remained in the United States that hadn't been dipped in concrete or smothered in asphalt. Others would be killed, but they would be killed anyway, or forced to live in zoos where they might be fed and medicated and gawked at, put on television by the likes of Leland Anders, but not loved.

No, he would release them and then release himself. He would offer himself up as a meal to his animals. "That's the way to do it, the way to get the world talking." That's what ego was all about, Sammy figured: getting others to talk about you with awe and wonder. The world didn't need to love him or even to respect him. They just needed to know him.

Opening the cages would be too easy, would allow the authorities to cage them back up and be done. Sammy cut the cages open. Still the master of his animals, Sammy knew he could open the cages without fear of being harmed by them immediately—he would have time. Not that they would harm him at all, really, unless given reason. They respected him. "I've spent so much time with you all in your cages," Sammy said as he unlocked the tiger's door. "Now it's your turn to spend some time with me on the outside."

Sammy cried as he embraced his tiger, as he bear-hugged his bear, as he opened the door to his second lion pride's cage and stepped back, inviting them out. Sammy took the lion's mane in his hands and gently, playfully shook the lion's head back and forth. As though the lion was heavily, lazily shaking his head and saying, *No, don't do it.*

Sammy lost all sense of time once the animals were released from their cages. He giddily roamed about them, still inside the warehouse, but in the common area between the cells. He felt like a shepherd watching over his sheep. Maybe he was a little crazy, but he was in love with his family. "Is love ever a rational animal?"

When all the animals had been free for some hours, after Sammy finished playing with them and saying goodbye, he went to the old fridge that he kept stocked in the warehouse with carcasses and scraps for the animals. He rubbed chicken innards all around him as a way to entice the animals to feed upon him.

"Come and get it!" He offered his body as a final sacrifice to the animals he spent his life caring for. He thought of his lovely Marielle and tears reappeared in his eyes. She'd forgotten and abandoned him.

Sammy watched his animals moving about the compound. Some—uncertain—remained in their open cages peering out. Others paced around the floor, looking to their master for direction, sniffing the fresh innards in the air. Wondering. Sammy dried his tears and put his mind to his task.

Sammy put the gun to his head. He knew the world would talk about him and his animals for years to come. He imagined the news stories, national television coverage, in-depth analysis, maybe even a novel or biography or made-for-television movie. He thought of Marielle and wondered whether she would remember him as he was when they first met, or as the person he'd become. He imagined that she would remember him as a lifelong series of gestures and actions, feelings and moods, and that she would not allow him to be defined by one moment. The thought made him smile. He looked at his animals and pulled the trigger.

Wide Open

The widow walked along the property that was now hers alone, a land full of blood and bone, dirt and sadness. Marielle would remember her husband. And she would remember the animals she loved. She did love them, all of them, the master and the beasts. She wished she hadn't left him without talking about it first, without letting him know that the separation may only have been temporary. She wished she'd considered what reaction her action might cause. She'd had no clue Sammy would take such a drastic plunge. She had needed time to find herself, but that didn't mean she wanted nothing to do with her partner in life. Now she believed she could have found herself again with him.

For the past year, she'd kept Sammy's ashes sealed airtight inside a plastic peanut-butter pail. She carried the pail now and had come to the mass grave, a mound much like the Native American mounds located less than an hour south of here. The Indian mounds were sacred places to the Native Americans, just as this mound had become a sacred place to her. But a place she would not often visit, being filled as it was with pain and regret.

Marielle opened the pail and released the ashes in the light autumn breeze. She cried as she watched the ashes dissipate over the mound of animals, a vague hint of peanut butter scenting the air. She forgave her husband for letting ego overpower love.

Marielle missed Sammy and the animals. Now, they were free. But she wasn't. She feared she would remain caged with these memories all her life.

As Marielle stood pondering whether she should go inside the house or go back to her car to leave this place for good, she spotted a figure walking her way along the path between her old home and the Thompson farm next door. It was Bobbie Anne Thompson, her old neighbor. The person who had first noticed something was amiss. The woman who had called the police and reported her animal family's release at the start of the massacre.

"Afternoon, Marielle," Bobbie Anne said as she came into speaking range. "Haven't seen you a spell."

"Hello, Bobbie Anne," Marielle replied somewhat coolly.

"Whatcha got there?"

Marielle looked down at the empty pail, the lid firmly back on top. "Recycling."

Bobbie Anne nodded, then glanced around. "I just put the kettle on. How about a cup of tea?"

Marielle glanced back to the place where she had lived with Sammy for so many years, then off to the Thompson house in the distance. Bobbie Anne had always been polite enough when they were both out in their yards, but she'd never invited her over for tea before.

Canada geese flocked overhead, their honks echoing across open fields. Bobbie Anne looked up at the geese, then back to Marielle. "Hot tea with pie will really hit the spot."

Marielle forced a smile. "I'm more of a coffee person."

Bobbie Anne nodded. "We have some instant in the cabinet. I'll make you a cup of coffee."

Marielle had a notion to yell at this woman, to give her a chunk of her mind. There had been moments over the past year that she imagined chewing her out or physically fighting her. She'd certainly wished the woman harm. Now, she put herself in Bobbie Anne's shoes, imagined looking out the window and seeing her pets being attacked. She supposed they had more in common than she wanted to admit.

"Sure." Marielle relented. She forced another smile. As Marielle walked with Bobbie Anne toward the warmth of the Thompson kitchen, she felt lighter than she had when she arrived. Neither ego, nor sorrow, nor regret would confine her. Bobbie Anne's coffee was bitter and the rhubarb pie looked to be several days beyond fresh, but the gesture mattered. Marielle felt, at least for the moment, that her cage door was wide open.

Acknowledgments

It takes an extended family of supportive and likeminded people to allow a novel like this one to be released into the world. I'd like to thank some of those who helped me in my pursuit of researching, writing, and polishing *Setting the Family Free*.

Thank you to early beta readers Nitin Jagdish, Lauren Beth Eisenberg Davis, Tom Glenn, Sherry Audette Morrow, Stephanie Senyak, Janet Knee, and Gregg Wilhelm for helping me to tame the wild metaphors and stray unnecessary words and to avoid distracting rabbit holes and the dangerous terrain of scenes and subplots that did not serve the story. I appreciate the later-draft input from readers Rafael Alvarez, Katherine Cottle, Charles Rammelkamp, Jerry Holt, Toby Devens, Lucrecia Gurrero, Bathsheba Monk, and Mark Mirabello. And thank you, Sheryl Morris, for your careful review and eagle's eye proofreading. I appreciate the attention to detail and dedicated efforts of Loyola's Apprentice House team to this book: Christina Damon, Claire Riley, Carmen Machalek and Kevin Atticks.

The original draft of *Setting the Family Free* was completed during my writing residency at the Ox-Bow School of Art, part of the School of the Art Institute of Chicago. Thank you, Ox-Bow, for providing an ideal environment for writing this novel.

About the Author

Eric D. Goodman is the author of *Womb: a novel in utero* (Merge Publishing, 2017) and *Tracks: A Novel in Stories* (Atticus Books, 2011), winner of the 2012 Gold Medal for Best Fiction in the Mid-Atlantic Region from the Independent Publisher Book Awards. He's also author of *Flightless Goose* (Writer's Lair Books, 2008), a storybook for children. More than a hundred of his stories and travelogues have been published in magazines, journals, and periodicals. He's curator and co-founder of the popular Lit and Art Reading Series and has read frequently from his fiction on Baltimore's NPR station, at book festivals and at literary events. Eric lives in Baltimore where he writes about wombs, trains, travel, and animals gone wild, among other things.

Learn more about Eric and connect via www.EricDGoodman.com, www.Facebook.com/EricDGoodman or www.Twitter.com/Edgewrite.

Apprentice
House Press
Loyola University Maryland

Apprentice House is the country's only campus-based, student-staffed book publishing company. Directed by professors and industry professionals, it is a nonprofit activity of the Communication Department at Loyola University Maryland.

Using state-of-the-art technology and an experiential learning model of education, Apprentice House publishes books in untraditional ways. This dual responsibility as publishers and educators creates an unprecedented collaborative environment among faculty and students, while teaching tomorrow's editors, designers, and marketers.

Outside of class, progress on book projects is carried forth by the AH Book Publishing Club, a co-curricular campus organization supported by Loyola University Maryland's Office of Student Activities.

Eclectic and provocative, Apprentice House titles intend to entertain as well as spark dialogue on a variety of topics. Financial contributions to sustain the press's work are welcomed. Contributions are tax deductible to the fullest extent allowed by the IRS.

To learn more about Apprentice House books or to obtain submission guidelines, please visit www.apprenticehouse.com.

Apprentice House
Communication Department
Loyola University Maryland
4501 N. Charles Street
Baltimore, MD 21210
Ph: 410-617-5265 • Fax: 410-617-2198
info@apprenticehouse.com • www.apprenticehouse.com